SONIC THE HEDGEHOG #27:
"Scrambled Hedgehog"
or years, the Freedom Fighters have relied on Sonic's speed and confidence
to get them through the worst situations. But where would they
be without their quick-footed friend, or worse yet, if he were fighting
for the other side? In this dramatic two-part tale, Sonic turns on his
friends after losing his memory and being
tricked by Robotnik to find Knothole and
give away its secret location!

SONIC THE HEDGEHOG #28:
"Saturday Night's Alright for a Fight"
Sonic, having lost his memory and being duped by Robotnik, has managed to
penetrate the defenses of Knothole and plans to
make quick work of his former allies. Is there anyone who can stand up to
our renegade rodent and help him see the error of his ways? Or has Sonic's
betrayal spelled the end for the good guys?!

"Growing Pains, Part I"
Angry at Sonic for turning against him, best friend Tails runs away
nd hops aboard his famous Sea Fox, the submarine which Rotor built for him.
Without the Freedom Fighters' permission, Tails sets course for an
uncharted island where he meets a helpless fox named
Fiona who has been captured by Robotnik. Tails' heart
skips a beat when he and Fiona Fox lock eyes,
but there's more to this "damsel in
distress" than meets the eye!

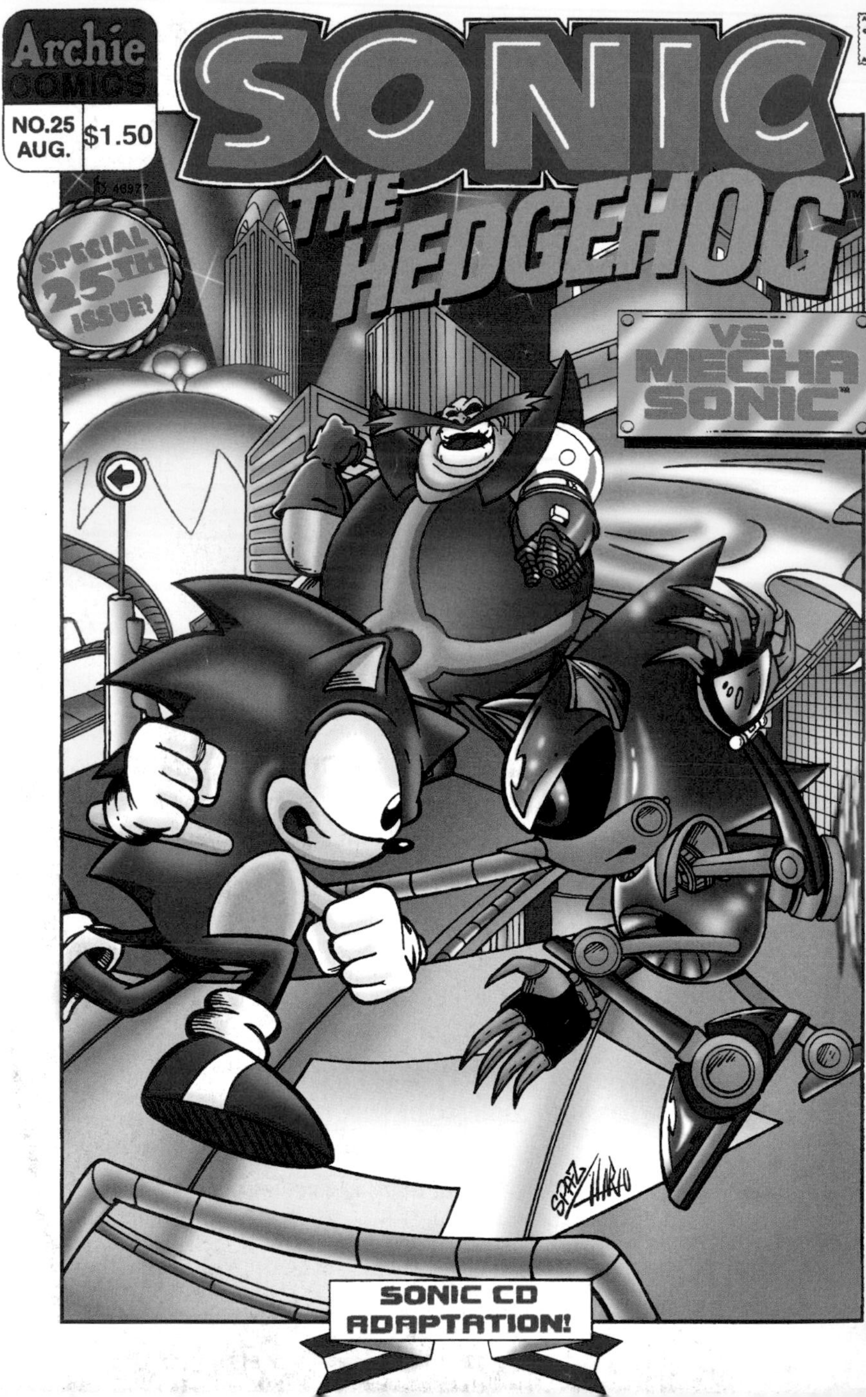
Archie
COMICS
NO.25
AUG.
$1.50
SONIC
THE
HEDGEHOG
SPECIAL
25TH
ISSUE!
VS.
MECHA
SONIC
SONIC CD
ADAPTATION!

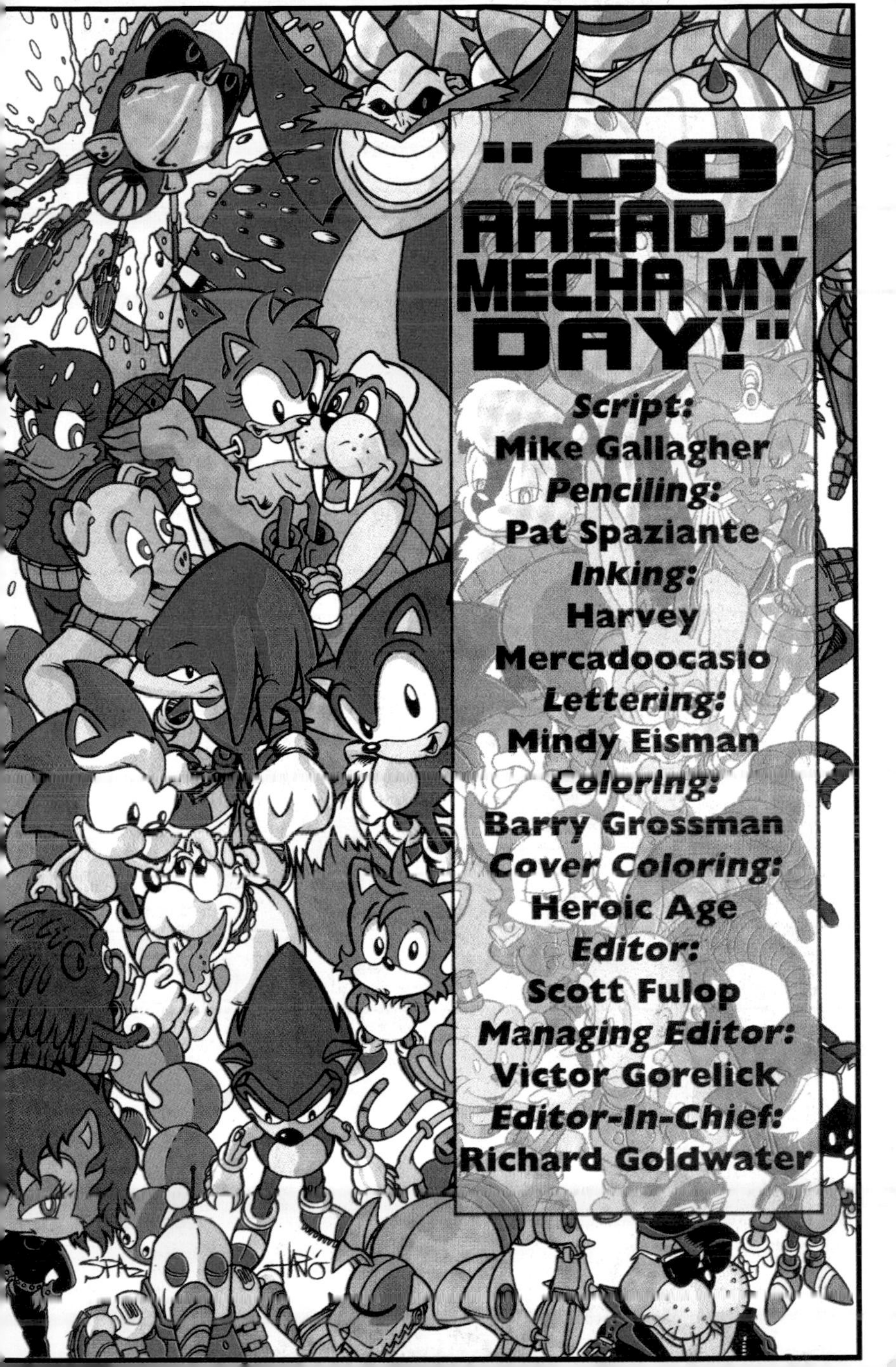
"GO AHEAD... MECHA MY DAY!"
Script:
Mike Gallagher
Penciling:
Pat Spaziante
Inking:
Harvey Mercadoocasio
Lettering:
Mindy Eisman
Coloring:
Barry Grossman
Cover Coloring:
Heroic Age
Editor:
Scott Fulop
Managing Editor:
Victor Gorelick
Editor-In-Chief:
Richard Goldwater

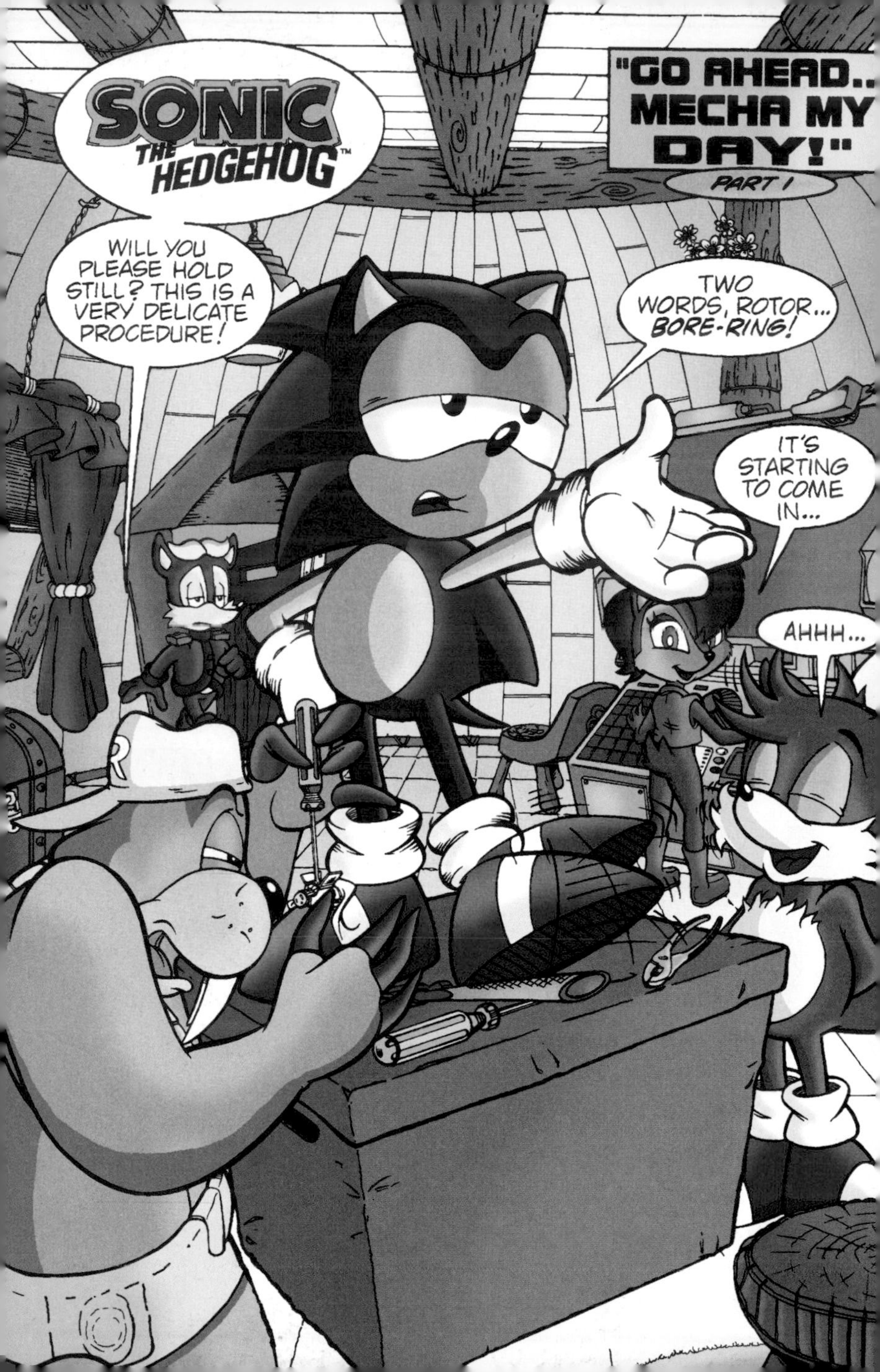
SONIC THE HEDGEHOG™
"GO AHEAD.. MECHA MY DAY!"
PART 1
WILL YOU PLEASE HOLD STILL? THIS IS A VERY DELICATE PROCEDURE!
TWO WORDS, ROTOR... BORE-RING!
IT'S STARTING TO COME IN...
AHHH...

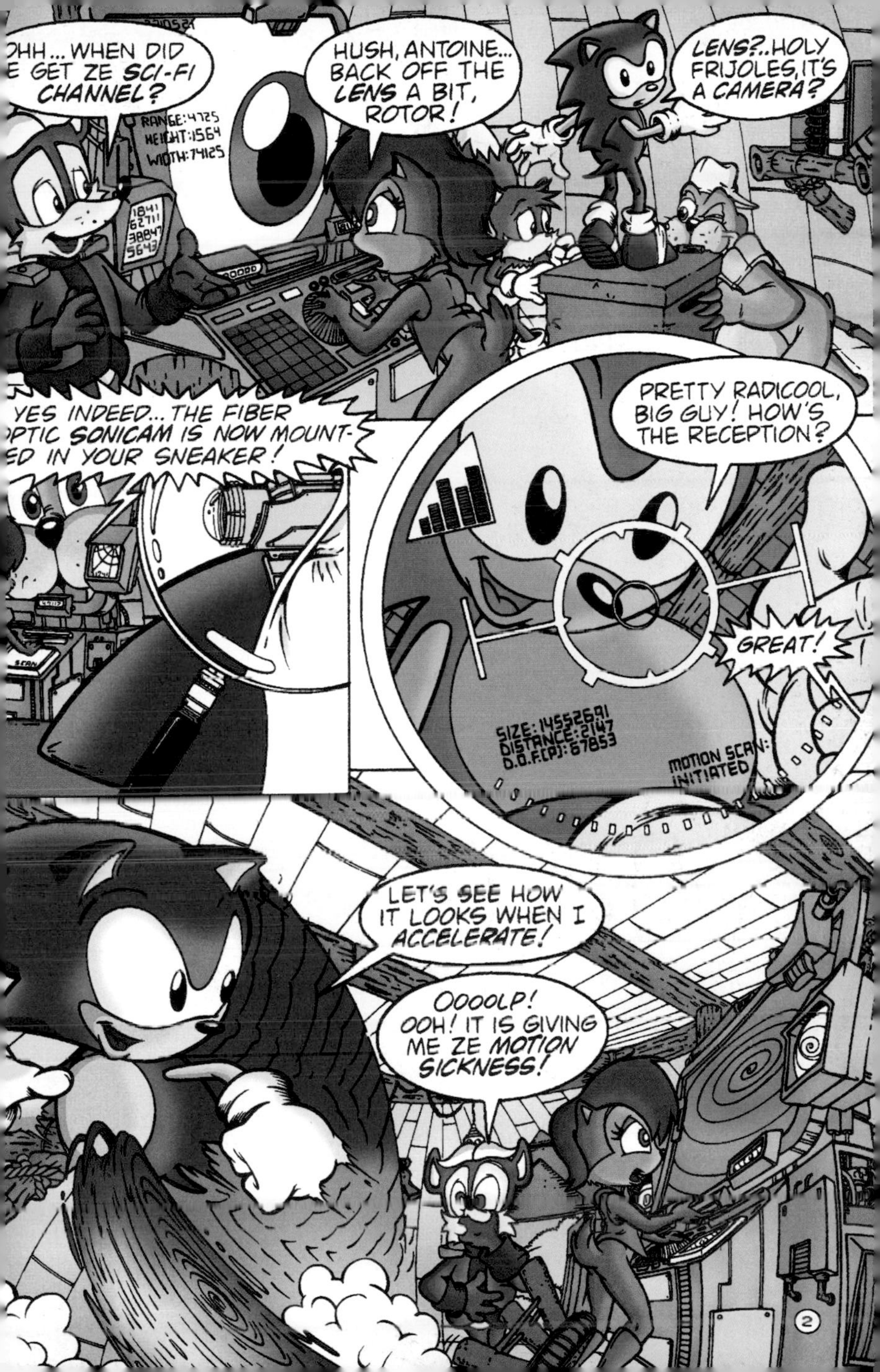

OHH... WHEN DID E GET ZE SCI-FI CHANNEL?
HUSH, ANTOINE... BACK OFF THE LENS A BIT, ROTOR!
LENS?..HOLY FRIJOLES, IT'S A CAMERA?
RANGE: 4725
HEIGHT: 1564
WIDTH: 74125
YES INDEED... THE FIBER PTIC SONICAM IS NOW MOUNT-ED IN YOUR SNEAKER!
PRETTY RADICOOL, BIG GUY! HOW'S THE RECEPTION?
GREAT!
SIZE: 14552691
DISTANCE: 2147
D.O.F.(P): 67853
MOTION SCAN: INITIATED
LET'S SEE HOW IT LOOKS WHEN I ACCELERATE!
OOOOLP! OOH! IT IS GIVING ME ZE MOTION SICKNESS!
2

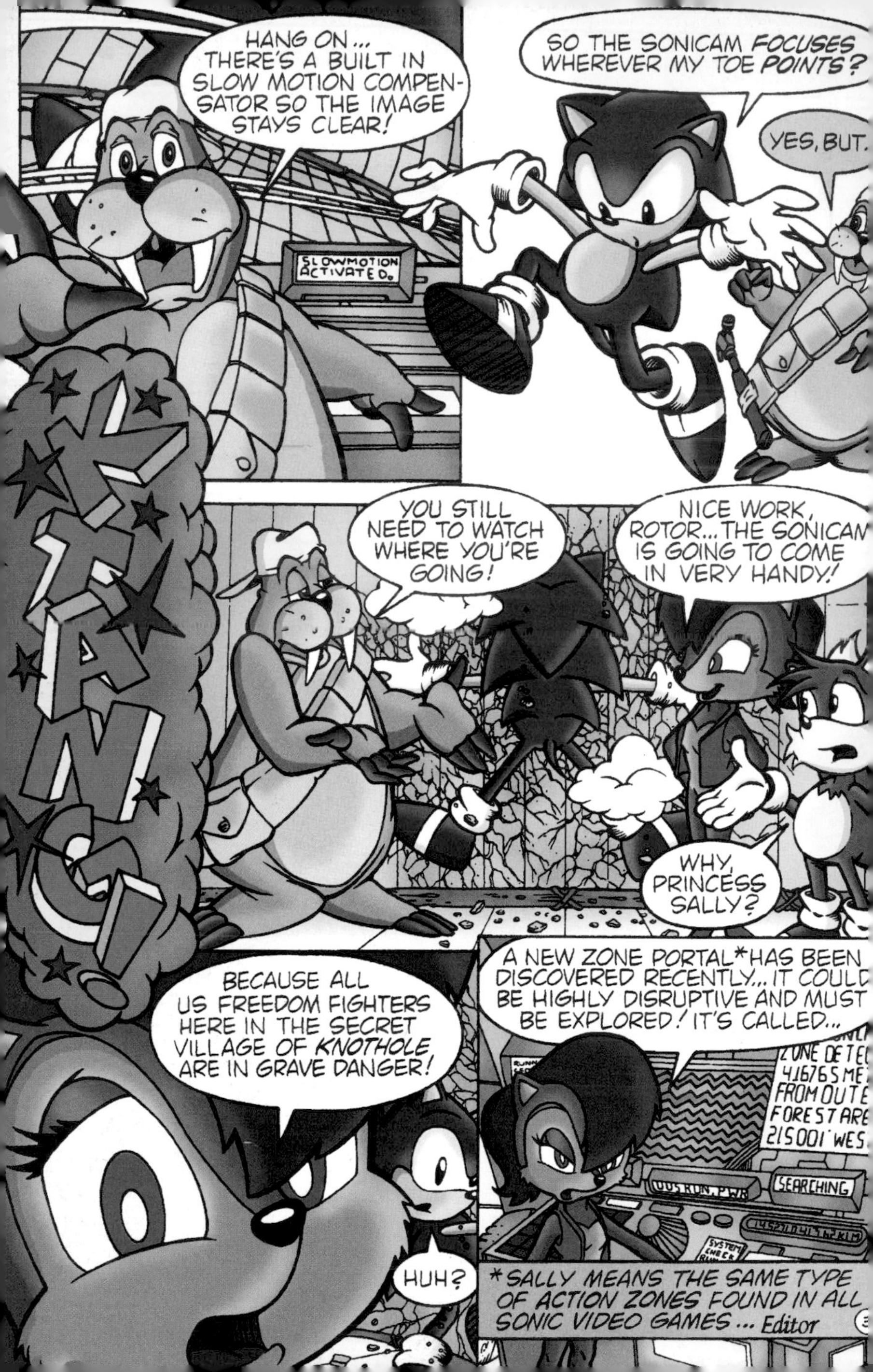
HANG ON... THERE'S A BUILT IN SLOW MOTION COMPEN-SATOR SO THE IMAGE STAYS CLEAR!
SLOWMOTION ACTIVATED.
SO THE SONICAM FOCUSES WHEREVER MY TOE POINTS?
YES, BUT...
YOU STILL NEED TO WATCH WHERE YOU'RE GOING!
NICE WORK, ROTOR... THE SONICAM IS GOING TO COME IN VERY HANDY!
WHY, PRINCESS SALLY?
BECAUSE ALL US FREEDOM FIGHTERS HERE IN THE SECRET VILLAGE OF KNOTHOLE ARE IN GRAVE DANGER!
HUH?
A NEW ZONE PORTAL* HAS BEEN DISCOVERED RECENTLY... IT COULD BE HIGHLY DISRUPTIVE AND MUST BE EXPLORED! IT'S CALLED...
SEARCHING
*SALLY MEANS THE SAME TYPE OF ACTION ZONES FOUND IN ALL SONIC VIDEO GAMES ... Editor

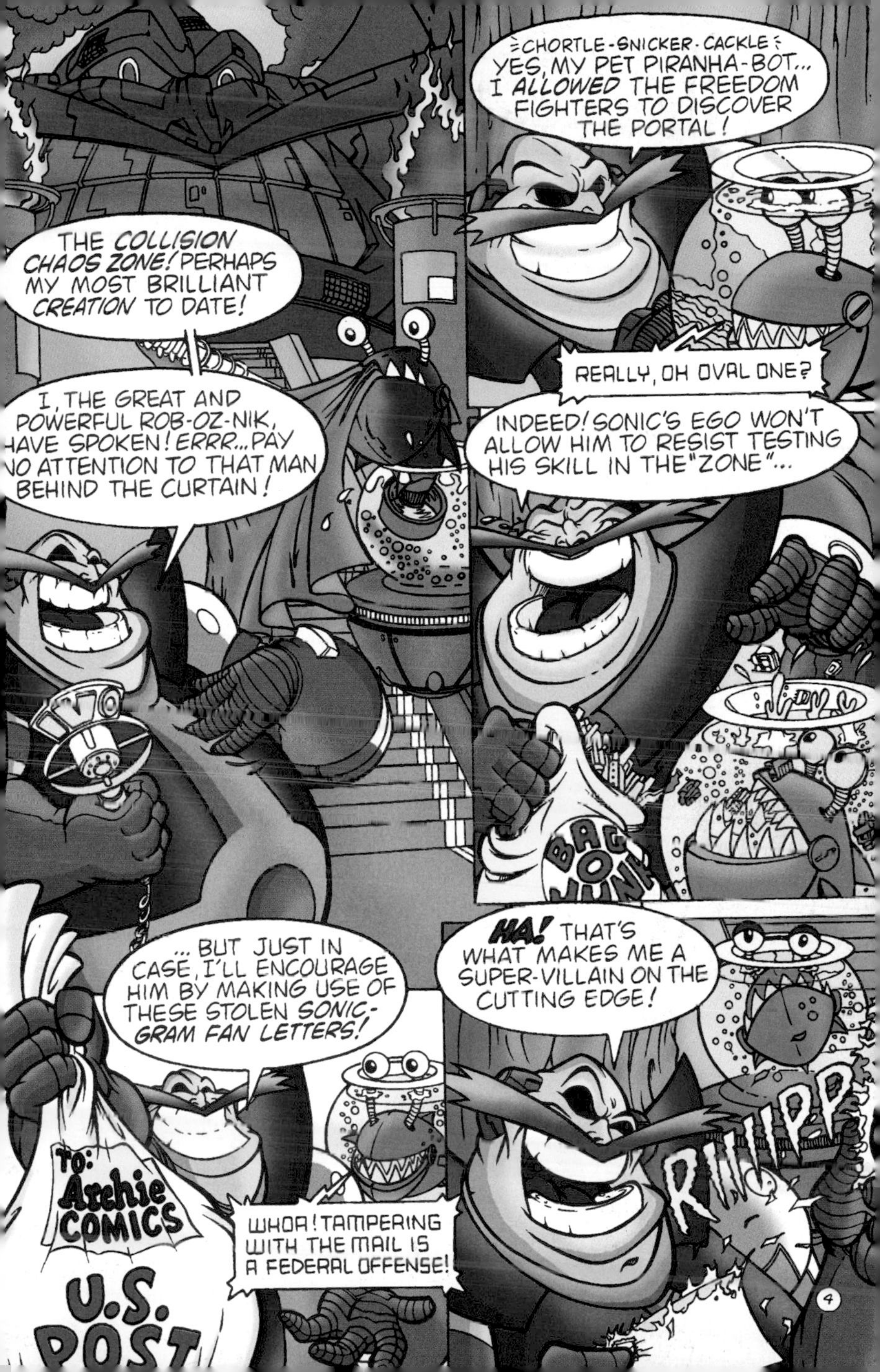
THE COLLISION CHAOS ZONE! PERHAPS MY MOST BRILLIANT CREATION TO DATE!
I, THE GREAT AND POWERFUL ROB-OZ-NIK, HAVE SPOKEN! ERRR...PAY NO ATTENTION TO THAT MAN BEHIND THE CURTAIN!
CHORTLE-SNICKER-CACKLE
YES, MY PET PIRANHA-BOT... I ALLOWED THE FREEDOM FIGHTERS TO DISCOVER THE PORTAL!
REALLY, OH OVAL ONE?
INDEED! SONIC'S EGO WON'T ALLOW HIM TO RESIST TESTING HIS SKILL IN THE "ZONE"...
BAG O JUNK
... BUT JUST IN CASE, I'LL ENCOURAGE HIM BY MAKING USE OF THESE STOLEN SONIC-GRAM FAN LETTERS!
To: Archie COMICS
U.S. POST
WHOA! TAMPERING WITH THE MAIL IS A FEDERAL OFFENSE!
HA! THAT'S WHAT MAKES ME A SUPER-VILLAIN ON THE CUTTING EDGE!
RIIIPP

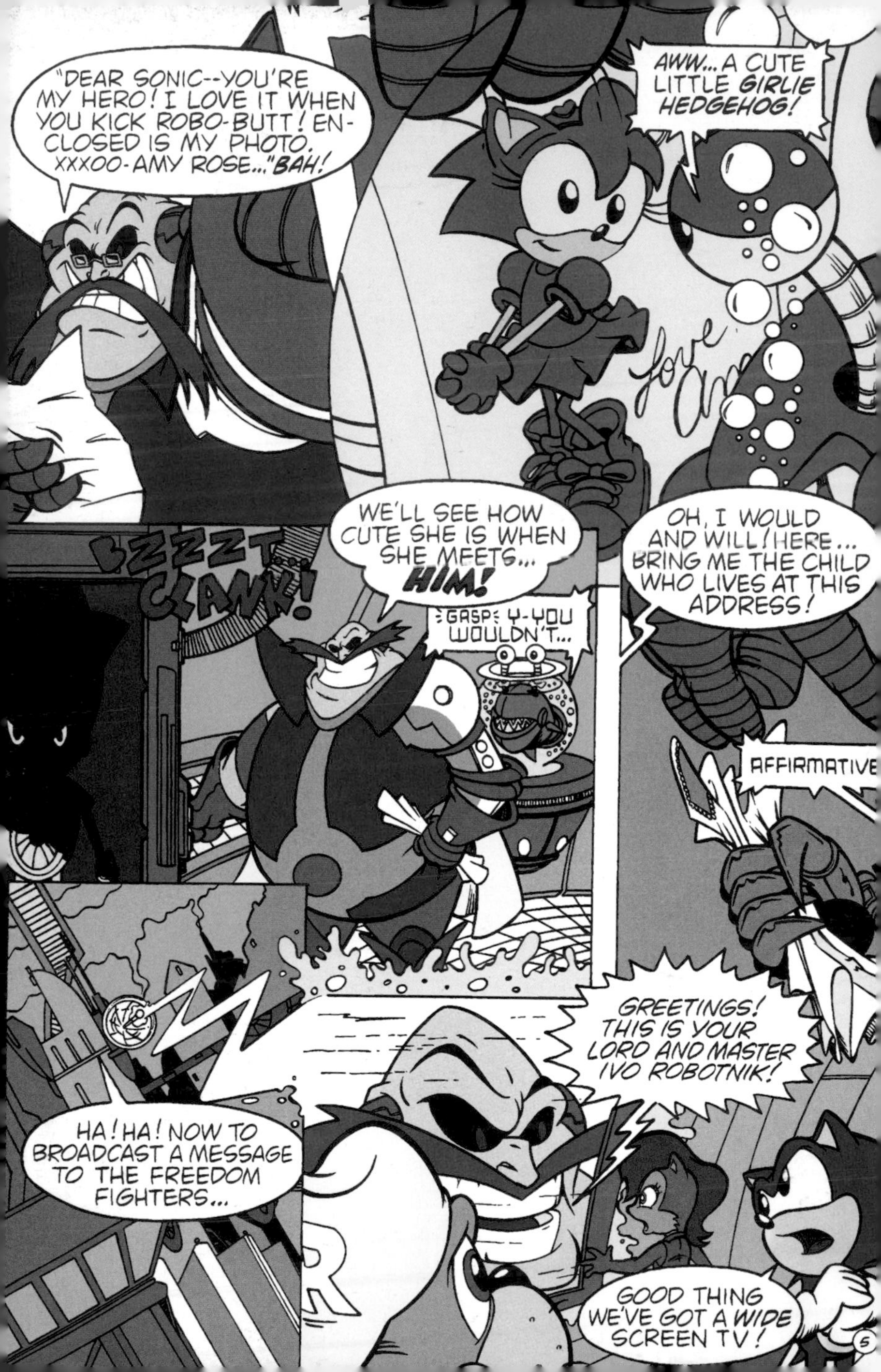
"DEAR SONIC--YOU'RE MY HERO! I LOVE IT WHEN YOU KICK ROBO-BUTT! EN-CLOSED IS MY PHOTO. XXXOO-AMY ROSE..." BAH!
AWW...A CUTE LITTLE GIRLIE HEDGEHOG!
Love Am
BZZZT... CLANK!
WE'LL SEE HOW CUTE SHE IS WHEN SHE MEETS... HIM!
GASP Y-YOU WOULDN'T...
OH, I WOULD AND WILL! HERE... BRING ME THE CHILD WHO LIVES AT THIS ADDRESS!
AFFIRMATIVE
HA! HA! NOW TO BROADCAST A MESSAGE TO THE FREEDOM FIGHTERS...
GREETINGS! THIS IS YOUR LORD AND MASTER IVO ROBOTNIK!
GOOD THING WE'VE GOT A WIDE SCREEN TV!

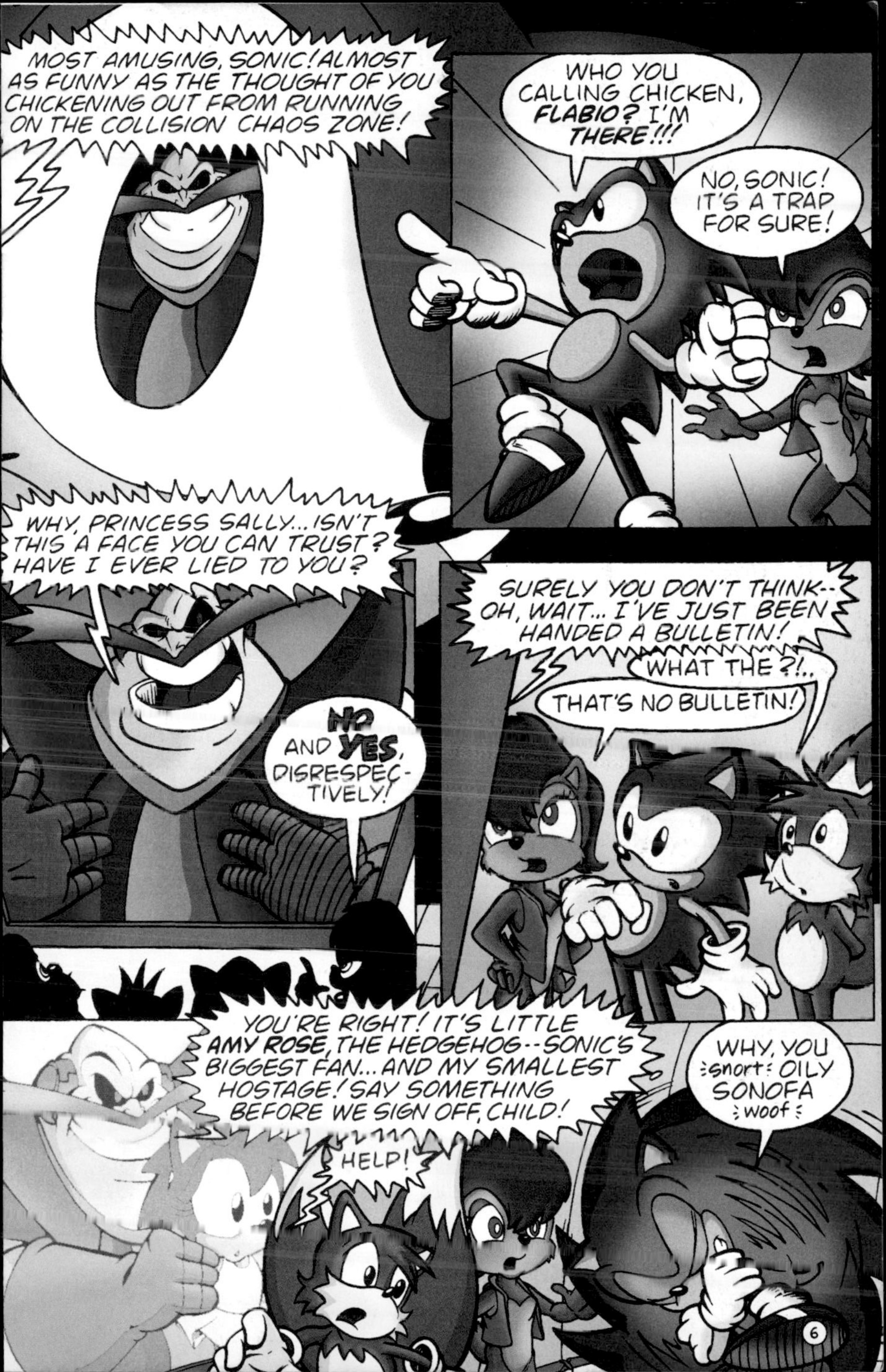
MOST AMUSING, SONIC! ALMOST AS FUNNY AS THE THOUGHT OF YOU CHICKENING OUT FROM RUNNING ON THE COLLISION CHAOS ZONE!
WHO YOU CALLING CHICKEN, FLABIO? I'M THERE!!!
NO, SONIC! IT'S A TRAP FOR SURE!
WHY, PRINCESS SALLY... ISN'T THIS A FACE YOU CAN TRUST? HAVE I EVER LIED TO YOU?
NO AND YES, DISRESPEC-TIVELY!
SURELY YOU DON'T THINK-- OH, WAIT... I'VE JUST BEEN HANDED A BULLETIN!
WHAT THE ?!..
THAT'S NO BULLETIN!
YOU'RE RIGHT! IT'S LITTLE AMY ROSE, THE HEDGEHOG--SONIC'S BIGGEST FAN... AND MY SMALLEST HOSTAGE! SAY SOMETHING BEFORE WE SIGN OFF, CHILD!
HELP!
WHY, YOU snort OILY SONOFA woof
6

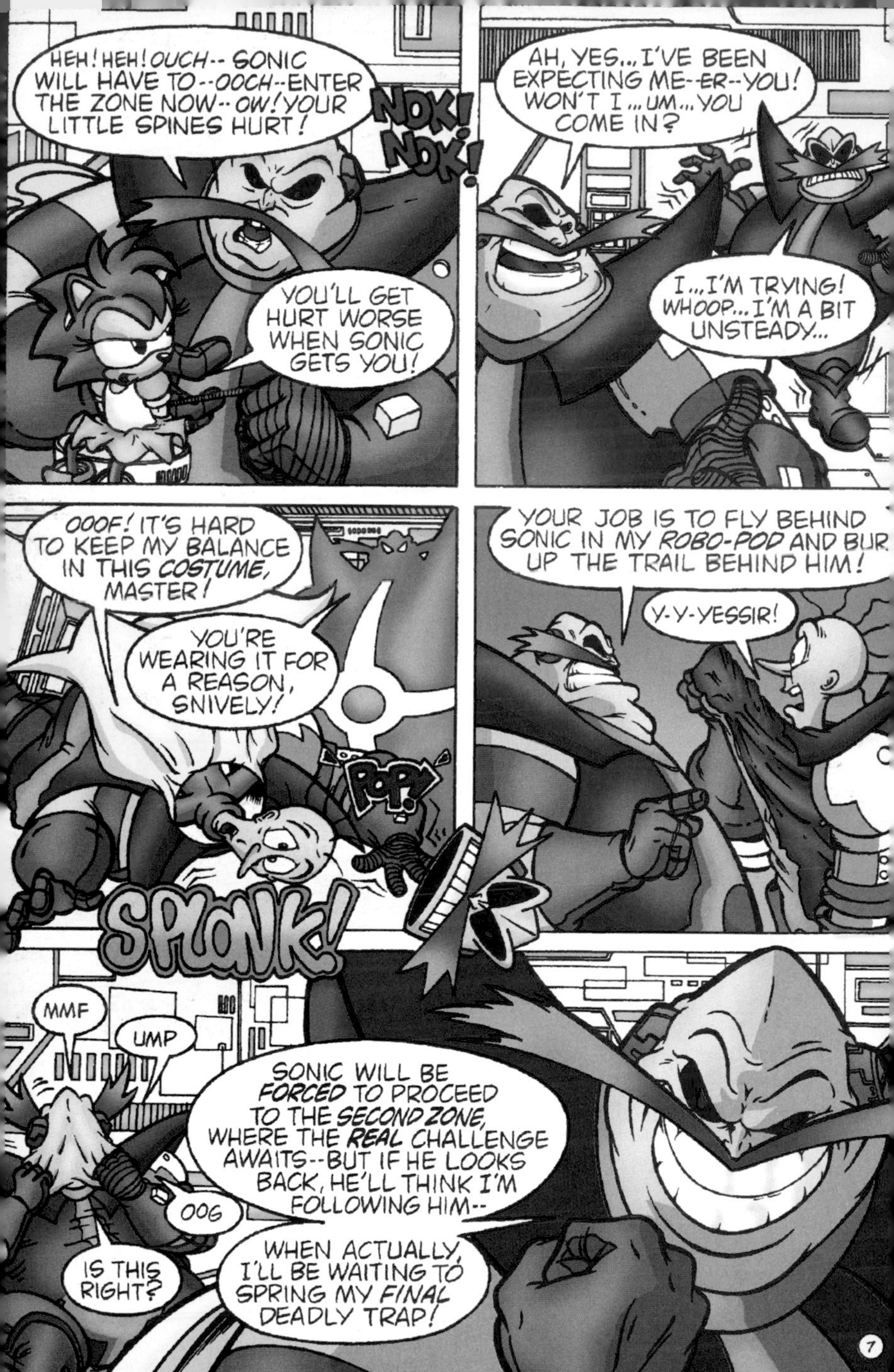

HEH! HEH! OUCH-- SONIC WILL HAVE TO--OOCH--ENTER THE ZONE NOW--OW! YOUR LITTLE SPINES HURT!
YOU'LL GET HURT WORSE WHEN SONIC GETS YOU!
NOK! NOK!
AH, YES... I'VE BEEN EXPECTING ME--ER--YOU! WON'T I... UM... YOU COME IN?
I... I'M TRYING! WHOOP... I'M A BIT UNSTEADY...
OOOF! IT'S HARD TO KEEP MY BALANCE IN THIS COSTUME, MASTER!
YOU'RE WEARING IT FOR A REASON, SNIVELY!
POP!
SPLONK!
YOUR JOB IS TO FLY BEHIND SONIC IN MY ROBO-POD AND BUR UP THE TRAIL BEHIND HIM!
Y-Y-YESSIR!
MMF
UMP
SONIC WILL BE FORCED TO PROCEED TO THE SECOND ZONE, WHERE THE REAL CHALLENGE AWAITS--BUT IF HE LOOKS BACK, HE'LL THINK I'M FOLLOWING HIM--
OOG
IS THIS RIGHT?
WHEN ACTUALLY, I'LL BE WAITING TO SPRING MY FINAL DEADLY TRAP!

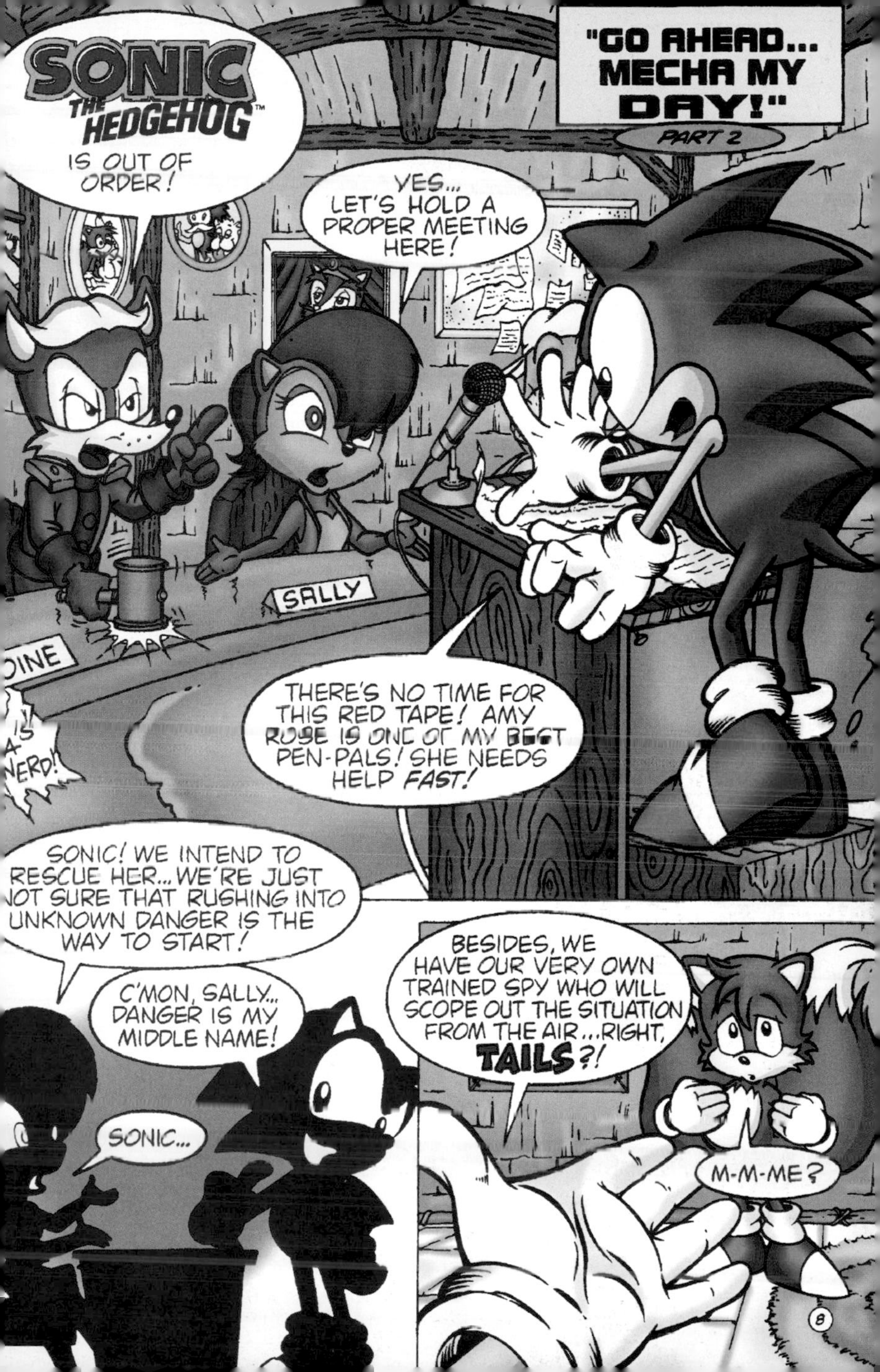
SONIC THE HEDGEHOG IS OUT OF ORDER!
"GO AHEAD... MECHA MY DAY!"
PART 2
YES... LET'S HOLD A PROPER MEETING HERE!
SALLY
THERE'S NO TIME FOR THIS RED TAPE! AMY ROSE IS ONE OF MY BEST PEN-PALS! SHE NEEDS HELP FAST!
SONIC! WE INTEND TO RESCUE HER... WE'RE JUST NOT SURE THAT RUSHING INTO UNKNOWN DANGER IS THE WAY TO START!
C'MON, SALLY... DANGER IS MY MIDDLE NAME!
SONIC...
BESIDES, WE HAVE OUR VERY OWN TRAINED SPY WHO WILL SCOPE OUT THE SITUATION FROM THE AIR... RIGHT, TAILS?!
M-M-ME?

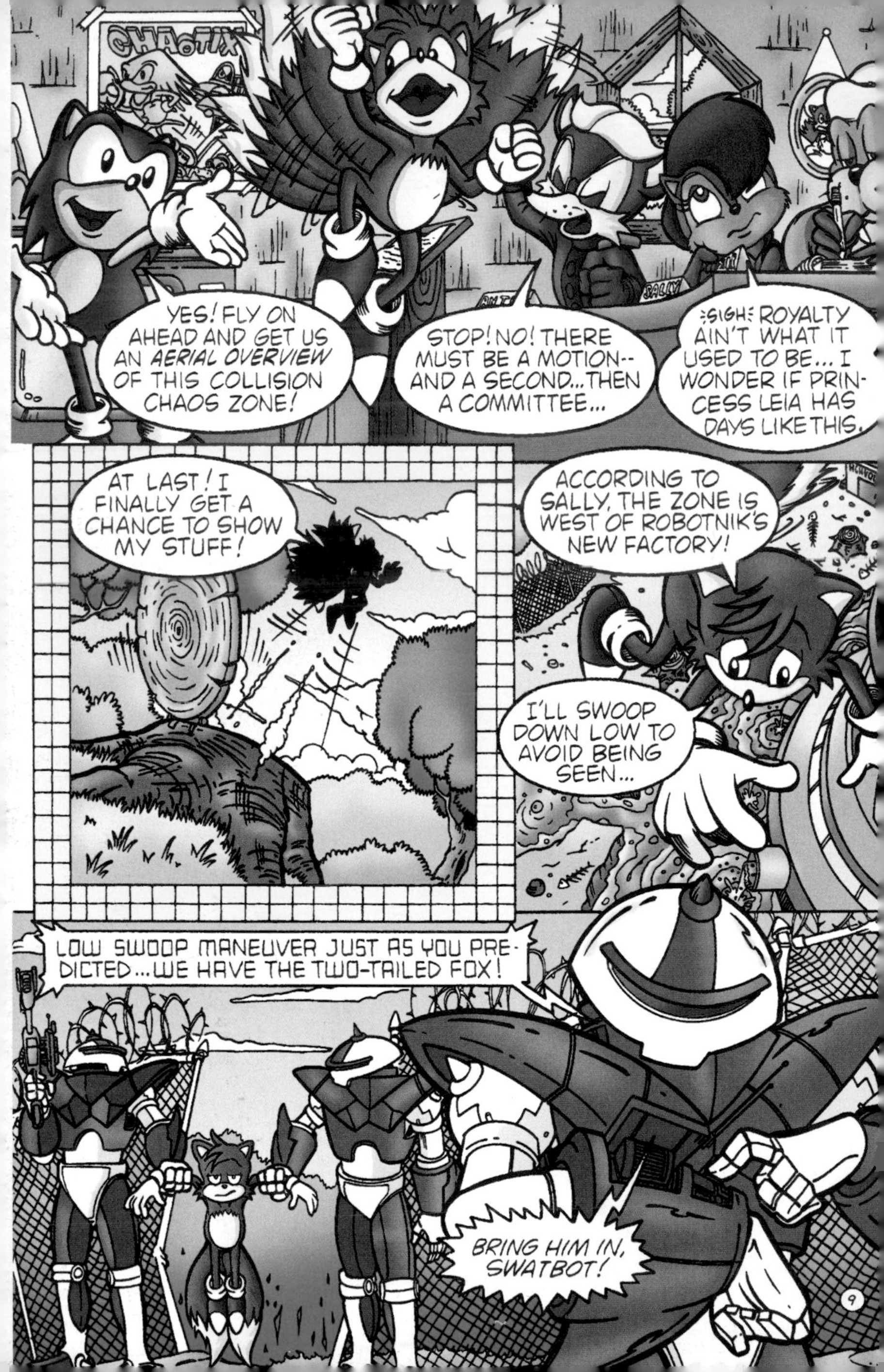
YES! FLY ON AHEAD AND GET US AN *AERIAL OVERVIEW* OF THIS COLLISION CHAOS ZONE!
STOP! NO! THERE MUST BE A MOTION-- AND A SECOND...THEN A COMMITTEE...
SIGH ROYALTY AIN'T WHAT IT USED TO BE... I WONDER IF PRINCESS LEIA HAS DAYS LIKE THIS.
SALLY
AT LAST! I FINALLY GET A CHANCE TO SHOW MY STUFF!
ACCORDING TO SALLY, THE ZONE IS WEST OF ROBOTNIK'S NEW FACTORY!
I'LL SWOOP DOWN LOW TO AVOID BEING SEEN...
LOW SWOOP MANEUVER JUST AS YOU PREDICTED...WE HAVE THE TWO-TAILED FOX!
BRING HIM IN, SWATBOT!

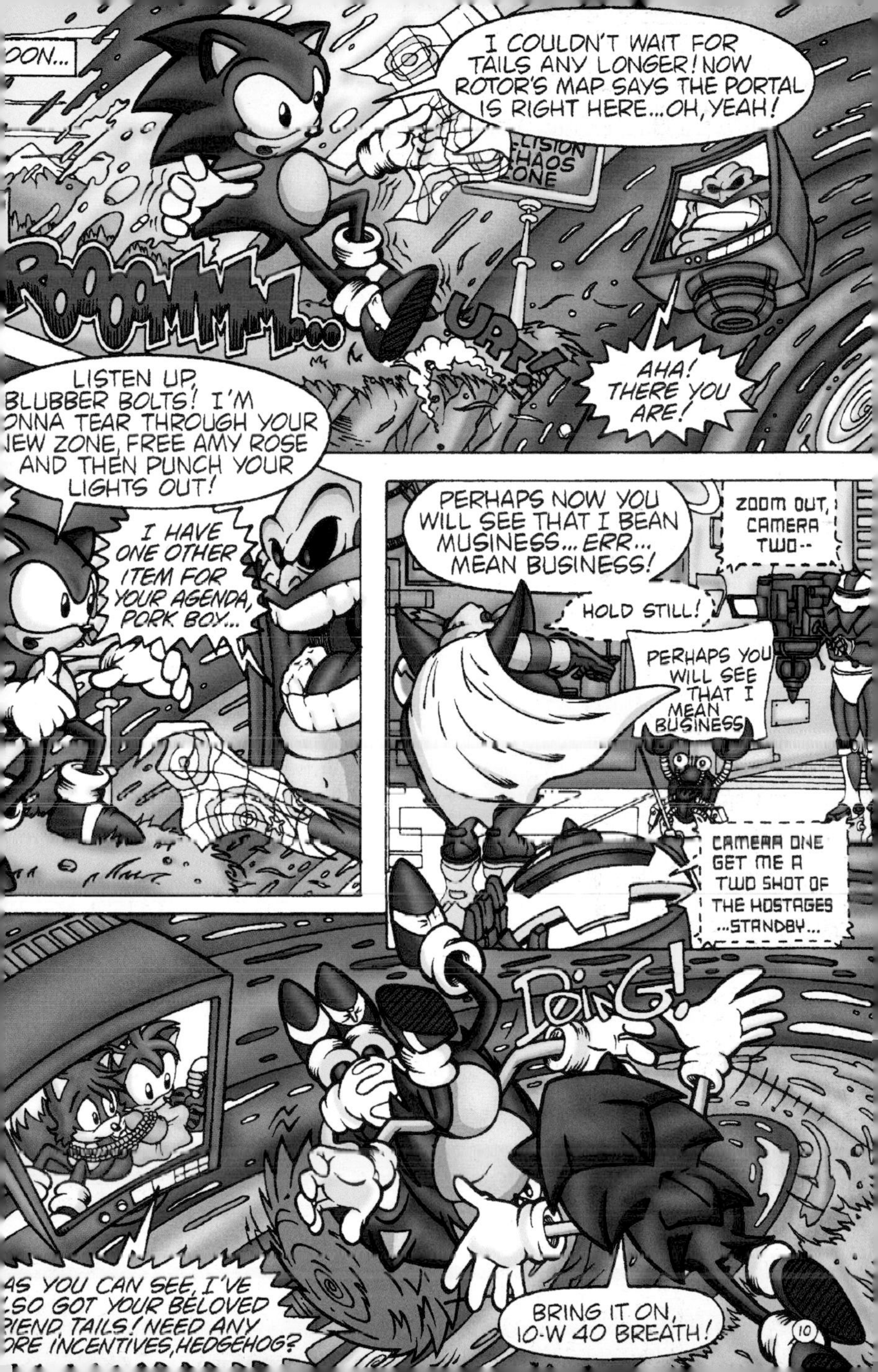

OON...
I COULDN'T WAIT FOR TAILS ANY LONGER! NOW ROTOR'S MAP SAYS THE PORTAL IS RIGHT HERE...OH, YEAH!
ELISION HAOS ZONE
ROOOMMM...
URK!
AHA! THERE YOU ARE!
LISTEN UP, BLUBBER BOLTS! I'M ONNA TEAR THROUGH YOUR JEW ZONE, FREE AMY ROSE AND THEN PUNCH YOUR LIGHTS OUT!
I HAVE ONE OTHER ITEM FOR YOUR AGENDA, PORK BOY...
PERHAPS NOW YOU WILL SEE THAT I BEAN MUSINESS... ERR... MEAN BUSINESS!
ZOOM OUT, CAMERA TWO--
HOLD STILL!
PERHAPS YOU WILL SEE THAT I MEAN BUSINESS
CAMERA ONE GET ME A TWO SHOT OF THE HOSTAGES ...STANDBY...
DOING!
AS YOU CAN SEE, I'VE SO GOT YOUR BELOVED RIEND TAILS! NEED ANY ORE INCENTIVES, HEDGEHOG?
BRING IT ON, 10-W 40 BREATH!

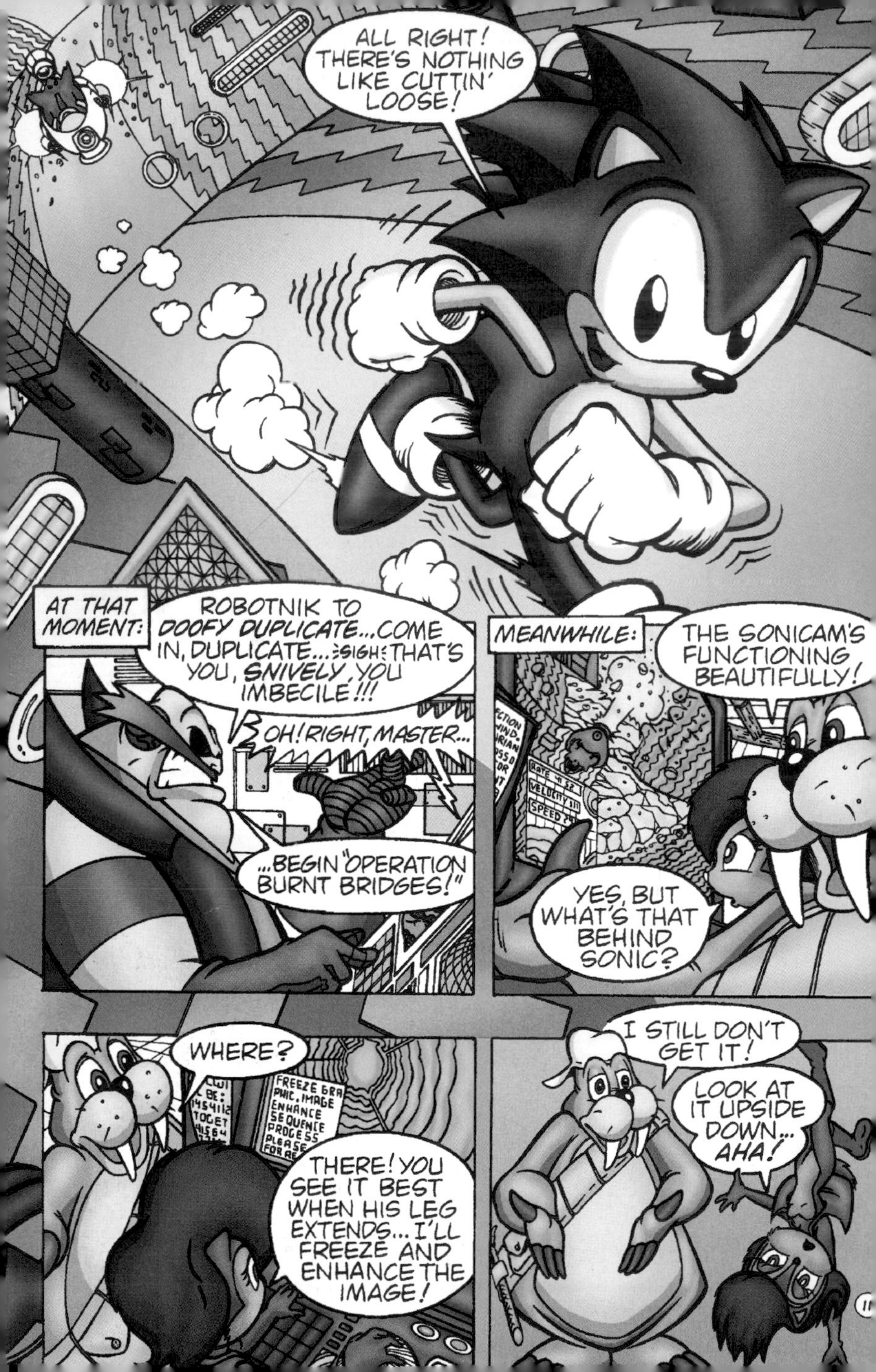

ALL RIGHT! THERE'S NOTHING LIKE CUTTIN' LOOSE!
AT THAT MOMENT:
ROBOTNIK TO DOOFY DUPLICATE...COME IN, DUPLICATE...SIGH THAT'S YOU, SNIVELY, YOU IMBECILE!!!
OH! RIGHT, MASTER...
...BEGIN "OPERATION BURNT BRIDGES!"
MEANWHILE:
THE SONICAM'S FUNCTIONING BEAUTIFULLY!
YES, BUT WHAT'S THAT BEHIND SONIC?
WHERE?
FREEZE GRAPHIC IMAGE ENHANCE SEQUENCE PROGRESS PLEASE
THERE! YOU SEE IT BEST WHEN HIS LEG EXTENDS... I'LL FREEZE AND ENHANCE THE IMAGE!
I STILL DON'T GET IT!
LOOK AT IT UPSIDE DOWN... AHA!

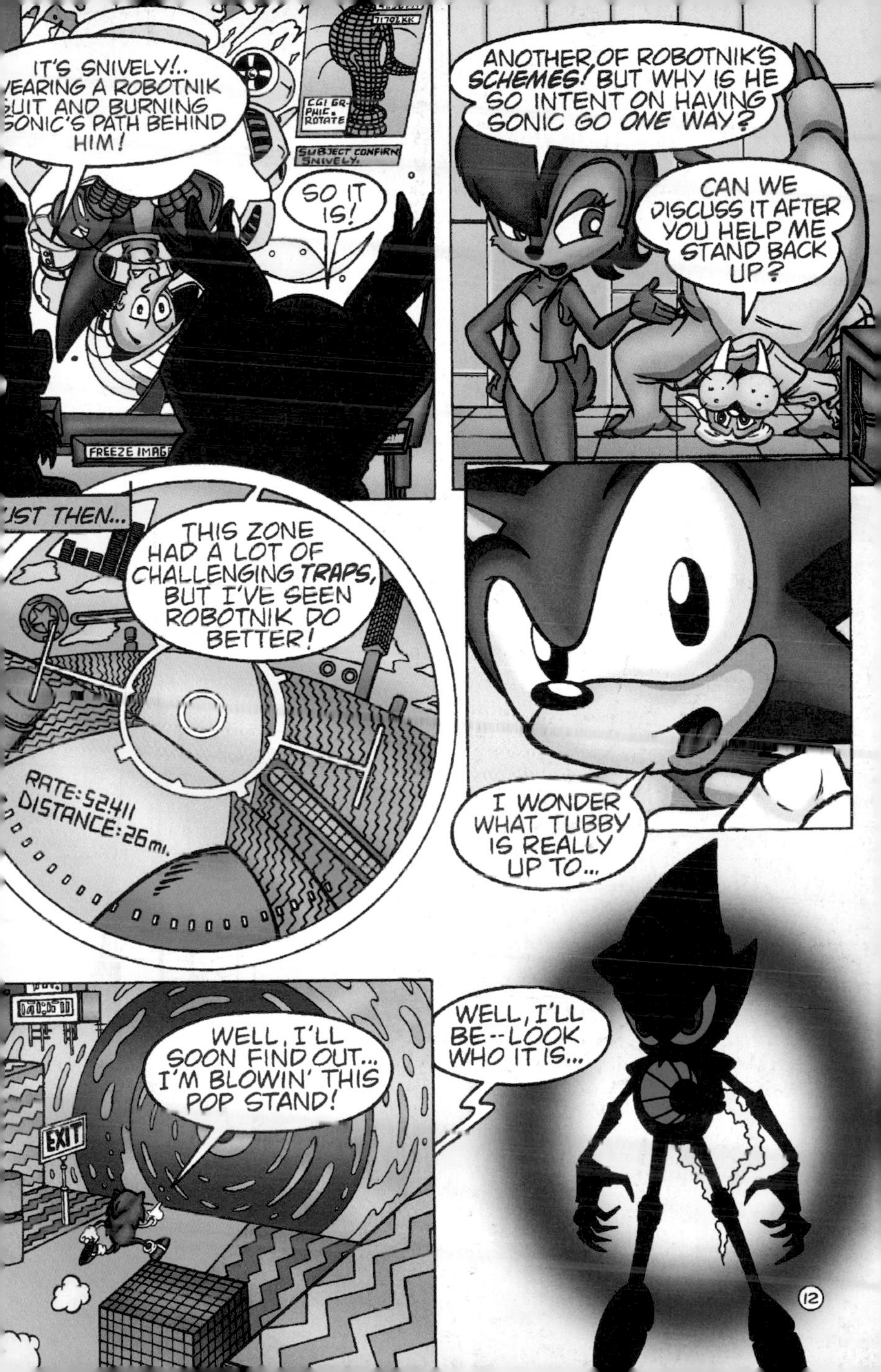

IT'S SNIVELY!.. WEARING A ROBOTNIK SUIT AND BURNING SONIC'S PATH BEHIND HIM!
CGI GRAPHIC ROTATE
SUBJECT CONFIRM SNIVELY.
SO IT IS!
FREEZE IMAGE
ANOTHER OF ROBOTNIK'S SCHEMES! BUT WHY IS HE SO INTENT ON HAVING SONIC GO ONE WAY?
CAN WE DISCUSS IT AFTER YOU HELP ME STAND BACK UP?
JUST THEN...
THIS ZONE HAD A LOT OF CHALLENGING TRAPS, BUT I'VE SEEN ROBOTNIK DO BETTER!
RATE: 52.411
DISTANCE: 26 mi.
I WONDER WHAT TUBBY IS REALLY UP TO...
WELL, I'LL SOON FIND OUT... I'M BLOWIN' THIS POP STAND!
EXIT
WELL, I'LL BE--LOOK WHO IT IS...

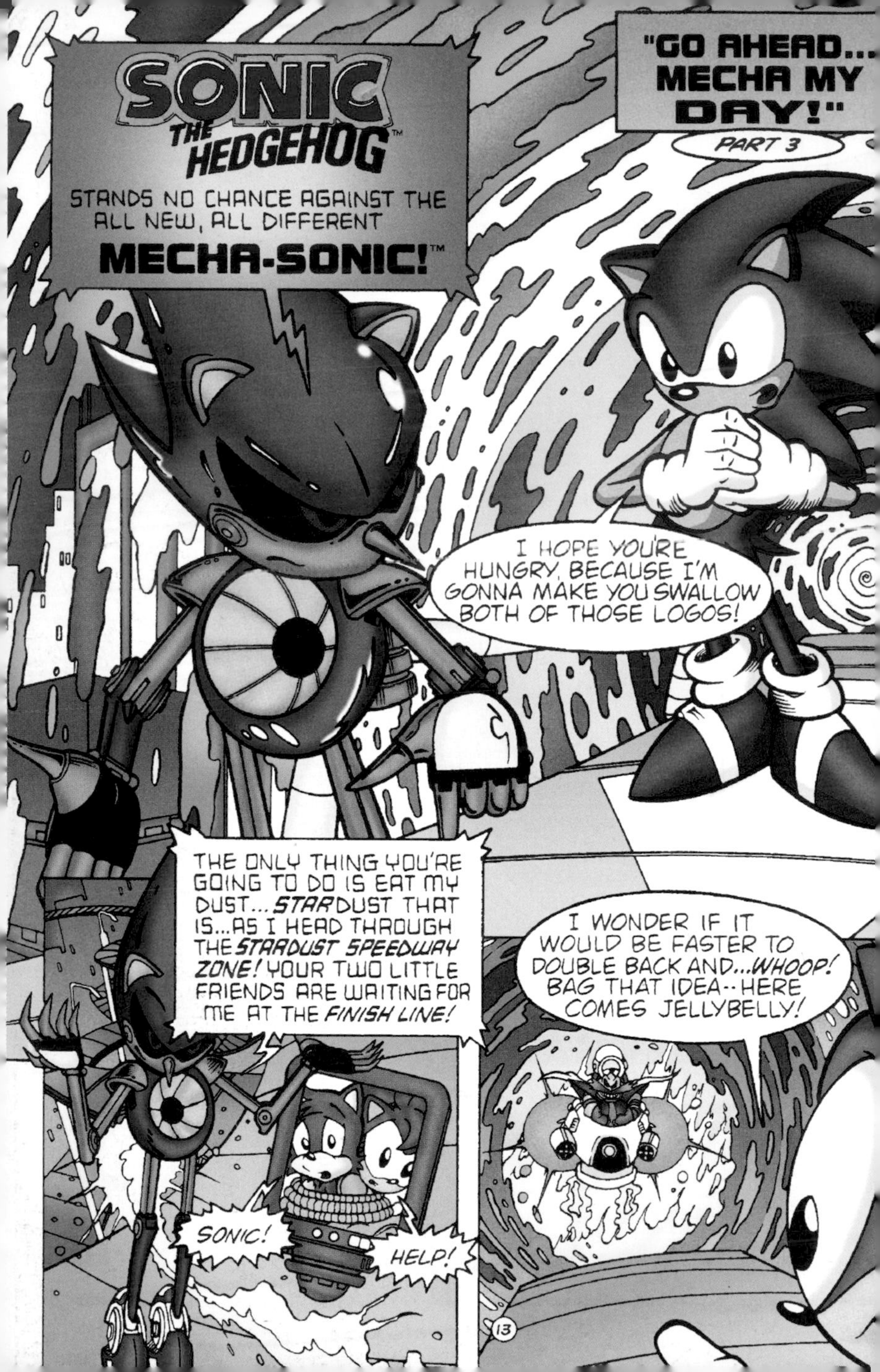
SONIC THE HEDGEHOG™
STANDS NO CHANCE AGAINST THE ALL NEW, ALL DIFFERENT
MECHA-SONIC!™
"GO AHEAD... MECHA MY DAY!"
PART 3
I HOPE YOU'RE HUNGRY, BECAUSE I'M GONNA MAKE YOU SWALLOW BOTH OF THOSE LOGOS!
THE ONLY THING YOU'RE GOING TO DO IS EAT MY DUST... STARDUST THAT IS...AS I HEAD THROUGH THE STARDUST SPEEDWAY ZONE! YOUR TWO LITTLE FRIENDS ARE WAITING FOR ME AT THE FINISH LINE!
SONIC!
HELP!
I WONDER IF IT WOULD BE FASTER TO DOUBLE BACK AND...WHOOP! BAG THAT IDEA-- HERE COMES JELLYBELLY!

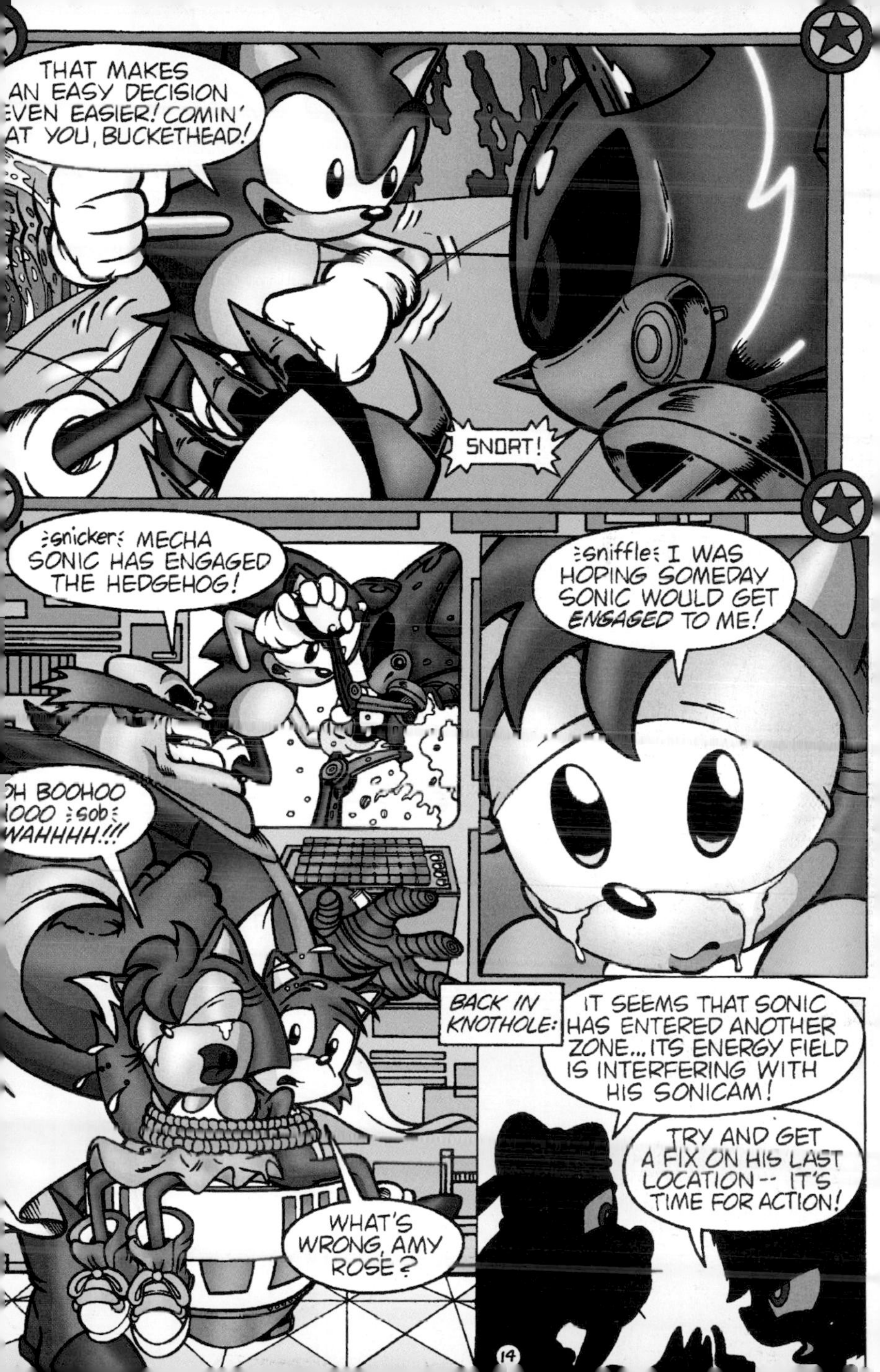
THAT MAKES AN EASY DECISION EVEN EASIER! COMIN' AT YOU, BUCKETHEAD!
SNORT!
snicker MECHA SONIC HAS ENGAGED THE HEDGEHOG!
sniffle I WAS HOPING SOMEDAY SONIC WOULD GET ENGAGED TO ME!
OH BOOHOO HOOO sob WAHHHH!!!
WHAT'S WRONG, AMY ROSE?
BACK IN KNOTHOLE:
IT SEEMS THAT SONIC HAS ENTERED ANOTHER ZONE...ITS ENERGY FIELD IS INTERFERING WITH HIS SONICAM!
TRY AND GET A FIX ON HIS LAST LOCATION -- IT'S TIME FOR ACTION!
14

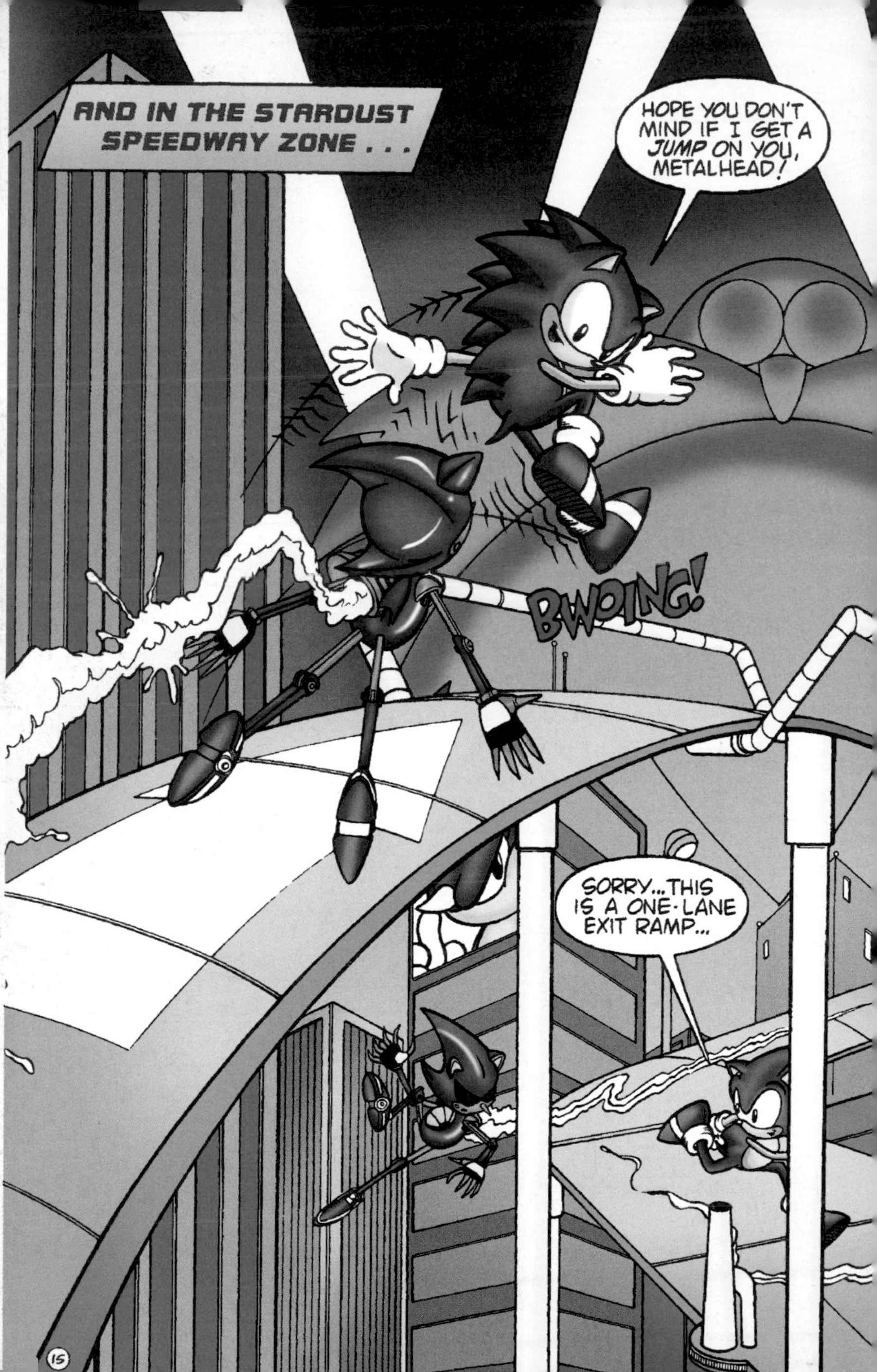
AND IN THE STARDUST SPEEDWAY ZONE . . .
HOPE YOU DON'T MIND IF I GET A JUMP ON YOU, METALHEAD!
BWOING!
SORRY...THIS IS A ONE-LANE EXIT RAMP...

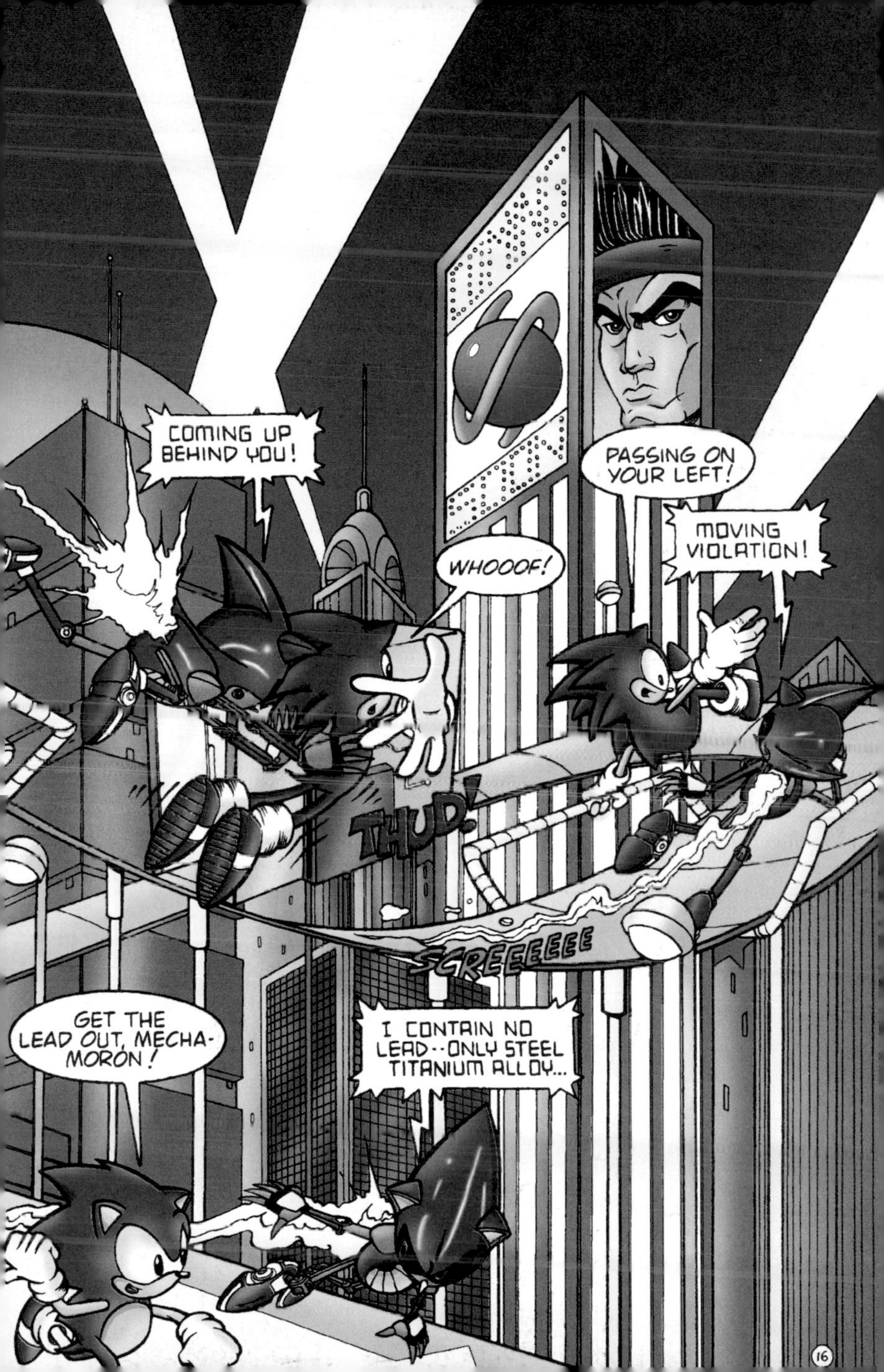
COMING UP BEHIND YOU!
PASSING ON YOUR LEFT!
MOVING VIOLATION!
WHOOOF!
THUD!
SCREEEEEE
GET THE LEAD OUT, MECHA-MORON!
I CONTAIN NO LEAD--ONLY STEEL TITANIUM ALLOY...

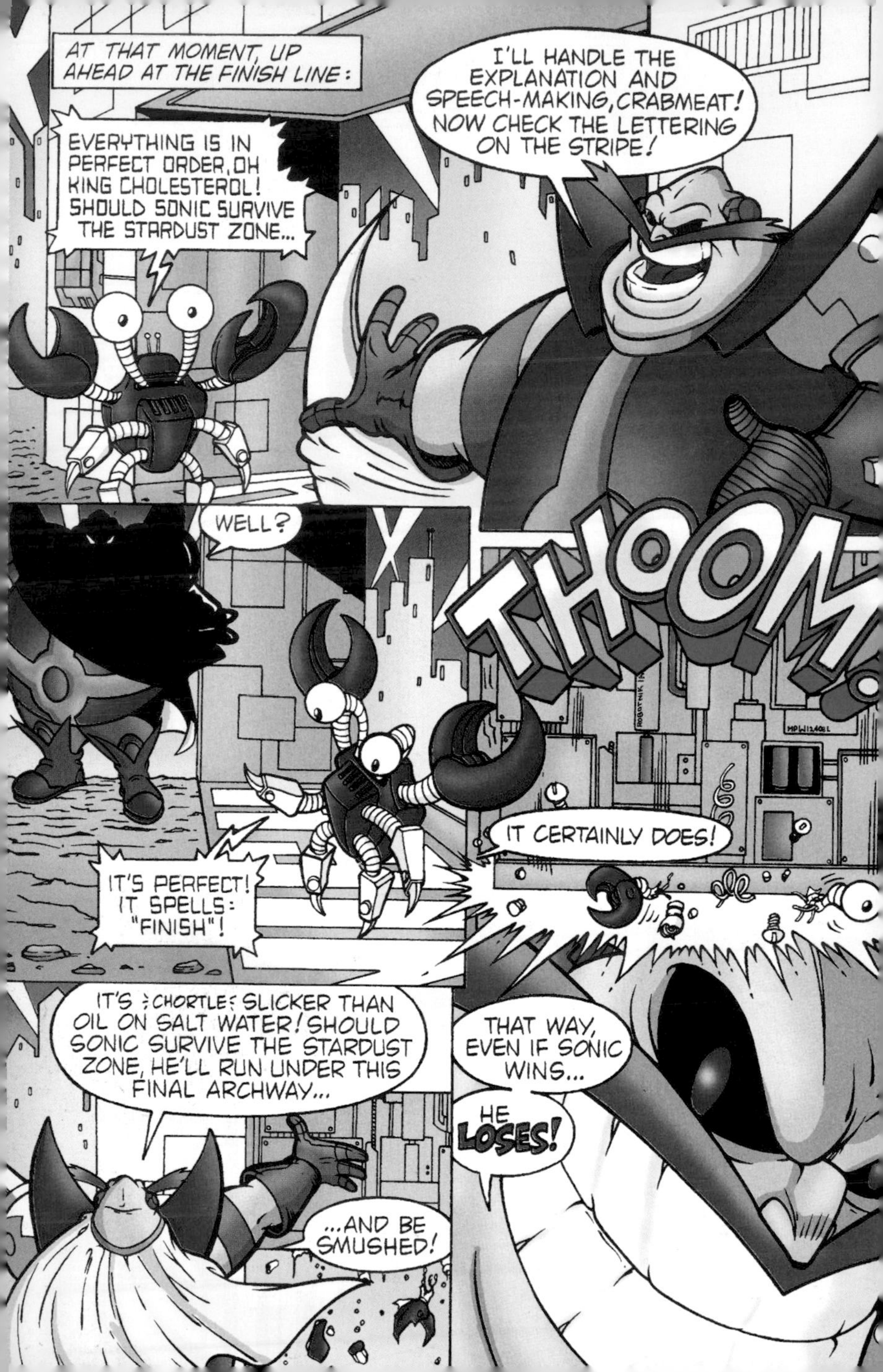
AT THAT MOMENT, UP AHEAD AT THE FINISH LINE:
EVERYTHING IS IN PERFECT ORDER, OH KING CHOLESTEROL! SHOULD SONIC SURVIVE THE STARDUST ZONE...
I'LL HANDLE THE EXPLANATION AND SPEECH-MAKING, CRABMEAT! NOW CHECK THE LETTERING ON THE STRIPE!
WELL?
IT'S PERFECT! IT SPELLS: "FINISH"!
THOOM!
IT CERTAINLY DOES!
IT'S ⋮CHORTLE⋮ SLICKER THAN OIL ON SALT WATER! SHOULD SONIC SURVIVE THE STARDUST ZONE, HE'LL RUN UNDER THIS FINAL ARCHWAY...
...AND BE SMUSHED!
THAT WAY, EVEN IF SONIC WINS...
HE LOSES!

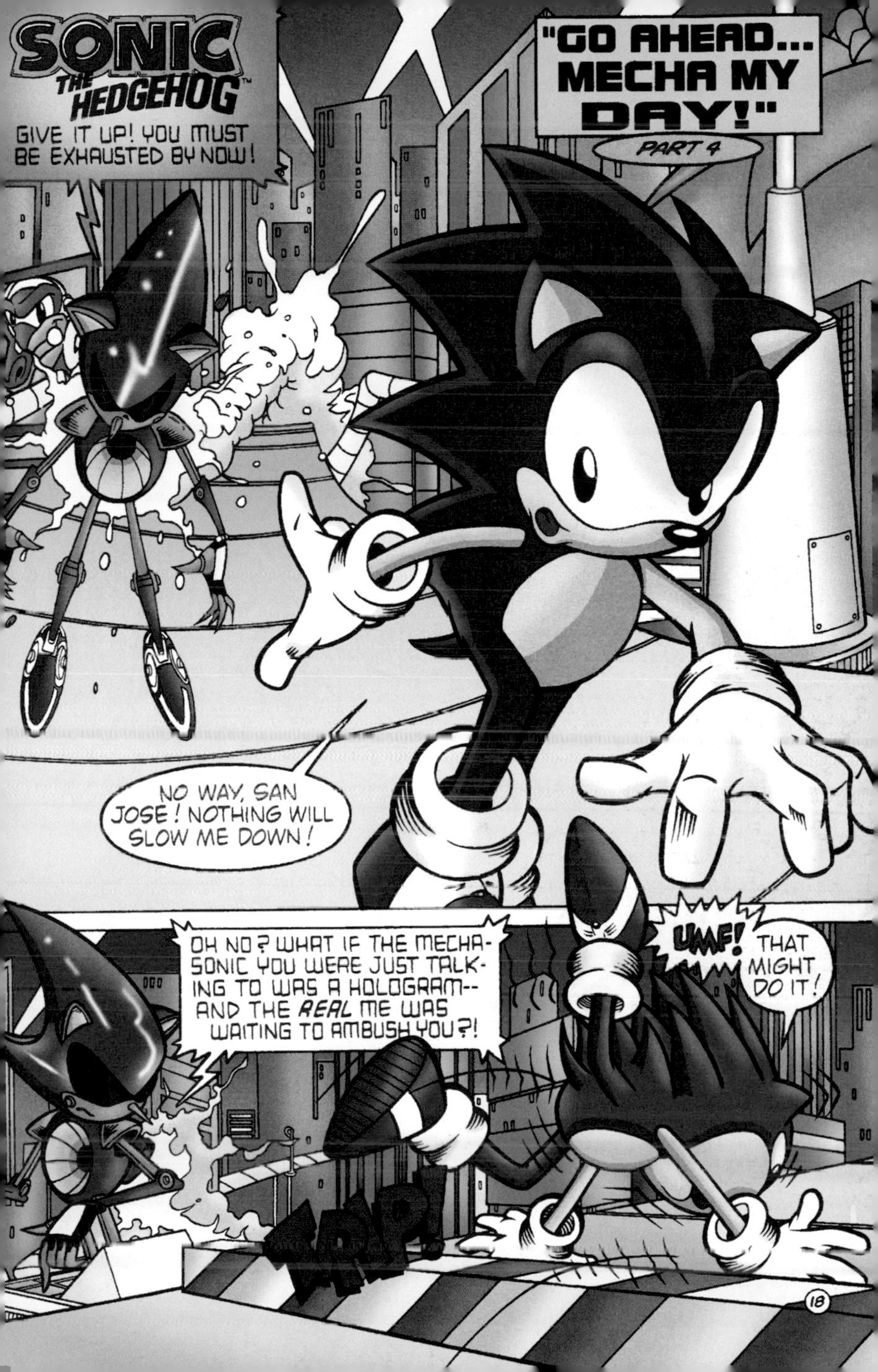
SONIC THE HEDGEHOG™
"GO AHEAD... MECHA MY DAY!"
PART 4
GIVE IT UP! YOU MUST BE EXHAUSTED BY NOW!
NO WAY, SAN JOSE! NOTHING WILL SLOW ME DOWN!
OH NO? WHAT IF THE MECHA-SONIC YOU WERE JUST TALKING TO WAS A HOLOGRAM-- AND THE REAL ME WAS WAITING TO AMBUSH YOU?!
UMF!
THAT MIGHT DO IT!
18

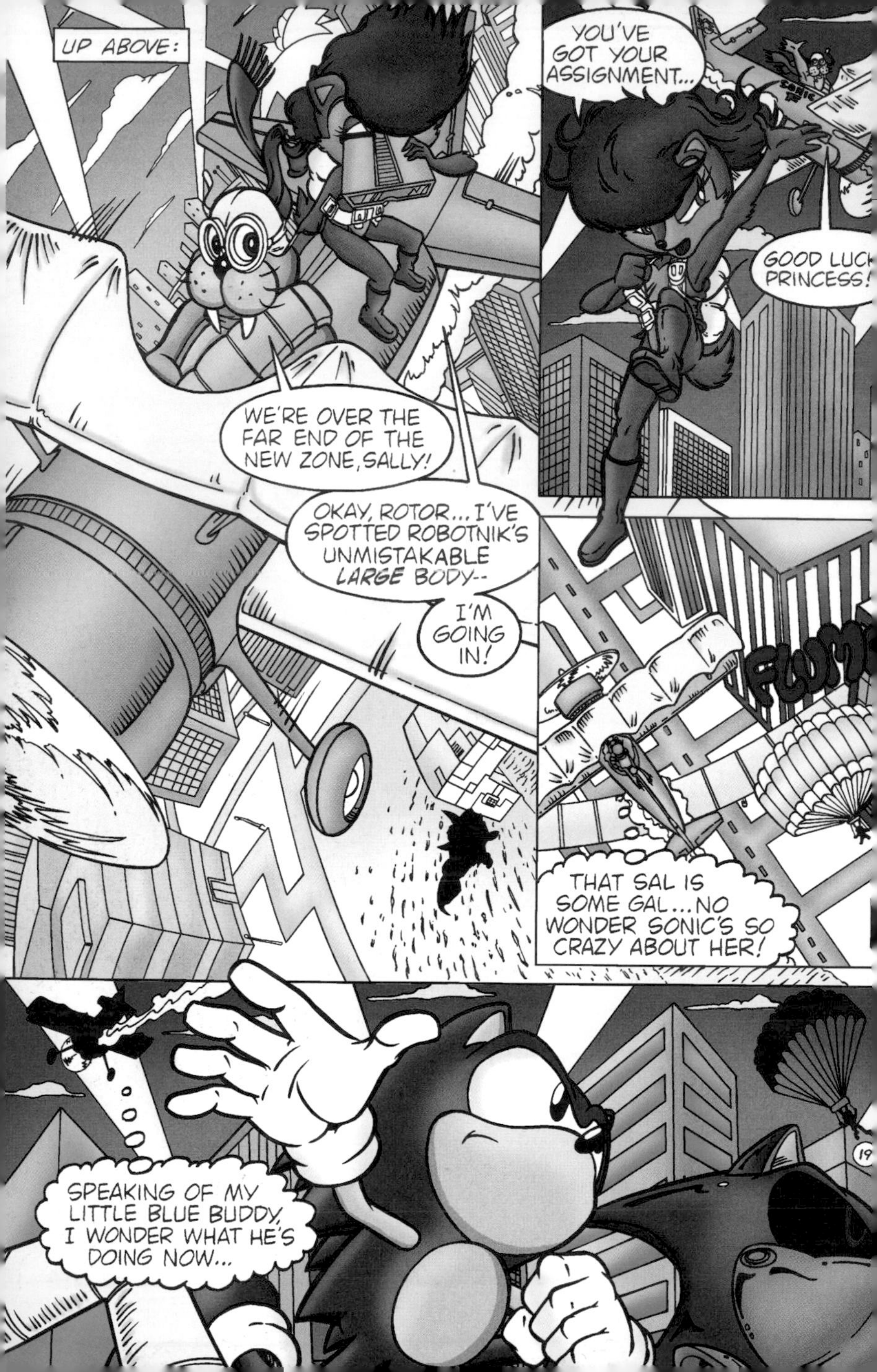
UP ABOVE:
WE'RE OVER THE FAR END OF THE NEW ZONE, SALLY!
OKAY, ROTOR... I'VE SPOTTED ROBOTNIK'S UNMISTAKABLE LARGE BODY--
I'M GOING IN!
YOU'VE GOT YOUR ASSIGNMENT...
GOOD LUCK PRINCESS!
FLUM
THAT SAL IS SOME GAL...NO WONDER SONIC'S SO CRAZY ABOUT HER!
SPEAKING OF MY LITTLE BLUE BUDDY, I WONDER WHAT HE'S DOING NOW...
19

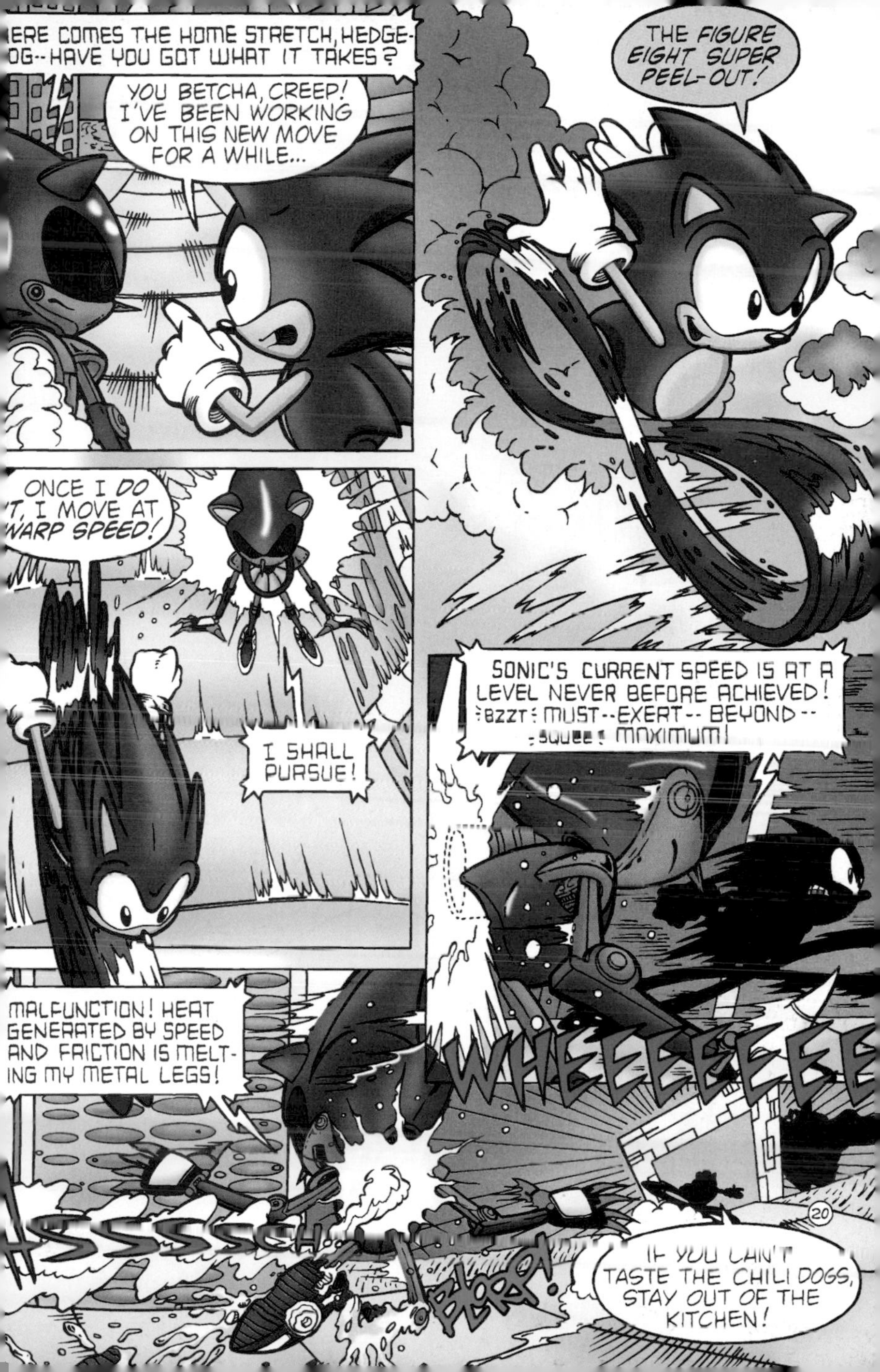

IERE COMES THE HOME STRETCH, HEDGE-
OG--HAVE YOU GOT WHAT IT TAKES?
YOU BETCHA, CREEP! I'VE BEEN WORKING ON THIS NEW MOVE FOR A WHILE...
THE FIGURE EIGHT SUPER PEEL-OUT!
ONCE I DO IT, I MOVE AT WARP SPEED!
I SHALL PURSUE!
SONIC'S CURRENT SPEED IS AT A LEVEL NEVER BEFORE ACHIEVED! BZZT! MUST--EXERT--BEYOND--SQUEE! MAXIMUM!
MALFUNCTION! HEAT GENERATED BY SPEED AND FRICTION IS MELTING MY METAL LEGS!
WHEEEEEEE
SSSSSCH
BLORP!
IF YOU CAN'T TASTE THE CHILI DOGS, STAY OUT OF THE KITCHEN!

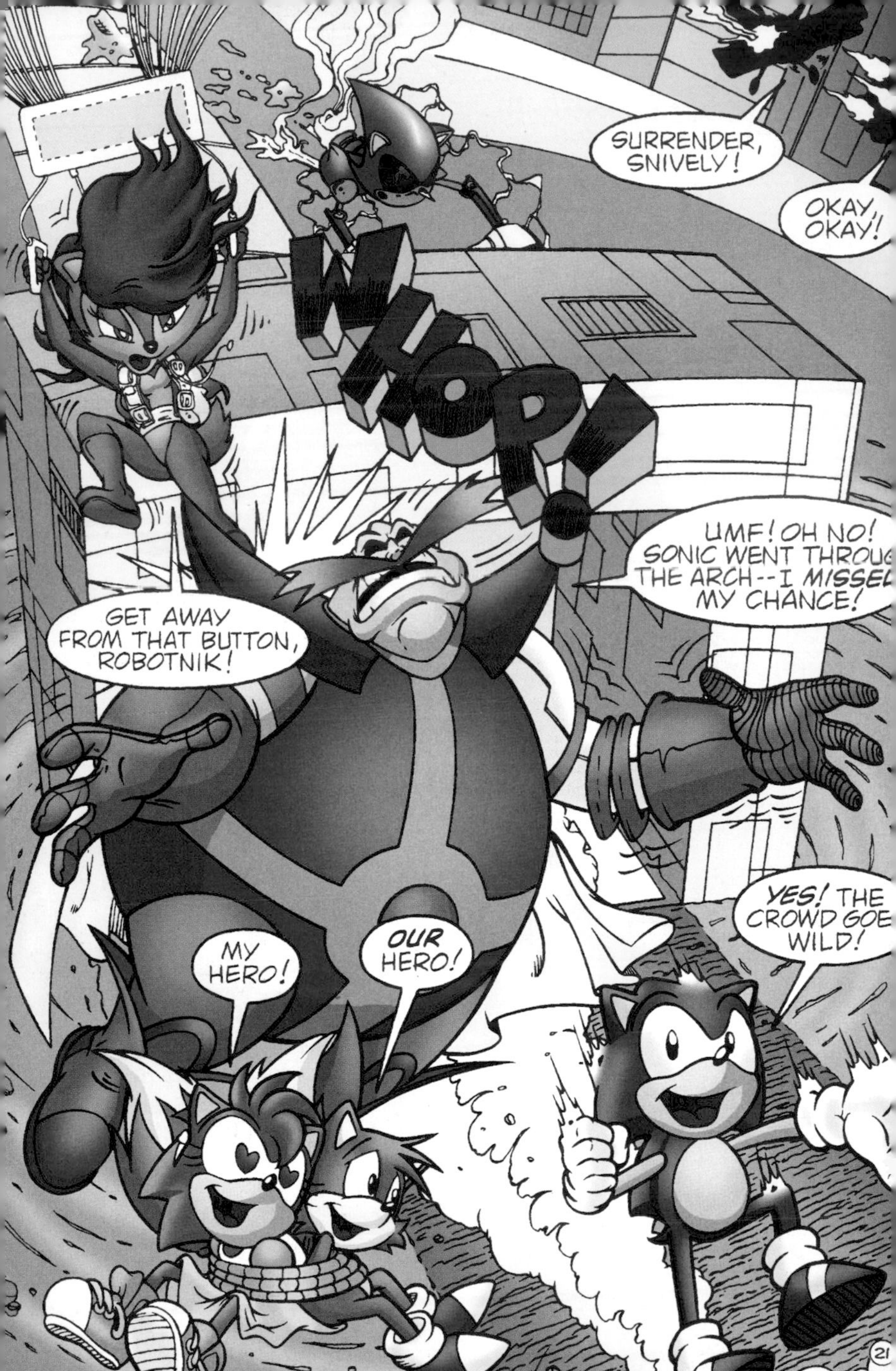
SURRENDER, SNIVELY!
OKAY, OKAY!
WHOP!
UMF! OH NO! SONIC WENT THROUG THE ARCH--I MISSED MY CHANCE!
GET AWAY FROM THAT BUTTON, ROBOTNIK!
YES! THE CROWD GOE WILD!
MY HERO!
OUR HERO!

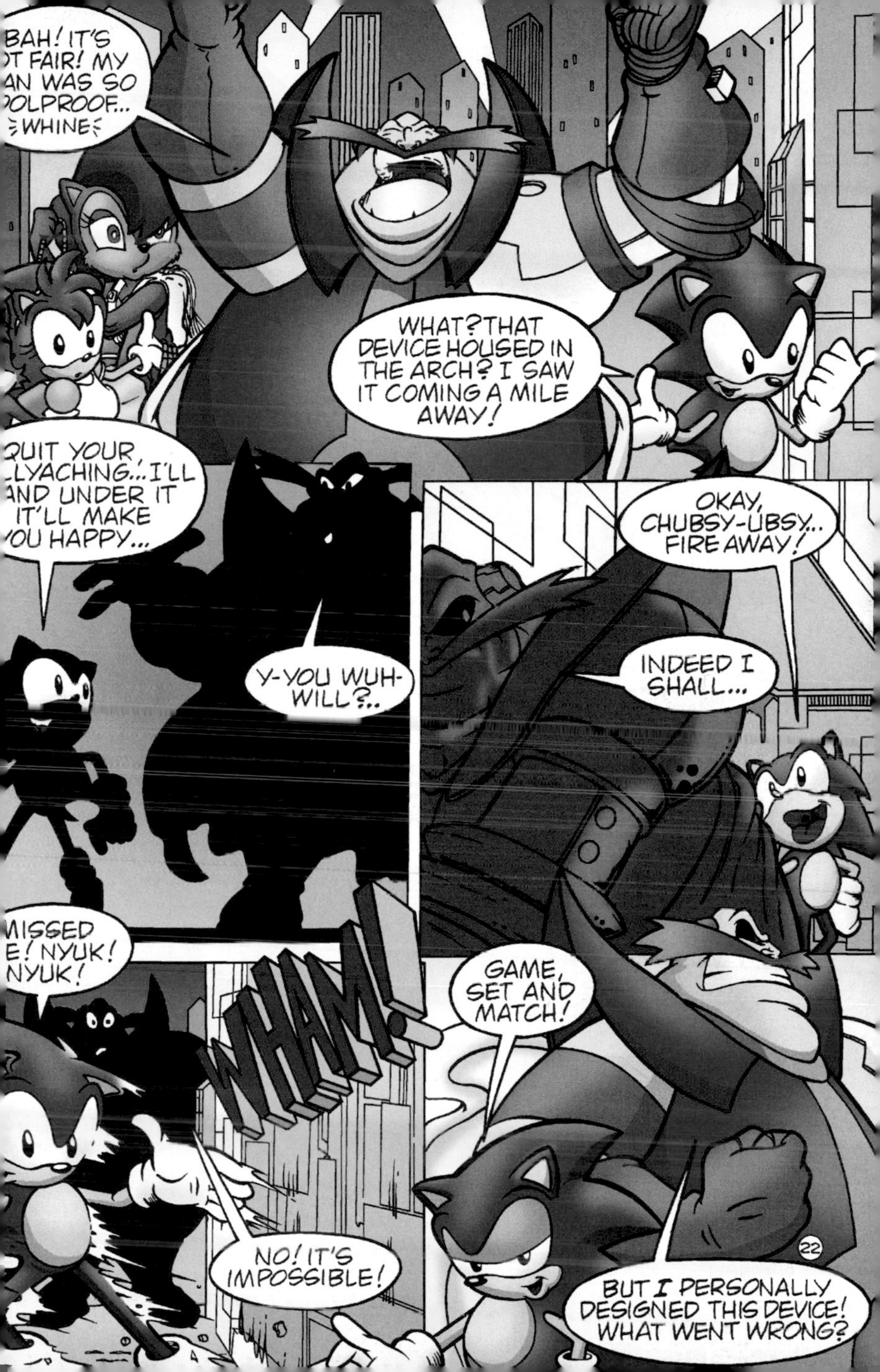
BAH! IT'S
T FAIR! MY
AN WAS SO
OLPROOF...
WHINE
WHAT? THAT DEVICE HOUSED IN THE ARCH? I SAW IT COMING A MILE AWAY!
QUIT YOUR
LYACHING... I'LL
AND UNDER IT
IT'LL MAKE
OU HAPPY...
Y-YOU WUH-WILL?..
OKAY, CHUBSY-UBSY... FIRE AWAY!
INDEED I SHALL...
MISSED
E! NYUK!
NYUK!
WHAM!
GAME, SET AND MATCH!
NO! IT'S IMPOSSIBLE!
BUT I PERSONALLY DESIGNED THIS DEVICE! WHAT WENT WRONG?
22

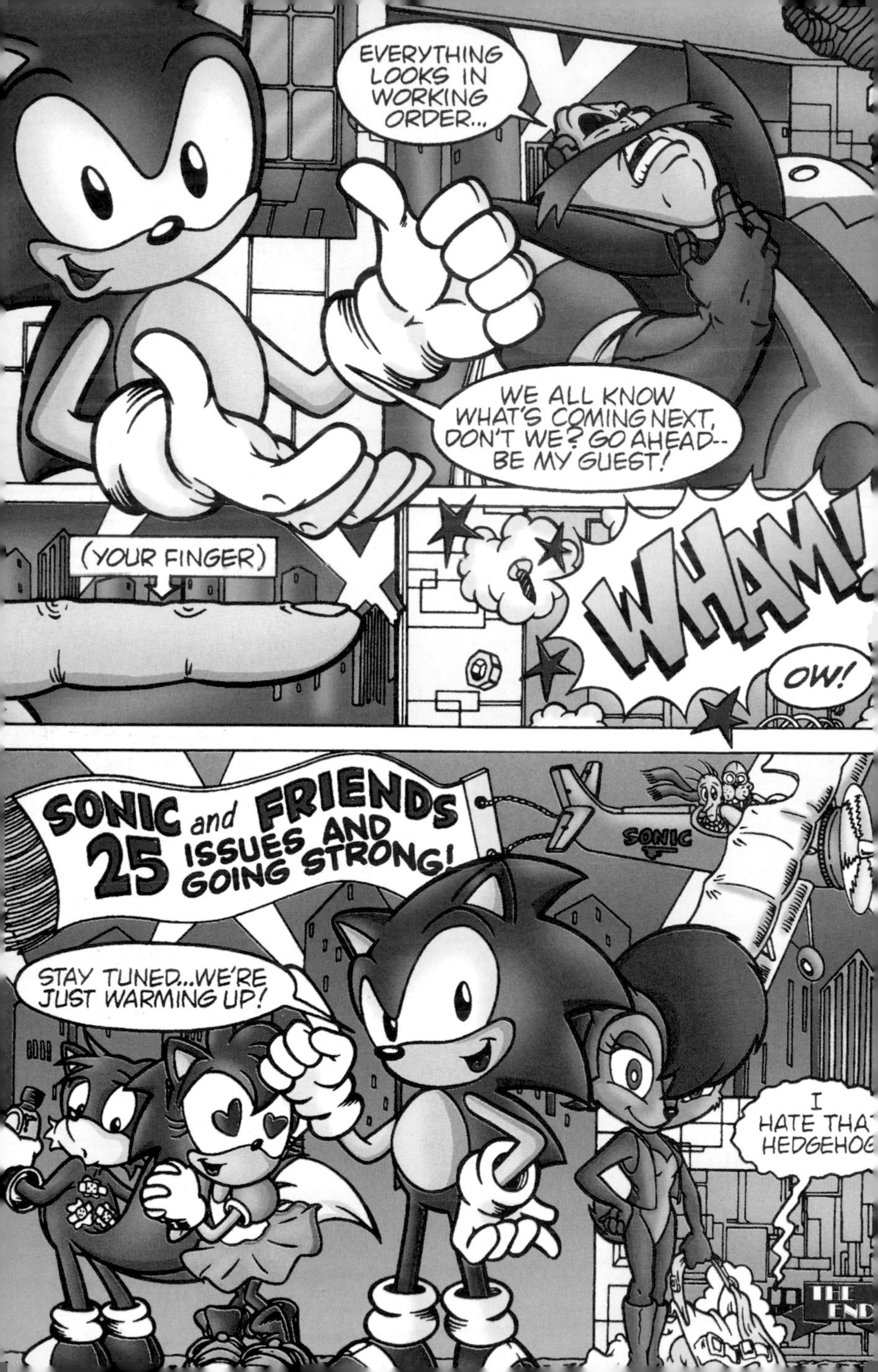
EVERYTHING LOOKS IN WORKING ORDER...
WE ALL KNOW WHAT'S COMING NEXT, DON'T WE? GO AHEAD-- BE MY GUEST!
(YOUR FINGER)
WHAM!
OW!
SONIC and FRIENDS 25 ISSUES AND GOING STRONG!
SONIC
STAY TUNED...WE'RE JUST WARMING UP!
I HATE THA
HEDGEHOG
THE END

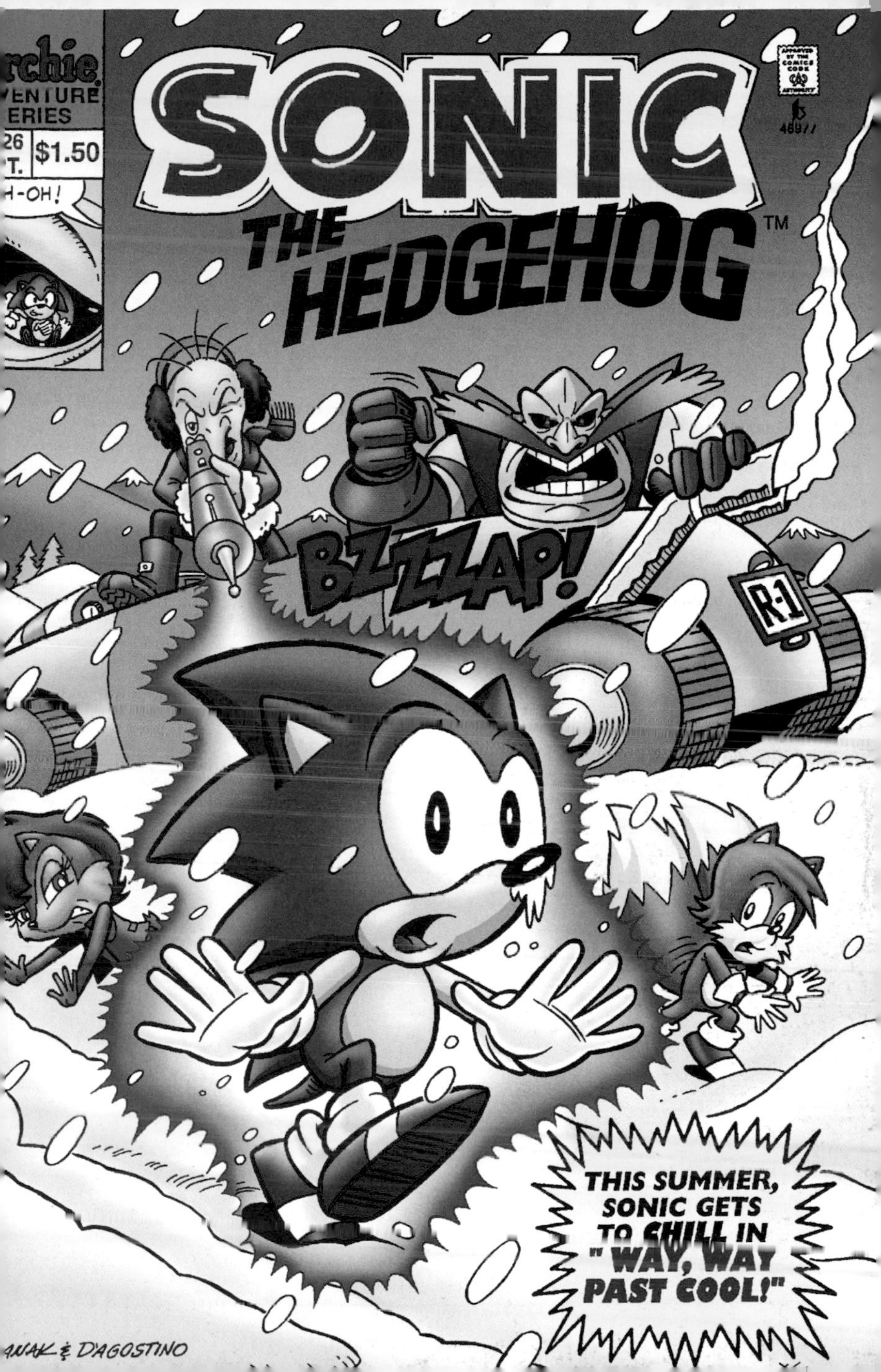
Archie
ADVENTURE SERIES
$1.50
SONIC THE HEDGEHOG™
H-OH!
BZZZAP!
R-1
THIS SUMMER, SONIC GETS TO CHILL IN "WAY, WAY PAST COOL!"
D'AGOSTINO

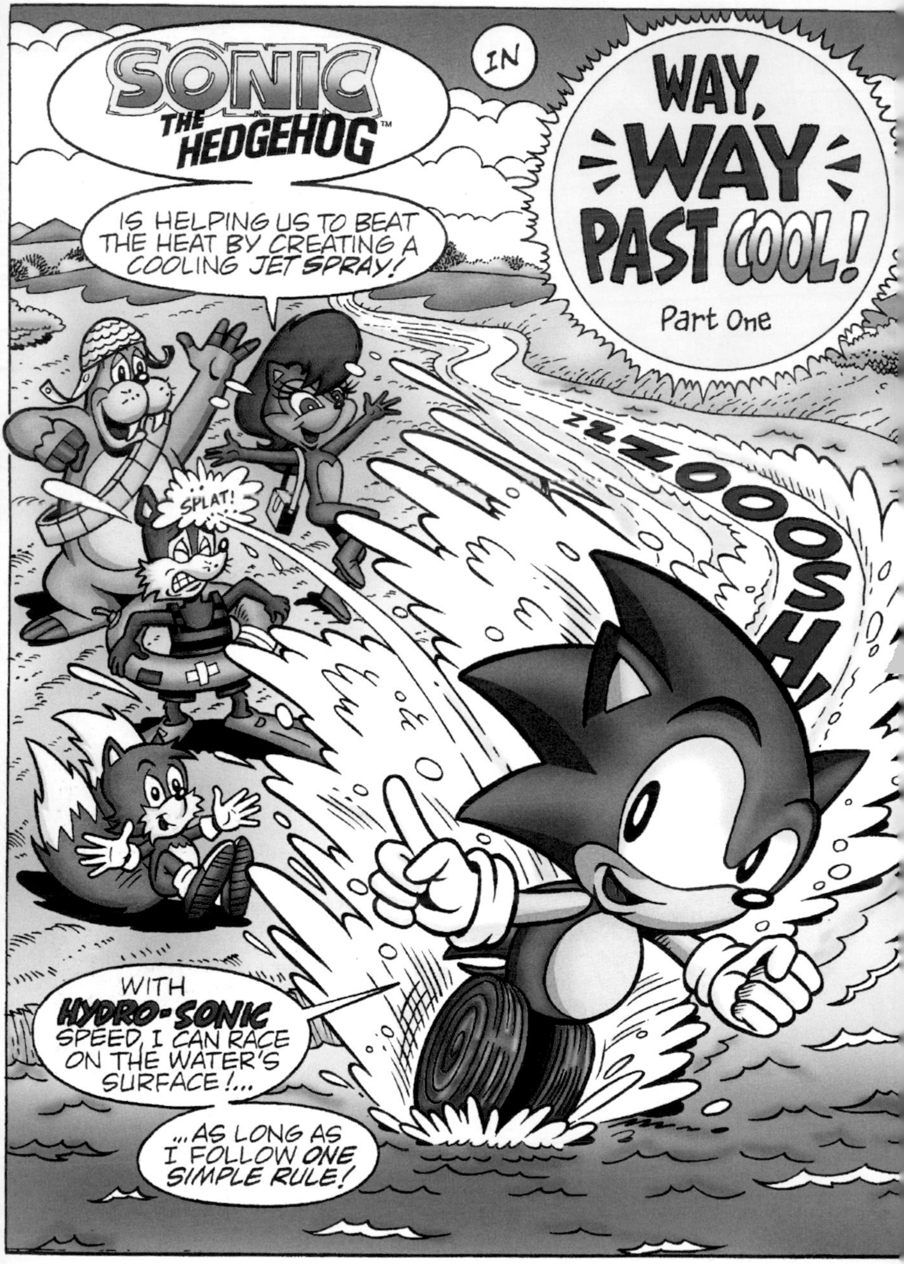
SONIC THE HEDGEHOG™
IN
WAY, WAY WAY PAST COOL!
Part One
IS HELPING US TO BEAT THE HEAT BY CREATING A COOLING JET SPRAY!
SPLAT!
ZZZOOOOOSH!
WITH HYDRO-SONIC SPEED, I CAN RACE ON THE WATER'S SURFACE!...
...AS LONG AS I FOLLOW ONE SIMPLE RULE!

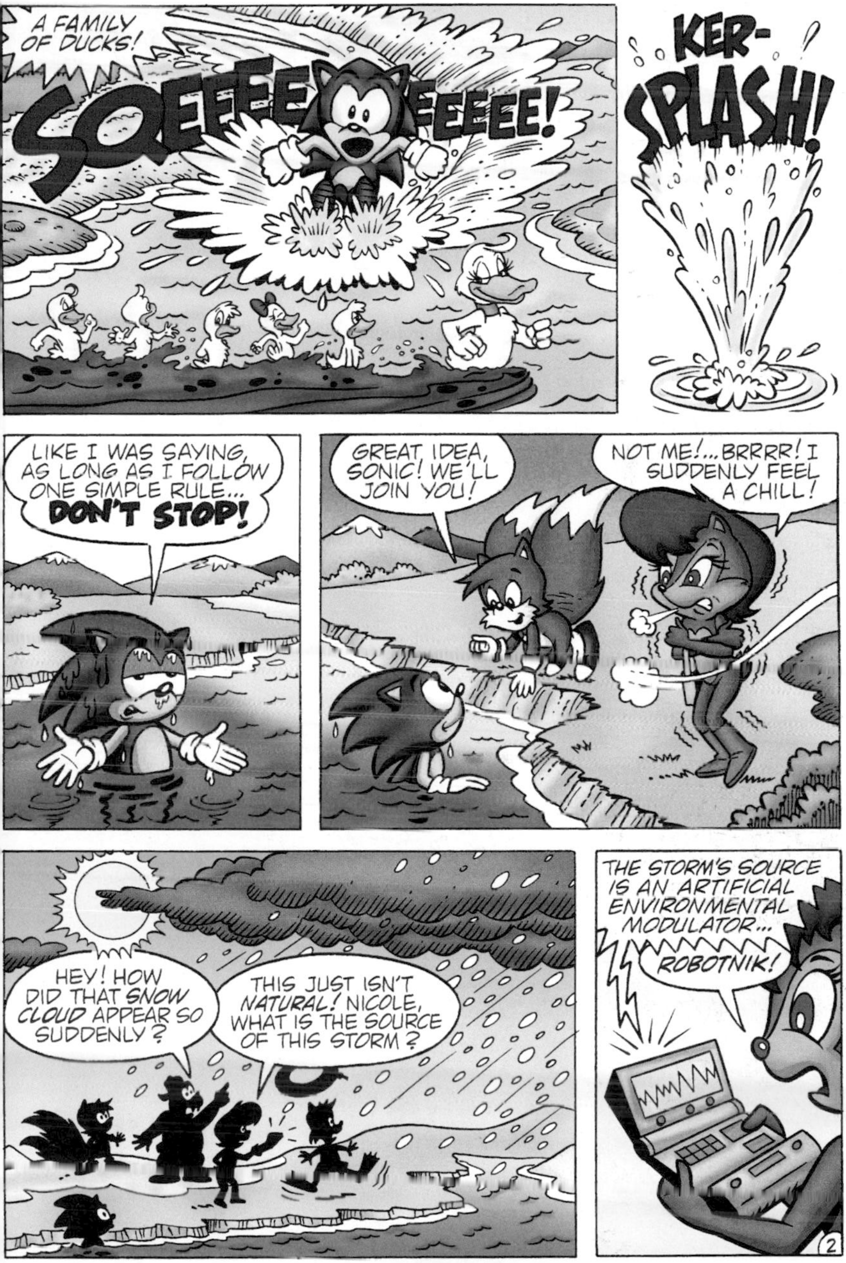
A FAMILY OF DUCKS!
SQEEEE EEEEE!
KER-SPLASH!
LIKE I WAS SAYING, AS LONG AS I FOLLOW ONE SIMPLE RULE... DON'T STOP!
GREAT IDEA, SONIC! WE'LL JOIN YOU!
NOT ME!... BRRRR! I SUDDENLY FEEL A CHILL!
HEY! HOW DID THAT SNOW CLOUD APPEAR SO SUDDENLY?
THIS JUST ISN'T NATURAL! NICOLE, WHAT IS THE SOURCE OF THIS STORM?
THE STORM'S SOURCE IS AN ARTIFICIAL ENVIRONMENTAL MODULATOR...
ROBOTNIK!
2

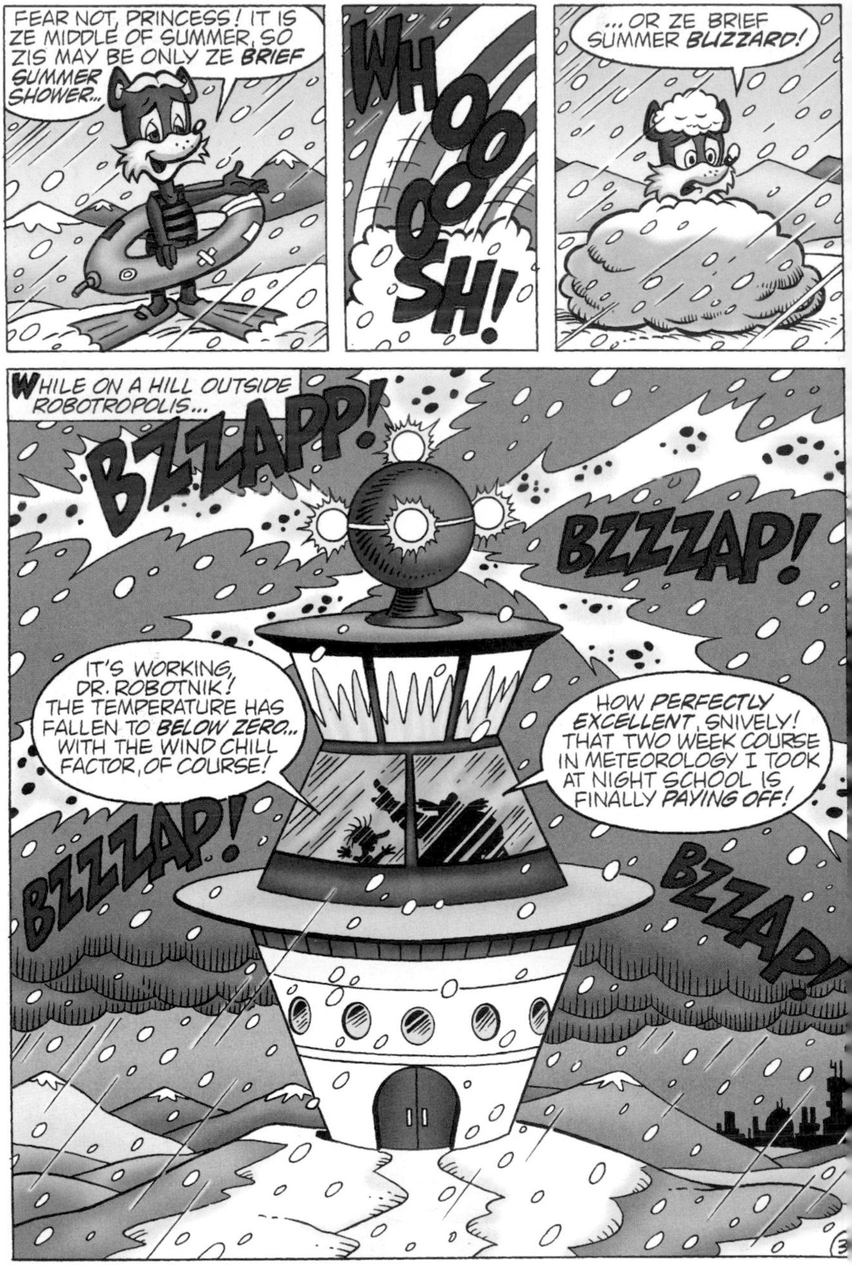
FEAR NOT, PRINCESS! IT IS ZE MIDDLE OF SUMMER, SO ZIS MAY BE ONLY ZE BRIEF SUMMER SHOWER...
WHOOOOOOSH!
...OR ZE BRIEF SUMMER BLIZZARD!
WHILE ON A HILL OUTSIDE ROBOTROPOLIS...
BZZZAPP!
BZZZAP!
IT'S WORKING, DR. ROBOTNIK! THE TEMPERATURE HAS FALLEN TO BELOW ZERO... WITH THE WIND CHILL FACTOR, OF COURSE!
HOW PERFECTLY EXCELLENT, SNIVELY! THAT TWO WEEK COURSE IN METEOROLOGY I TOOK AT NIGHT SCHOOL IS FINALLY PAYING OFF!
BZZZAP!
BZZAP!
3

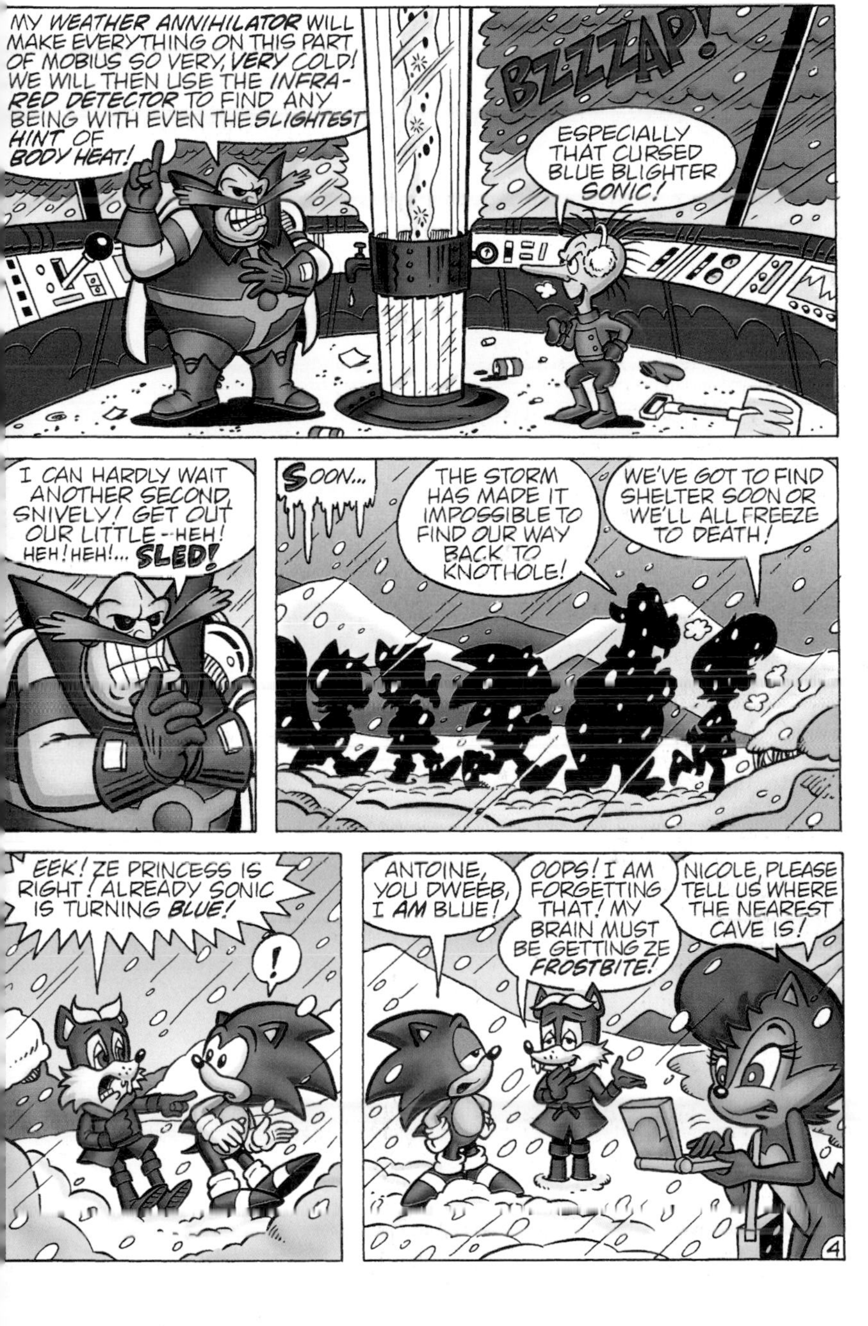
MY WEATHER ANNIHILATOR WILL MAKE EVERYTHING ON THIS PART OF MOBIUS SO VERY, VERY COLD! WE WILL THEN USE THE INFRA-RED DETECTOR TO FIND ANY BEING WITH EVEN THE SLIGHTEST HINT OF BODY HEAT!
BZZZZAP!
ESPECIALLY THAT CURSED BLUE BLIGHTER SONIC!
I CAN HARDLY WAIT ANOTHER SECOND, SNIVELY! GET OUT OUR LITTLE--HEH! HEH! HEH!... SLED!
SOON...
THE STORM HAS MADE IT IMPOSSIBLE TO FIND OUR WAY BACK TO KNOTHOLE!
WE'VE GOT TO FIND SHELTER SOON OR WE'LL ALL FREEZE TO DEATH!
EEK! ZE PRINCESS IS RIGHT! ALREADY SONIC IS TURNING BLUE!
!
ANTOINE, YOU DWEEB, I AM BLUE!
OOPS! I AM FORGETTING THAT! MY BRAIN MUST BE GETTING ZE FROSTBITE!
NICOLE, PLEASE TELL US WHERE THE NEAREST CAVE IS!

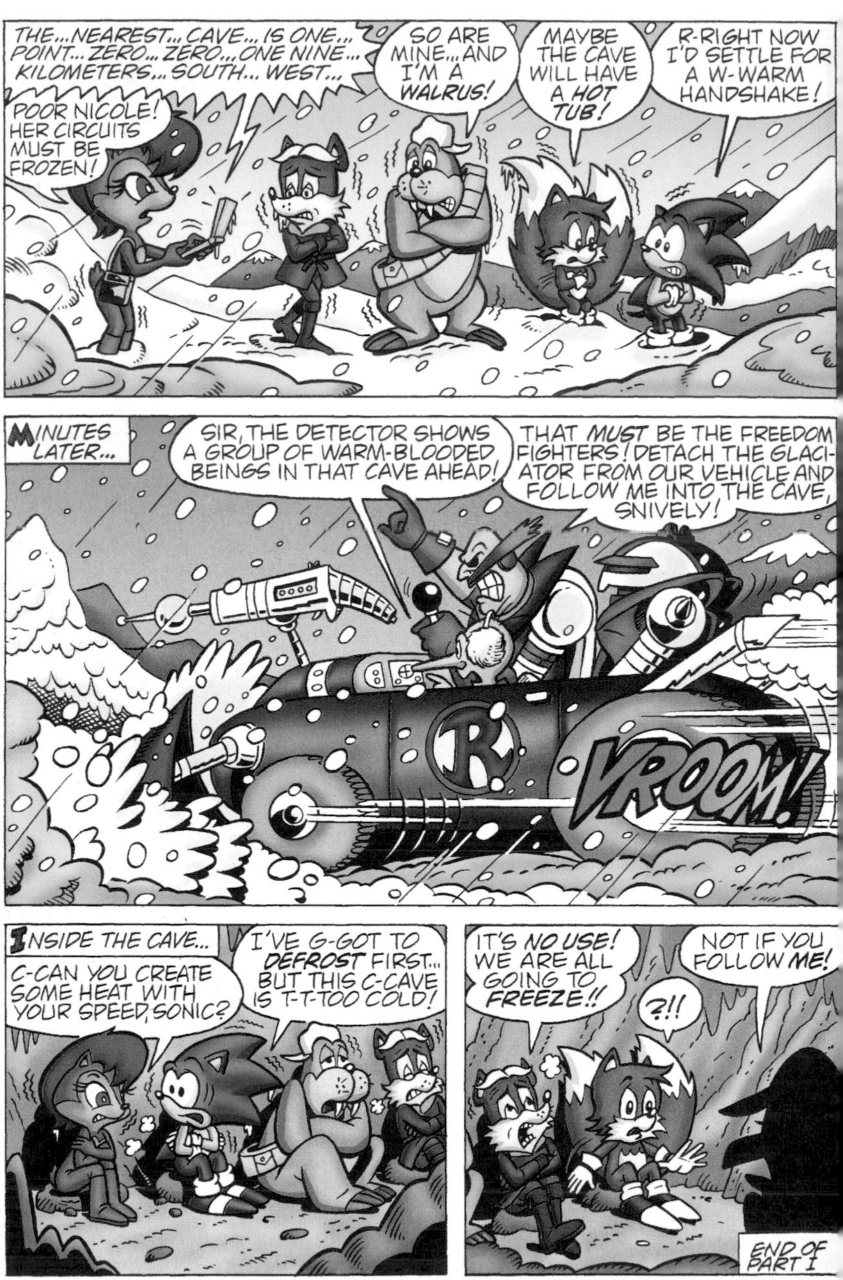
THE...NEAREST... CAVE... IS ONE... POINT... ZERO... ZERO... ONE NINE... KILOMETERS... SOUTH... WEST...
POOR NICOLE! HER CIRCUITS MUST BE FROZEN!
SO ARE MINE...AND I'M A WALRUS!
MAYBE THE CAVE WILL HAVE A HOT TUB!
R-RIGHT NOW I'D SETTLE FOR A W-WARM HANDSHAKE!
MINUTES LATER...
SIR, THE DETECTOR SHOWS A GROUP OF WARM-BLOODED BEINGS IN THAT CAVE AHEAD!
THAT MUST BE THE FREEDOM FIGHTERS! DETACH THE GLACIATOR FROM OUR VEHICLE AND FOLLOW ME INTO THE CAVE, SNIVELY!
VROOM!
INSIDE THE CAVE...
C-CAN YOU CREATE SOME HEAT WITH YOUR SPEED, SONIC?
I'VE G-GOT TO DEFROST FIRST... BUT THIS C-CAVE IS T-T-TOO COLD!
IT'S NO USE! WE ARE ALL GOING TO FREEZE!!
?!!
NOT IF YOU FOLLOW ME!
END OF PART I

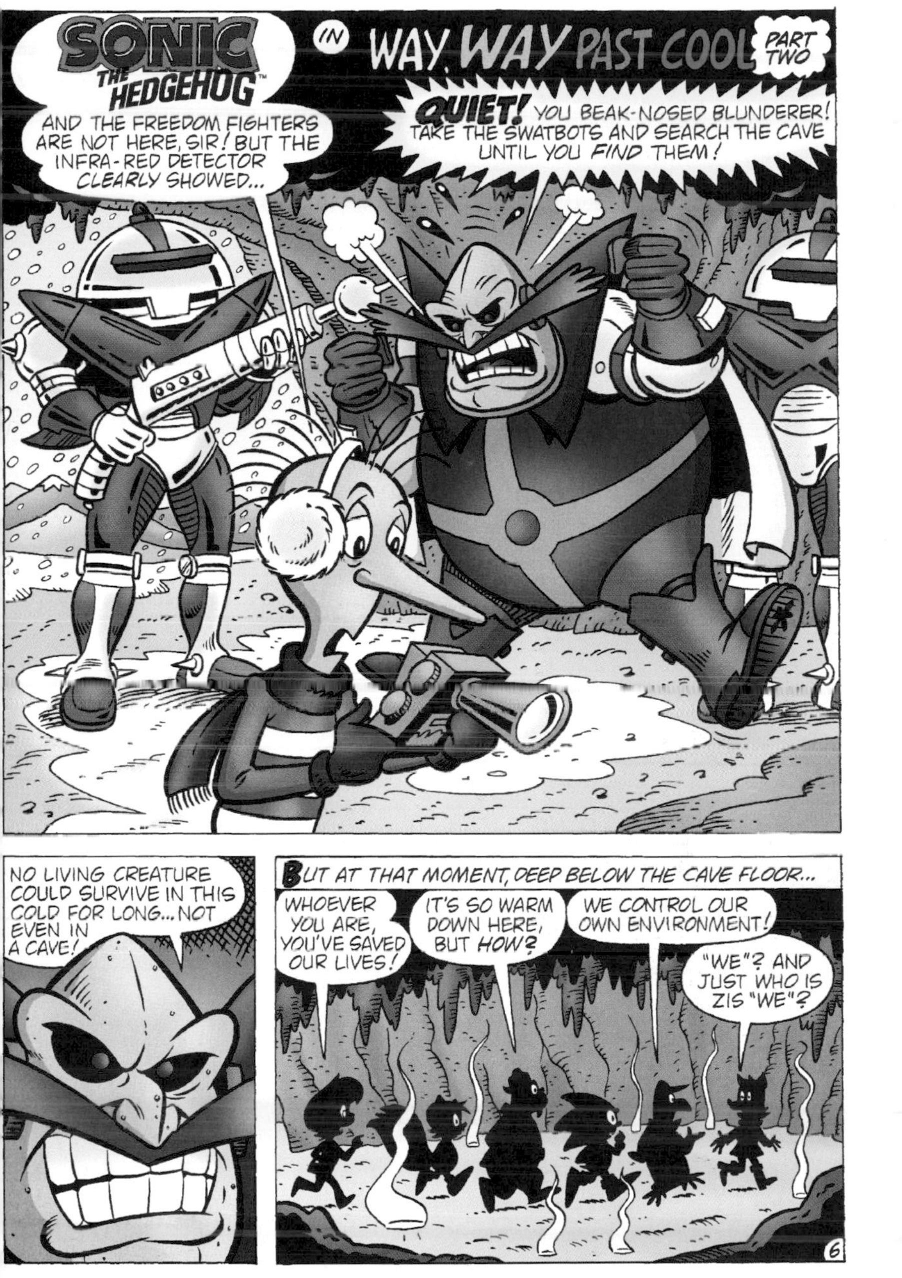
SONIC THE HEDGEHOG™
IN
WAY, WAY PAST COOL
PART TWO
AND THE FREEDOM FIGHTERS ARE NOT HERE, SIR! BUT THE INFRA-RED DETECTOR CLEARLY SHOWED...
QUIET! YOU BEAK-NOSED BLUNDERER! TAKE THE SWATBOTS AND SEARCH THE CAVE UNTIL YOU FIND THEM!
NO LIVING CREATURE COULD SURVIVE IN THIS COLD FOR LONG... NOT EVEN IN A CAVE!
BUT AT THAT MOMENT, DEEP BELOW THE CAVE FLOOR...
WHOEVER YOU ARE, YOU'VE SAVED OUR LIVES!
IT'S SO WARM DOWN HERE, BUT HOW?
WE CONTROL OUR OWN ENVIRONMENT!
"WE"? AND JUST WHO IS ZIS "WE"?
6

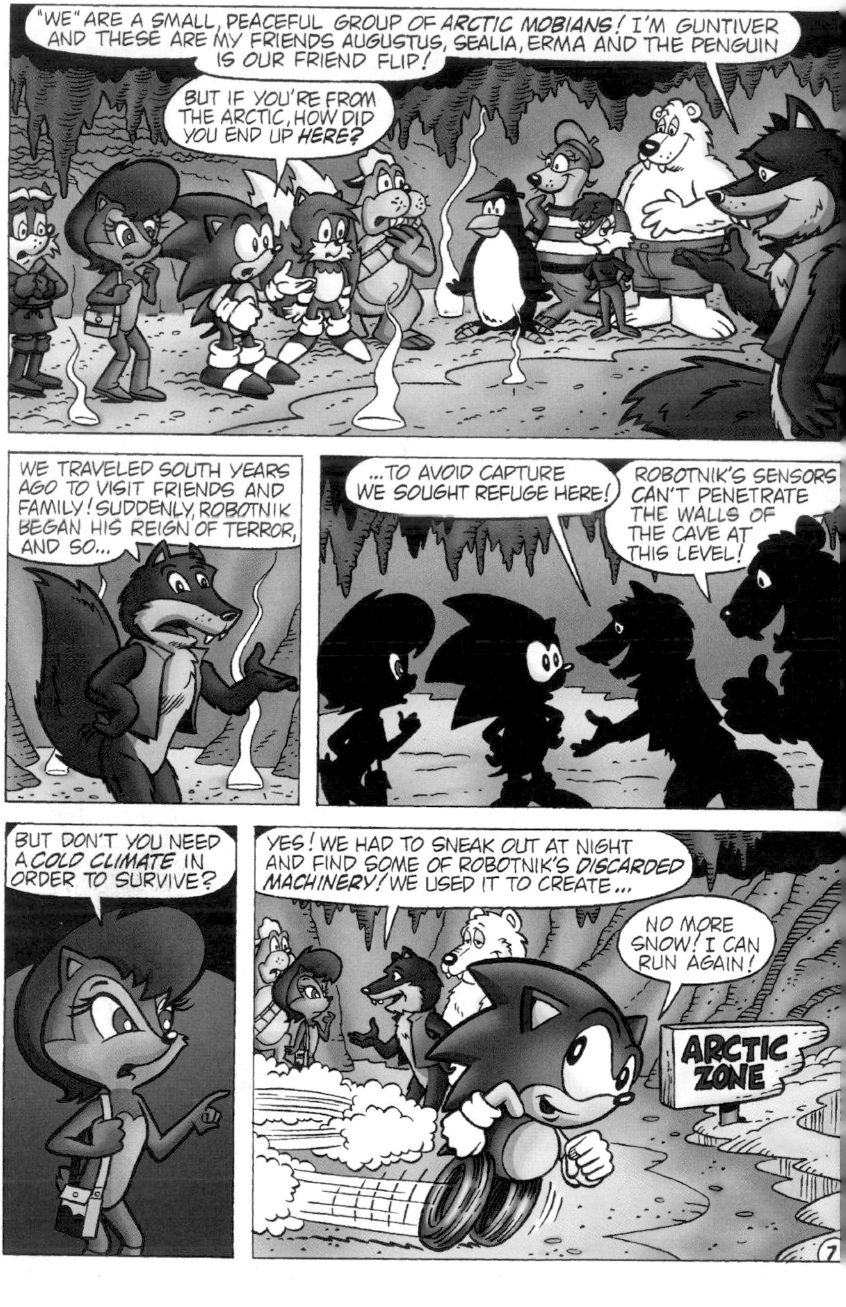
"WE" ARE A SMALL, PEACEFUL GROUP OF ARCTIC MOBIANS! I'M GUNTIVER AND THESE ARE MY FRIENDS AUGUSTUS, SEALIA, ERMA AND THE PENGUIN IS OUR FRIEND FLIP!
BUT IF YOU'RE FROM THE ARCTIC, HOW DID YOU END UP HERE?
WE TRAVELED SOUTH YEARS AGO TO VISIT FRIENDS AND FAMILY! SUDDENLY, ROBOTNIK BEGAN HIS REIGN OF TERROR, AND SO...
...TO AVOID CAPTURE WE SOUGHT REFUGE HERE!
ROBOTNIK'S SENSORS CAN'T PENETRATE THE WALLS OF THE CAVE AT THIS LEVEL!
BUT DON'T YOU NEED A COLD CLIMATE IN ORDER TO SURVIVE?
YES! WE HAD TO SNEAK OUT AT NIGHT AND FIND SOME OF ROBOTNIK'S DISCARDED MACHINERY! WE USED IT TO CREATE...
NO MORE SNOW! I CAN RUN AGAIN!
ARCTIC ZONE
7

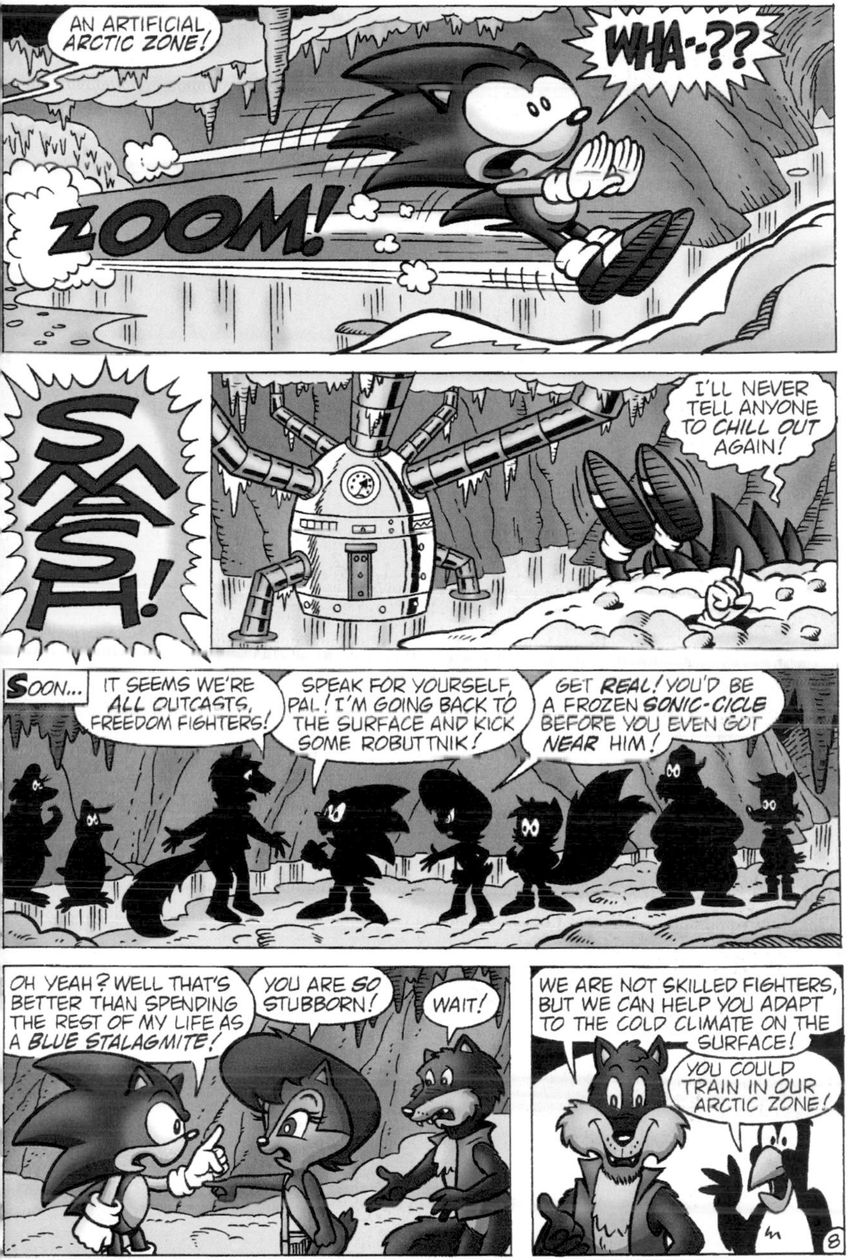
AN ARTIFICIAL ARCTIC ZONE!
WHA--??
ZOOM!
SMASH!
I'LL NEVER TELL ANYONE TO CHILL OUT AGAIN!
SOON...
IT SEEMS WE'RE ALL OUTCASTS, FREEDOM FIGHTERS!
SPEAK FOR YOURSELF, PAL! I'M GOING BACK TO THE SURFACE AND KICK SOME ROBUTTNIK!
GET REAL! YOU'D BE A FROZEN SONIC-CICLE BEFORE YOU EVEN GOT NEAR HIM!
OH YEAH? WELL THAT'S BETTER THAN SPENDING THE REST OF MY LIFE AS A BLUE STALAGMITE!
YOU ARE SO STUBBORN!
WAIT!
WE ARE NOT SKILLED FIGHTERS, BUT WE CAN HELP YOU ADAPT TO THE COLD CLIMATE ON THE SURFACE!
YOU COULD TRAIN IN OUR ARCTIC ZONE!
8

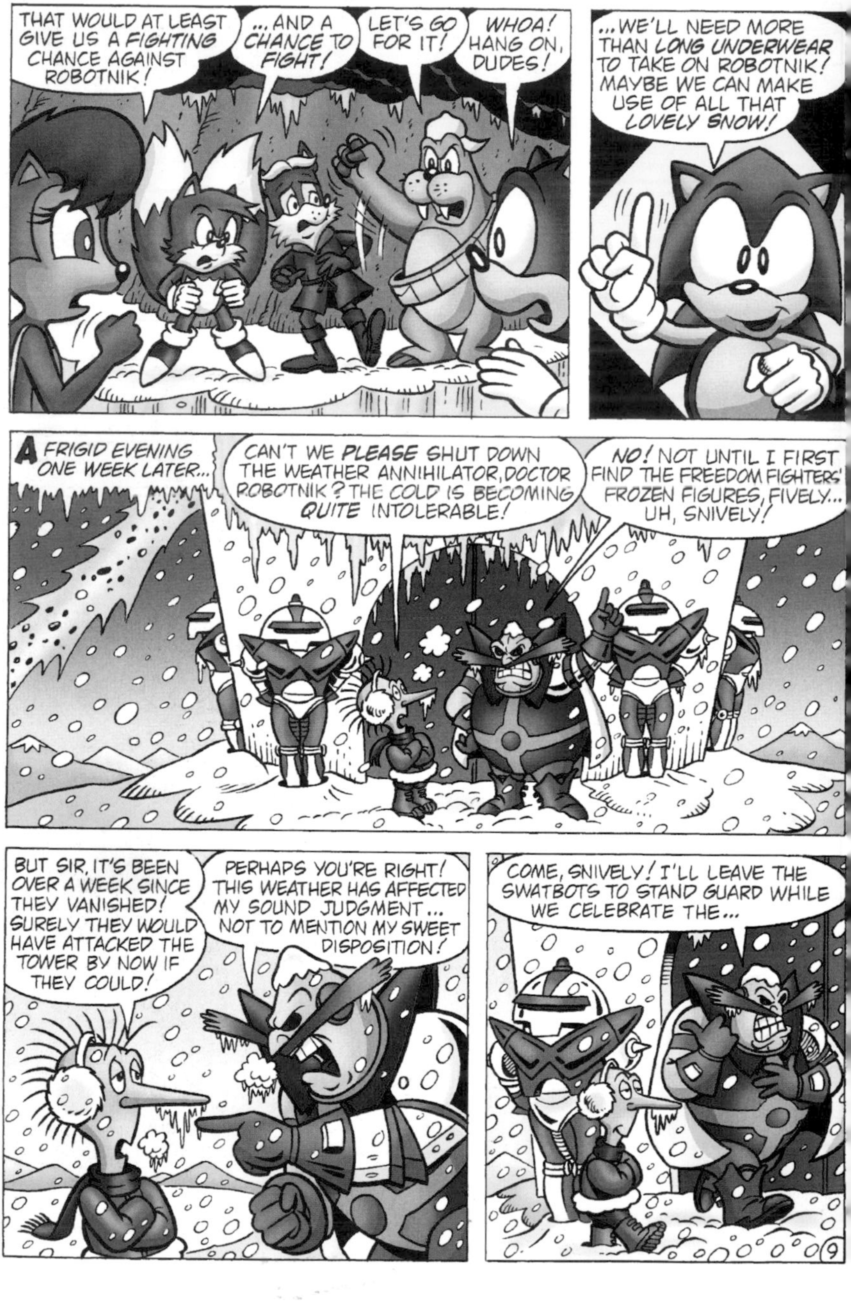

THAT WOULD AT LEAST GIVE US A FIGHTING CHANCE AGAINST ROBOTNIK!
...AND A CHANCE TO FIGHT!
LET'S GO FOR IT!
WHOA! HANG ON, DUDES!
...WE'LL NEED MORE THAN LONG UNDERWEAR TO TAKE ON ROBOTNIK! MAYBE WE CAN MAKE USE OF ALL THAT LOVELY SNOW!
A FRIGID EVENING ONE WEEK LATER...
CAN'T WE PLEASE SHUT DOWN THE WEATHER ANNIHILATOR, DOCTOR ROBOTNIK? THE COLD IS BECOMING QUITE INTOLERABLE!
NO! NOT UNTIL I FIRST FIND THE FREEDOM FIGHTERS' FROZEN FIGURES, FIVELY... UH, SNIVELY!
BUT SIR, IT'S BEEN OVER A WEEK SINCE THEY VANISHED! SURELY THEY WOULD HAVE ATTACKED THE TOWER BY NOW IF THEY COULD!
PERHAPS YOU'RE RIGHT! THIS WEATHER HAS AFFECTED MY SOUND JUDGMENT... NOT TO MENTION MY SWEET DISPOSITION!
COME, SNIVELY! I'LL LEAVE THE SWATBOTS TO STAND GUARD WHILE WE CELEBRATE THE...

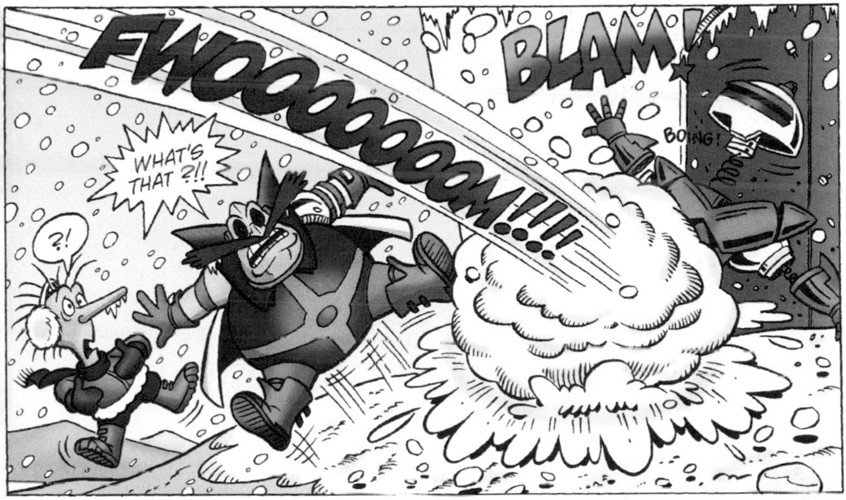
FWOOOOOOOOM!!!!
BLAM!
WHAT'S THAT ?!!
?!
BOING!

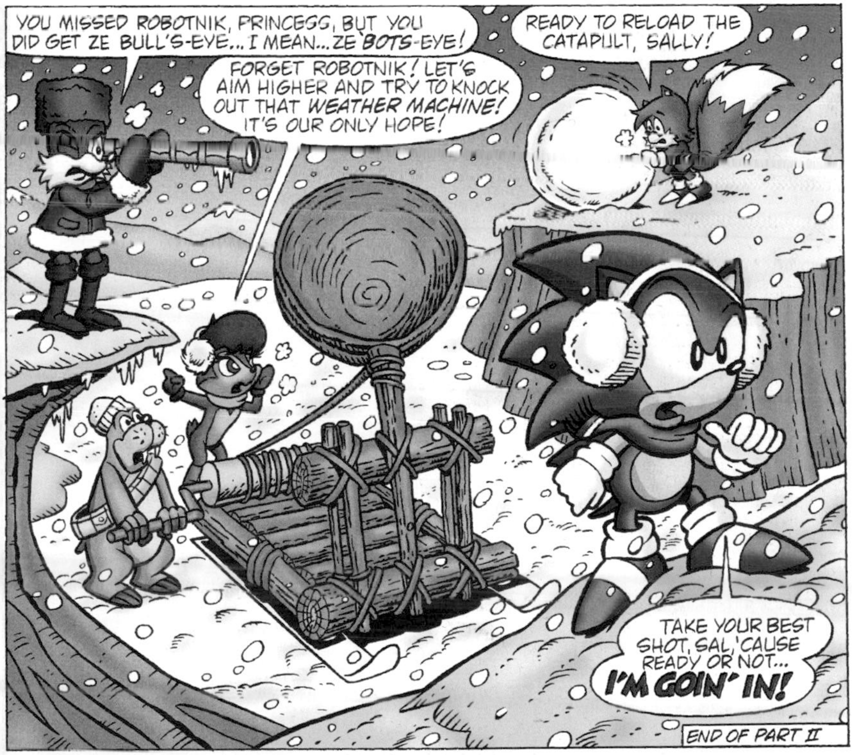
YOU MISSED ROBOTNIK, PRINCESS, BUT YOU DID GET ZE BULL'S-EYE... I MEAN... ZE BOTS-EYE!
FORGET ROBOTNIK! LET'S AIM HIGHER AND TRY TO KNOCK OUT THAT WEATHER MACHINE! IT'S OUR ONLY HOPE!
READY TO RELOAD THE CATAPULT, SALLY!
TAKE YOUR BEST SHOT, SAL, 'CAUSE READY OR NOT... I'M GOIN' IN!
END OF PART II

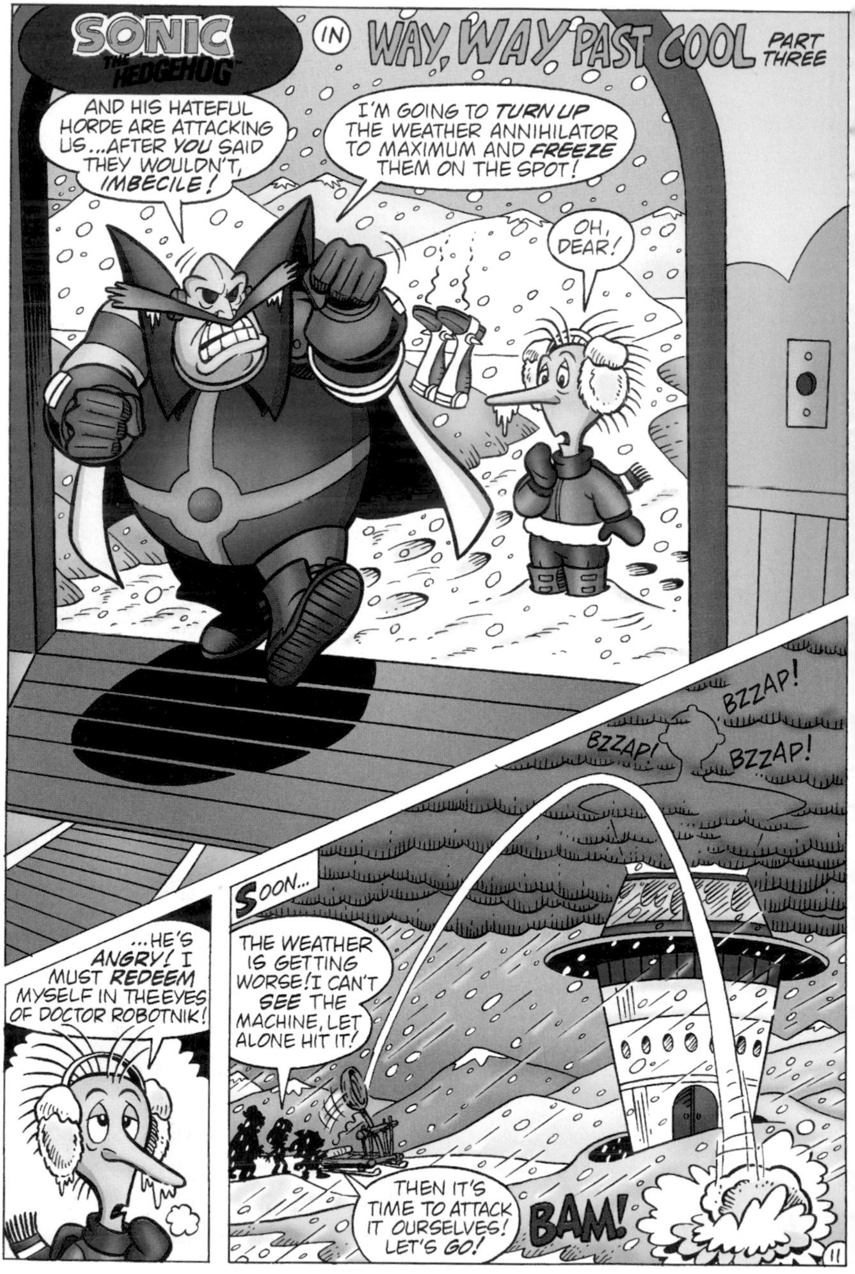
SONIC THE HEDGEHOG IN WAY, WAY PAST COOL PART THREE
AND HIS HATEFUL HORDE ARE ATTACKING US...AFTER YOU SAID THEY WOULDN'T, IMBECILE!
I'M GOING TO TURN UP THE WEATHER ANNIHILATOR TO MAXIMUM AND FREEZE THEM ON THE SPOT!
OH, DEAR!
BZZAP!
BZZAP!
BZZAP!
...HE'S ANGRY! I MUST REDEEM MYSELF IN THEEYES OF DOCTOR ROBOTNIK!
SOON...
THE WEATHER IS GETTING WORSE! I CAN'T SEE THE MACHINE, LET ALONE HIT IT!
THEN IT'S TIME TO ATTACK IT OURSELVES! LET'S GO!
BAM!

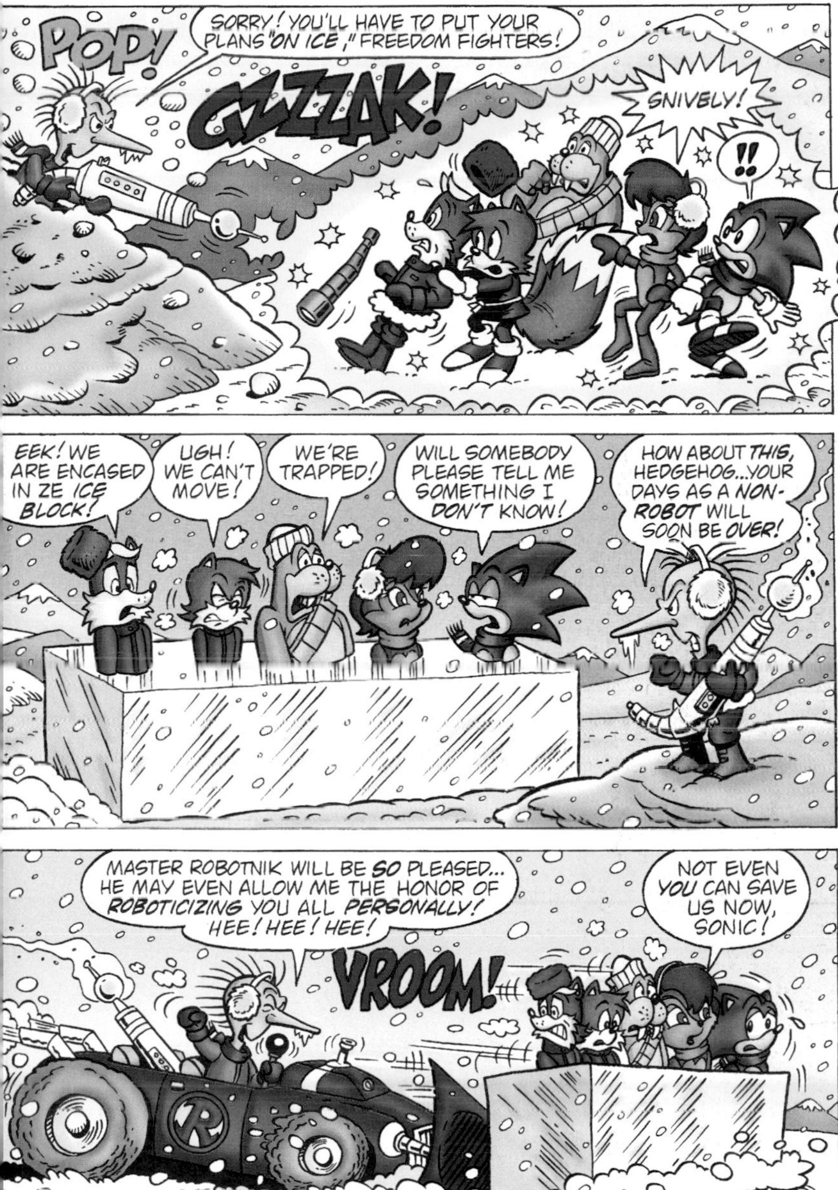
POP!
SORRY! YOU'LL HAVE TO PUT YOUR PLANS "ON ICE," FREEDOM FIGHTERS!
GZZZAK!
SNIVELY!
!!
EEK! WE ARE ENCASED IN ZE ICE BLOCK!
UGH! WE CAN'T MOVE!
WE'RE TRAPPED!
WILL SOMEBODY PLEASE TELL ME SOMETHING I DON'T KNOW!
HOW ABOUT THIS, HEDGEHOG...YOUR DAYS AS A NON-ROBOT WILL SOON BE OVER!
MASTER ROBOTNIK WILL BE SO PLEASED... HE MAY EVEN ALLOW ME THE HONOR OF ROBOTICIZING YOU ALL PERSONALLY! HEE! HEE! HEE!
VROOM!
NOT EVEN YOU CAN SAVE US NOW, SONIC!

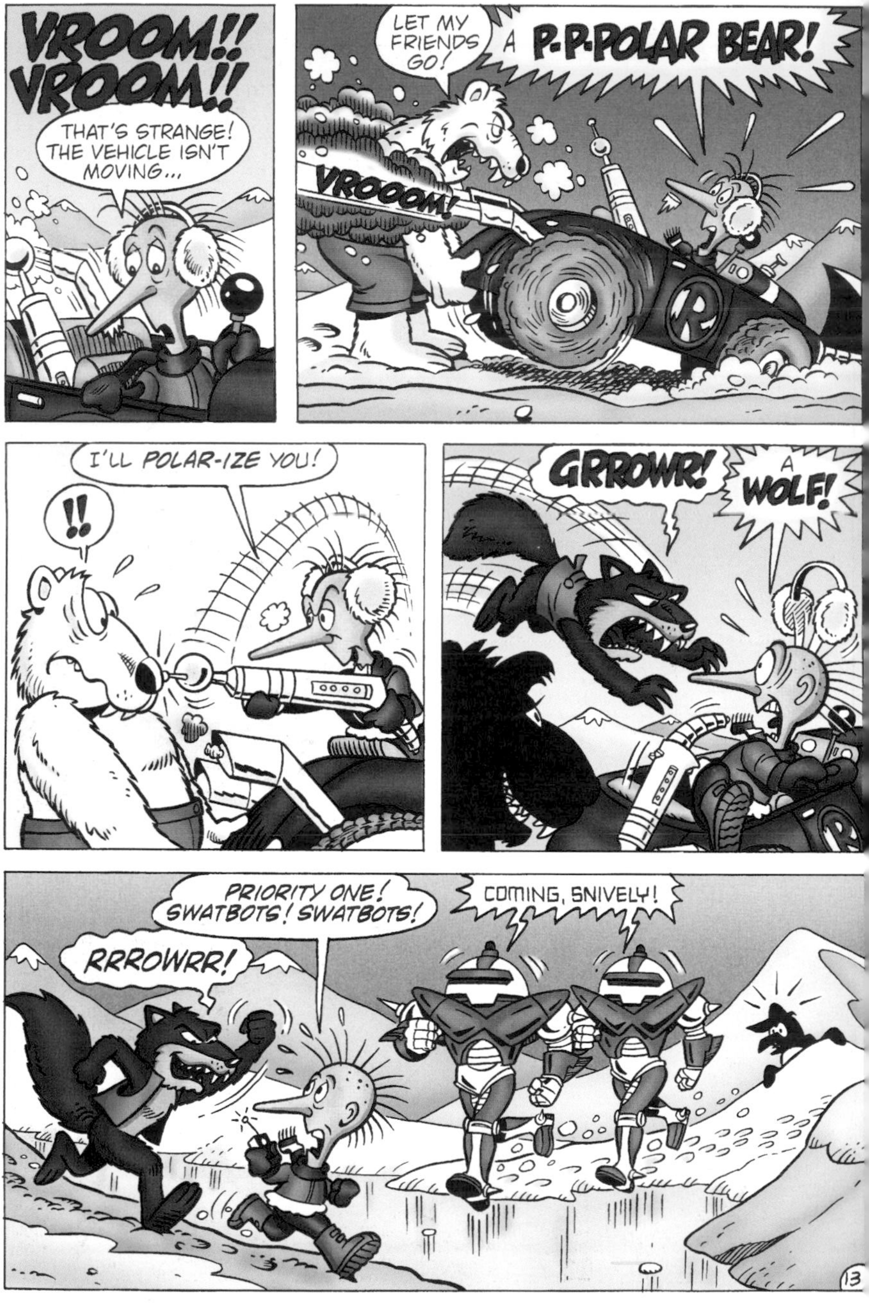
VROOM!! VROOM!!
THAT'S STRANGE! THE VEHICLE ISN'T MOVING...
LET MY FRIENDS GO!
A P-P-POLAR BEAR!
VROOOOM!
I'LL POLAR-IZE YOU!
!!
GRRROWR!
A WOLF!
PRIORITY ONE! SWATBOTS! SWATBOTS!
COMING, SNIVELY!
RRROWRR!

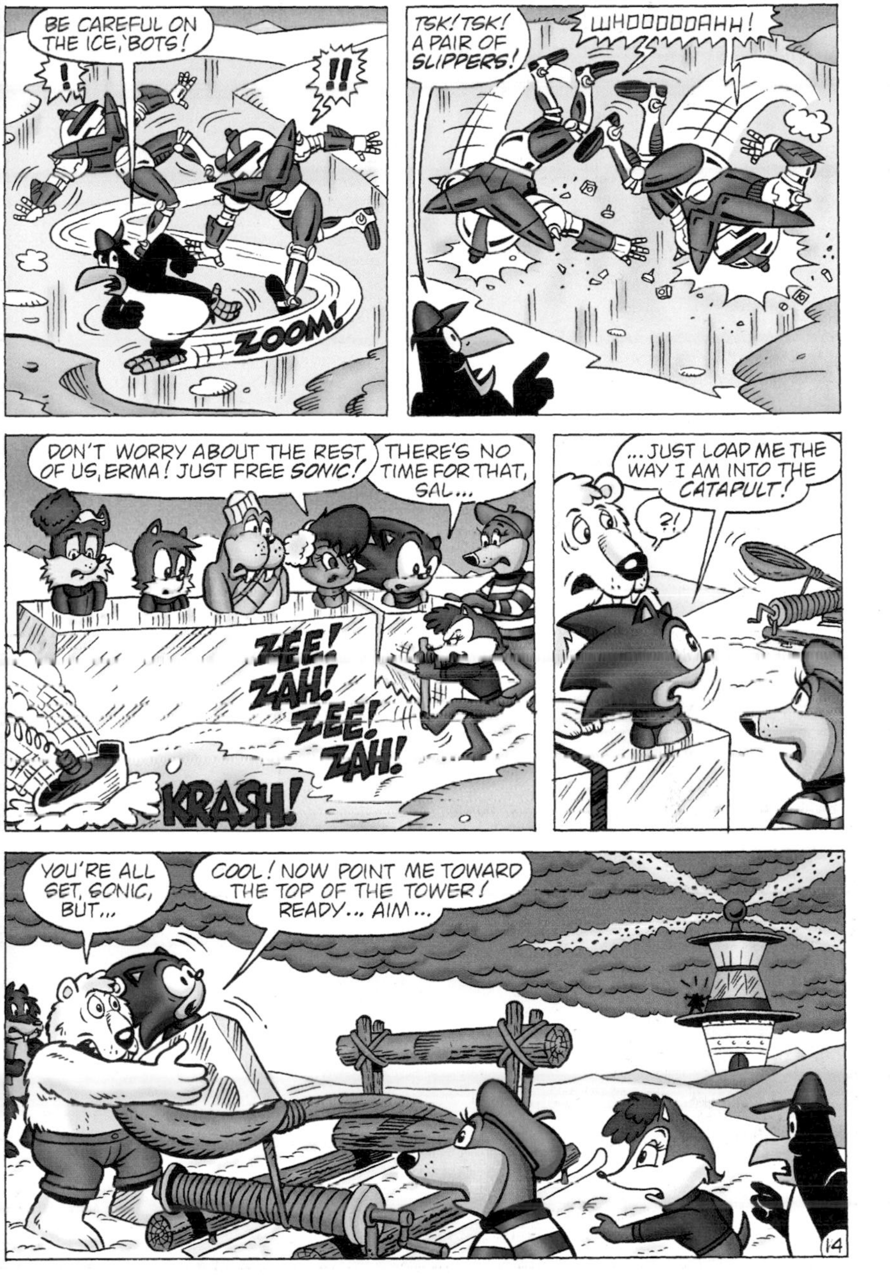
BE CAREFUL ON THE ICE, 'BOTS!
!
!!
ZOOM!
TSK! TSK! A PAIR OF SLIPPERS!
WHOOOOOAHH!
DON'T WORRY ABOUT THE REST OF US, ERMA! JUST FREE SONIC!
THERE'S NO TIME FOR THAT, SAL...
ZEE! ZAH! ZEE! ZAH!
KRASH!
...JUST LOAD ME THE WAY I AM INTO THE CATAPULT!
?!
YOU'RE ALL SET, SONIC, BUT...
COOL! NOW POINT ME TOWARD THE TOP OF THE TOWER! READY... AIM...
14

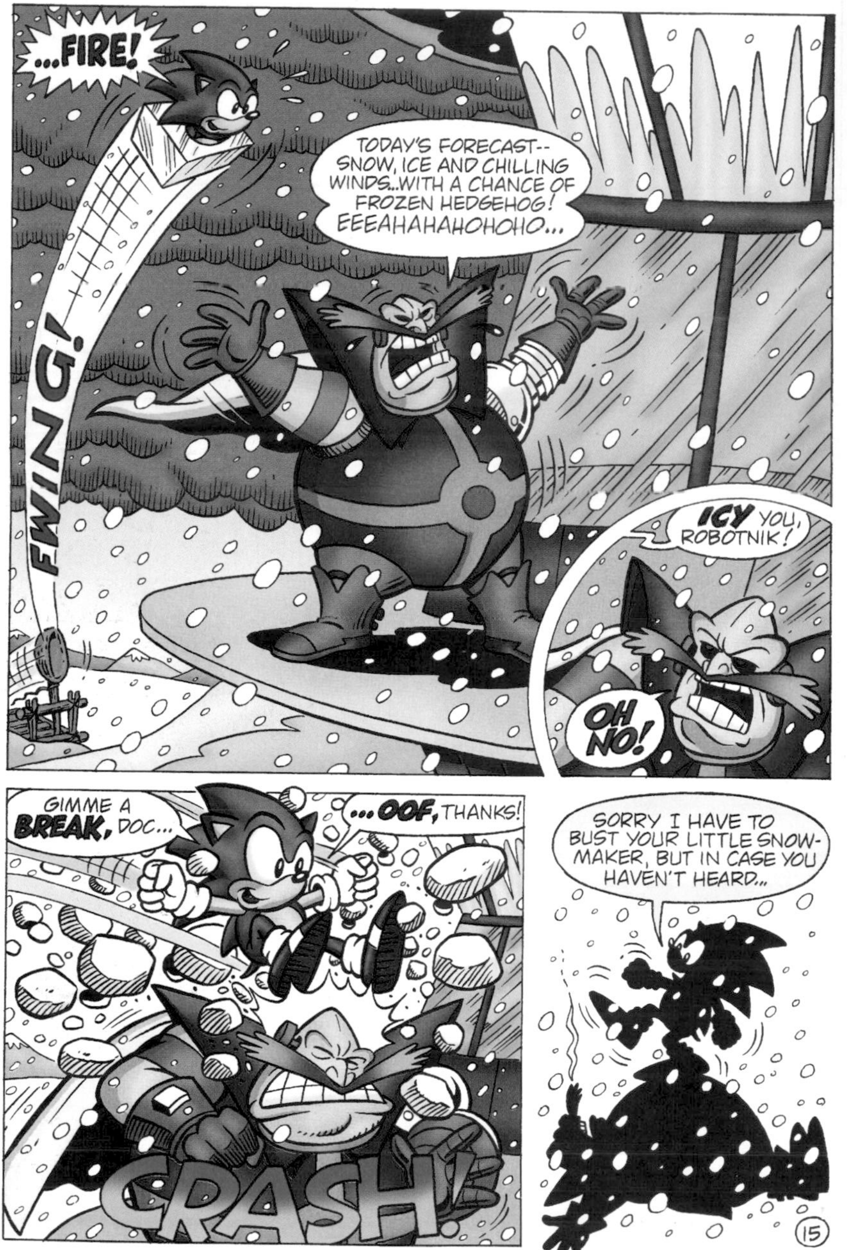
...FIRE!
TODAY'S FORECAST-- SNOW, ICE AND CHILLING WINDS...WITH A CHANCE OF FROZEN HEDGEHOG! EEEAHAHAHOHOHO...
FWING!
ICY YOU, ROBOTNIK!
OH NO!
GIMME A BREAK, DOC...
...OOF, THANKS!
CRASH!
SORRY I HAVE TO BUST YOUR LITTLE SNOW-MAKER, BUT IN CASE YOU HAVEN'T HEARD...

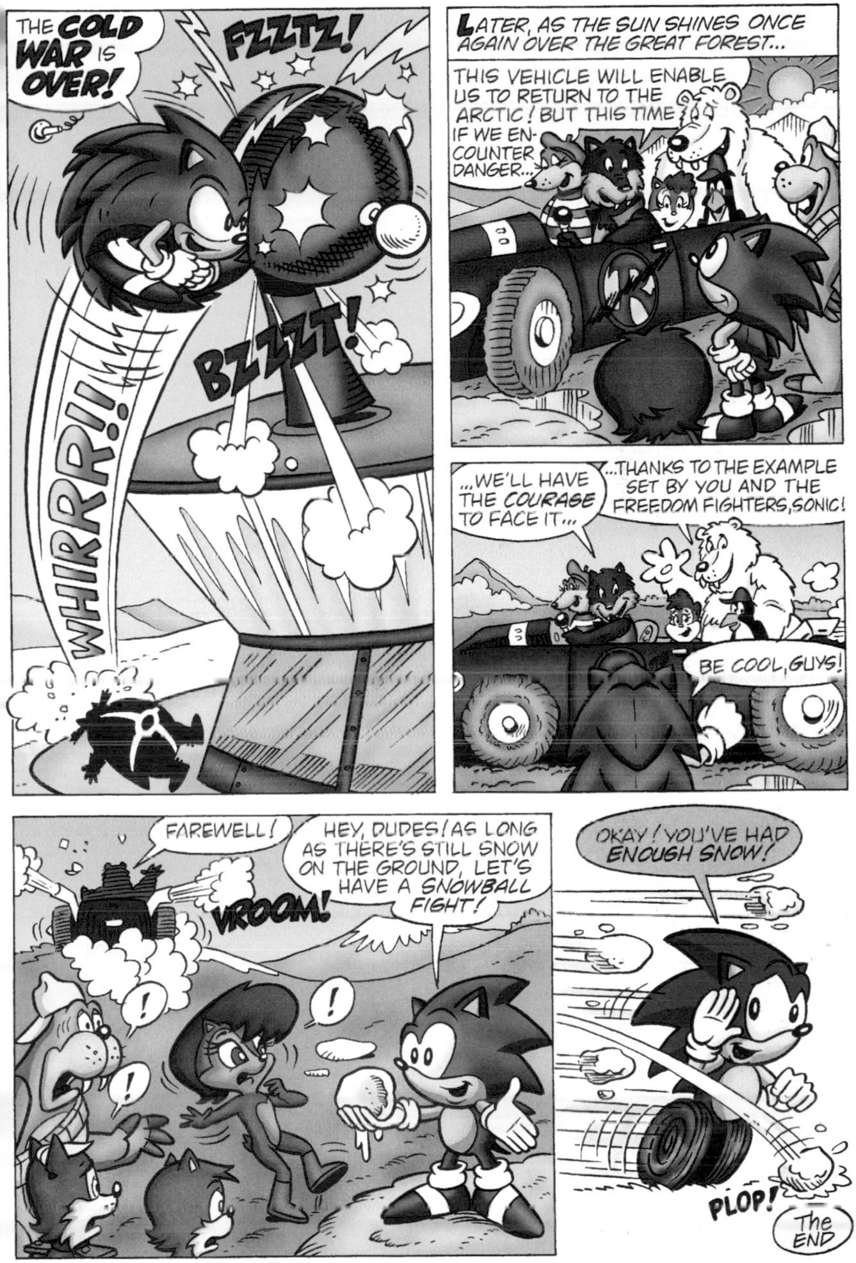
THE COLD WAR IS OVER!
FZZZTZ!
BZZZZT!
WHIRRR!!!
LATER, AS THE SUN SHINES ONCE AGAIN OVER THE GREAT FOREST...
THIS VEHICLE WILL ENABLE US TO RETURN TO THE ARCTIC! BUT THIS TIME IF WE ENCOUNTER DANGER...
...WE'LL HAVE THE COURAGE TO FACE IT...
...THANKS TO THE EXAMPLE SET BY YOU AND THE FREEDOM FIGHTERS, SONIC!
BE COOL, GUYS!
FAREWELL!
VROOM!
HEY, DUDES! AS LONG AS THERE'S STILL SNOW ON THE GROUND, LET'S HAVE A SNOWBALL FIGHT!
!
!
!
OKAY! YOU'VE HAD ENOUGH SNOW!
PLOP!
The END

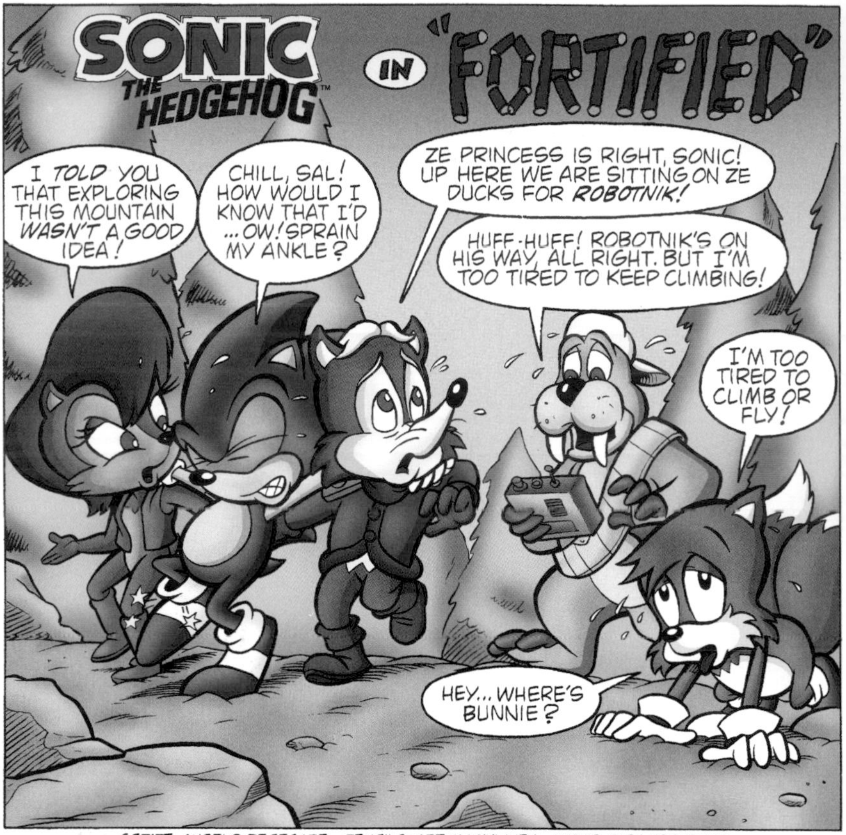
SONIC THE HEDGEHOG™
IN "FORTIFIED"
I *TOLD* YOU THAT EXPLORING THIS MOUNTAIN *WASN'T* A GOOD IDEA!
CHILL, SAL! HOW WOULD I KNOW THAT I'D ...OW! SPRAIN MY ANKLE?
ZE PRINCESS IS RIGHT, SONIC! UP HERE WE ARE SITTING ON ZE DUCKS FOR *ROBOTNIK!*
HUFF-HUFF! ROBOTNIK'S ON HIS WAY, ALL RIGHT. BUT I'M TOO TIRED TO KEEP CLIMBING!
I'M TOO TIRED TO CLIMB OR FLY!
HEY... WHERE'S BUNNIE?

SCRIPT: ANGELO DECESARE PENCILS: ART MAWHINNEY INKING: RICH KOSLOWSKI

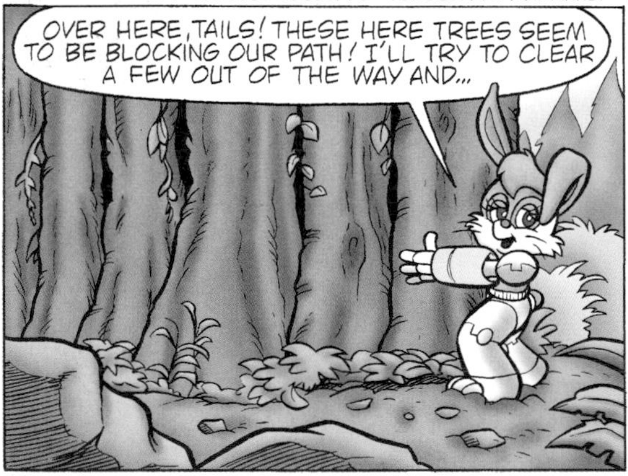
OVER HERE, TAILS! THESE HERE TREES SEEM TO BE BLOCKING OUR PATH! I'LL TRY TO CLEAR A FEW OUT OF THE WAY AND...

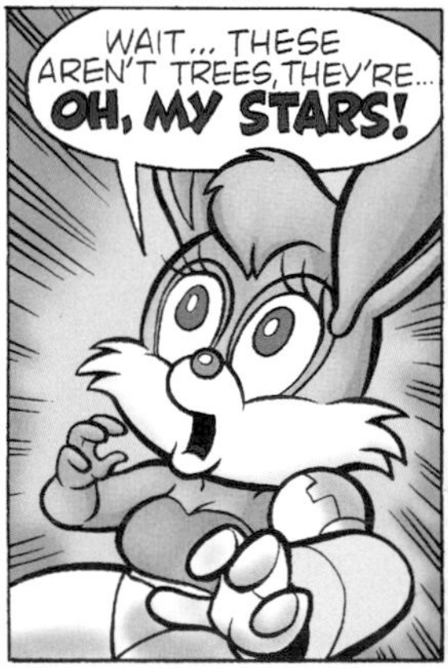
WAIT... THESE AREN'T TREES, THEY'RE... **OH, MY STARS!**

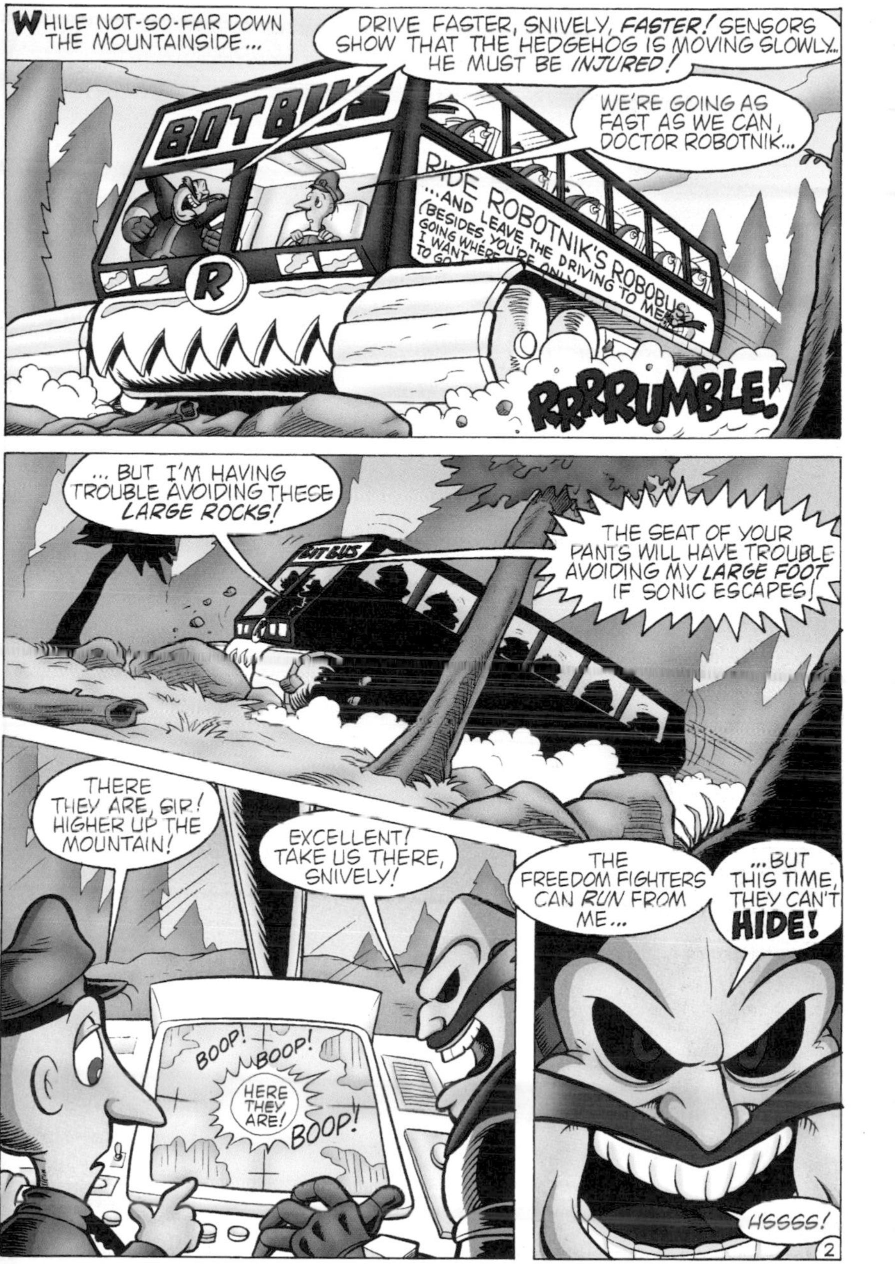
WHILE NOT-SO-FAR DOWN THE MOUNTAINSIDE...
DRIVE FASTER, SNIVELY, FASTER! SENSORS SHOW THAT THE HEDGEHOG IS MOVING SLOWLY... HE MUST BE INJURED!
WE'RE GOING AS FAST AS WE CAN, DOCTOR ROBOTNIK...
BOTBUS
RIDE ROBOTNIK'S ROBOBUS ...AND LEAVE THE DRIVING TO ME!
RRRRUMBLE!
... BUT I'M HAVING TROUBLE AVOIDING THESE LARGE ROCKS!
THE SEAT OF YOUR PANTS WILL HAVE TROUBLE AVOIDING MY LARGE FOOT IF SONIC ESCAPES!
BOT BUS
THERE THEY ARE, SIR! HIGHER UP THE MOUNTAIN!
EXCELLENT! TAKE US THERE, SNIVELY!
BOOP! BOOP!
HERE THEY ARE!
BOOP!
THE FREEDOM FIGHTERS CAN RUN FROM ME...
...BUT THIS TIME, THEY CAN'T HIDE!
HSSSS!

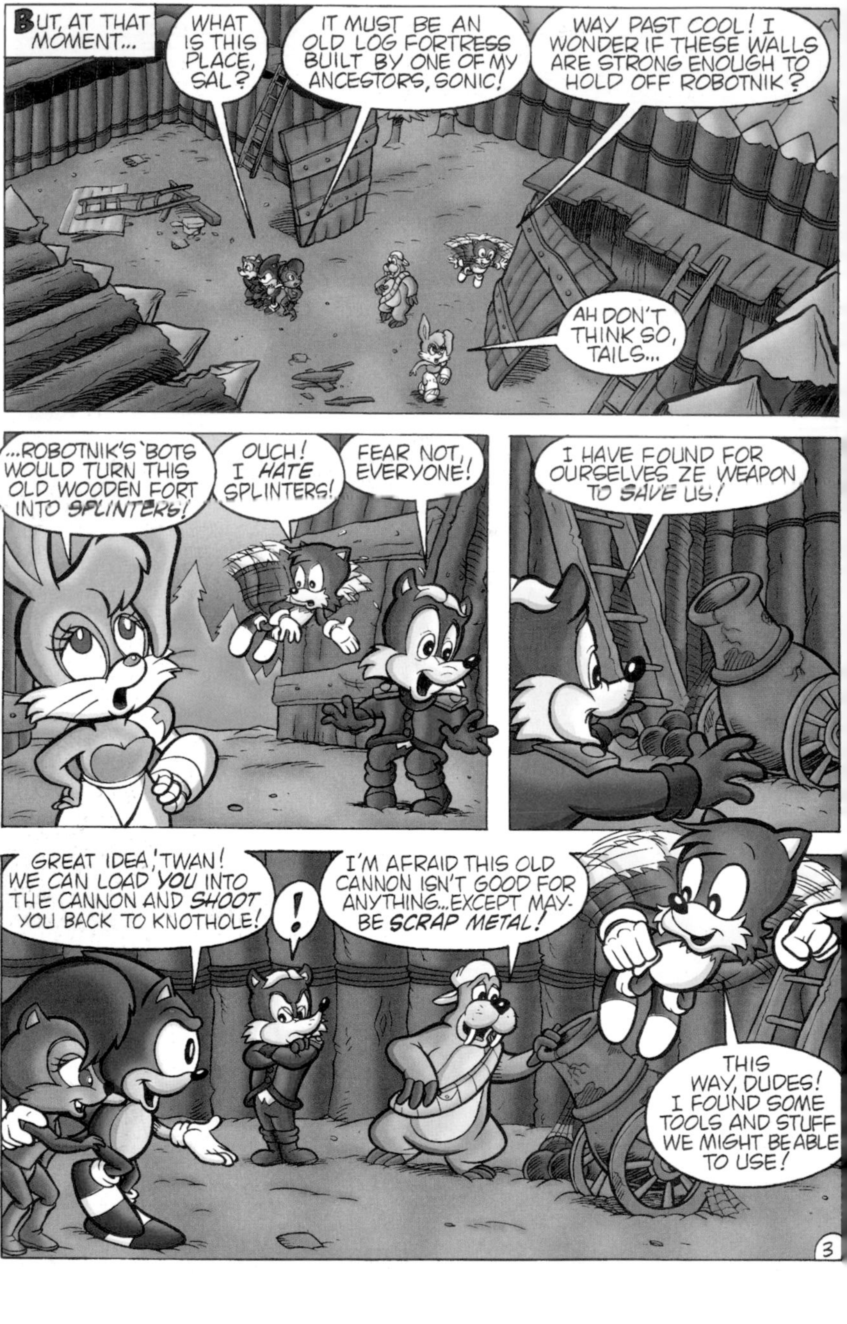
BUT, AT THAT MOMENT...
WHAT IS THIS PLACE, SAL?
IT MUST BE AN OLD LOG FORTRESS BUILT BY ONE OF MY ANCESTORS, SONIC!
WAY PAST COOL! I WONDER IF THESE WALLS ARE STRONG ENOUGH TO HOLD OFF ROBOTNIK?
AH DON'T THINK SO, TAILS...
...ROBOTNIK'S 'BOTS WOULD TURN THIS OLD WOODEN FORT INTO SPLINTERS!
OUCH! I HATE SPLINTERS!
FEAR NOT, EVERYONE!
I HAVE FOUND FOR OURSELVES ZE WEAPON TO SAVE US!
GREAT IDEA, TWAN! WE CAN LOAD YOU INTO THE CANNON AND SHOOT YOU BACK TO KNOTHOLE!
!
I'M AFRAID THIS OLD CANNON ISN'T GOOD FOR ANYTHING...EXCEPT MAY-BE SCRAP METAL!
THIS WAY, DUDES! I FOUND SOME TOOLS AND STUFF WE MIGHT BE ABLE TO USE!

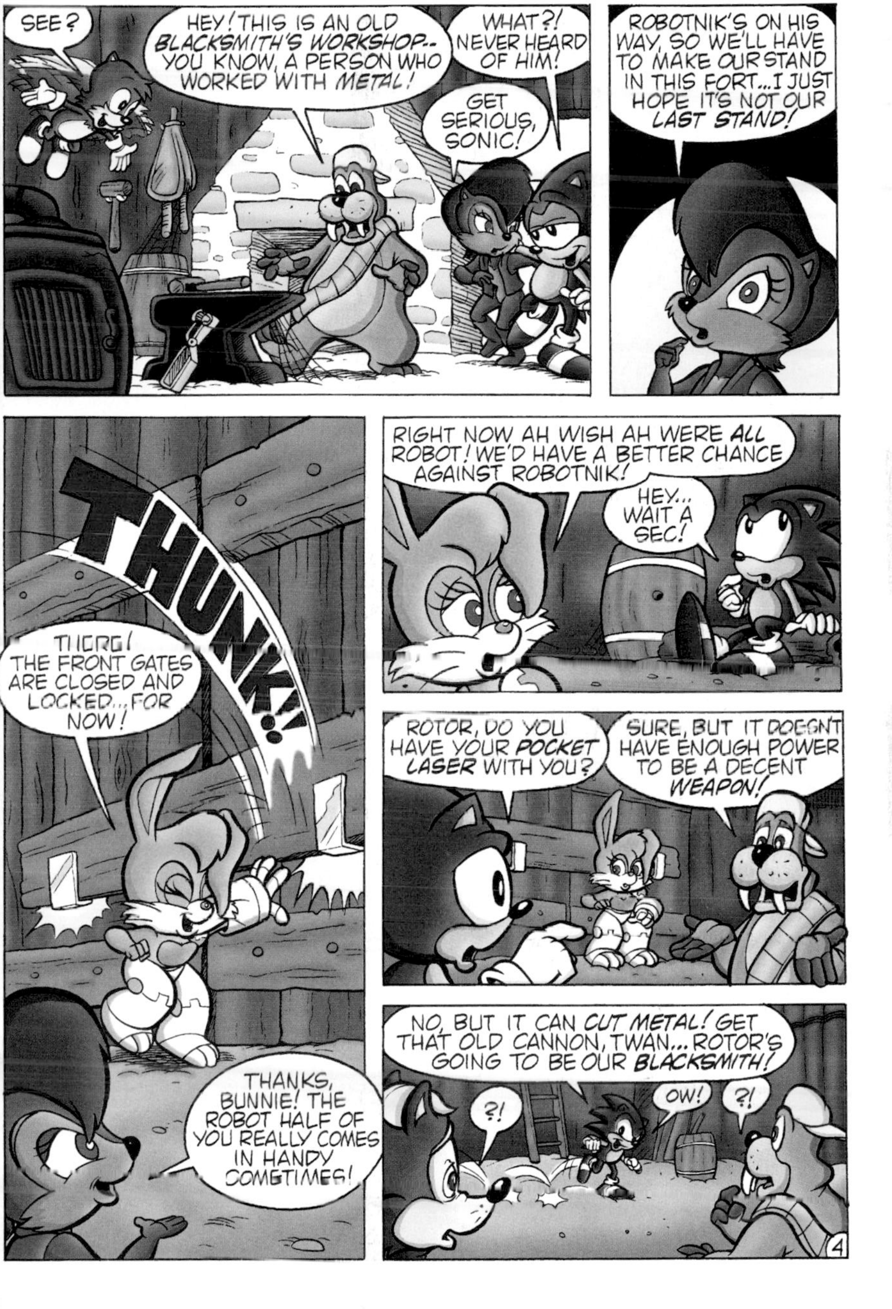
SEE?
HEY! THIS IS AN OLD BLACKSMITH'S WORKSHOP-- YOU KNOW, A PERSON WHO WORKED WITH METAL!
WHAT?! NEVER HEARD OF HIM!
GET SERIOUS, SONIC!
ROBOTNIK'S ON HIS WAY, SO WE'LL HAVE TO MAKE OUR STAND IN THIS FORT... I JUST HOPE IT'S NOT OUR LAST STAND!
THUNK!!
THERE! THE FRONT GATES ARE CLOSED AND LOCKED...FOR NOW!
THANKS, BUNNIE! THE ROBOT HALF OF YOU REALLY COMES IN HANDY SOMETIMES!
RIGHT NOW AH WISH AH WERE ALL ROBOT! WE'D HAVE A BETTER CHANCE AGAINST ROBOTNIK!
HEY... WAIT A SEC!
ROTOR, DO YOU HAVE YOUR POCKET LASER WITH YOU?
SURE, BUT IT DOESN'T HAVE ENOUGH POWER TO BE A DECENT WEAPON!
NO, BUT IT CAN CUT METAL! GET THAT OLD CANNON, TWAN... ROTOR'S GOING TO BE OUR BLACKSMITH!
?!
OW!
?!
4

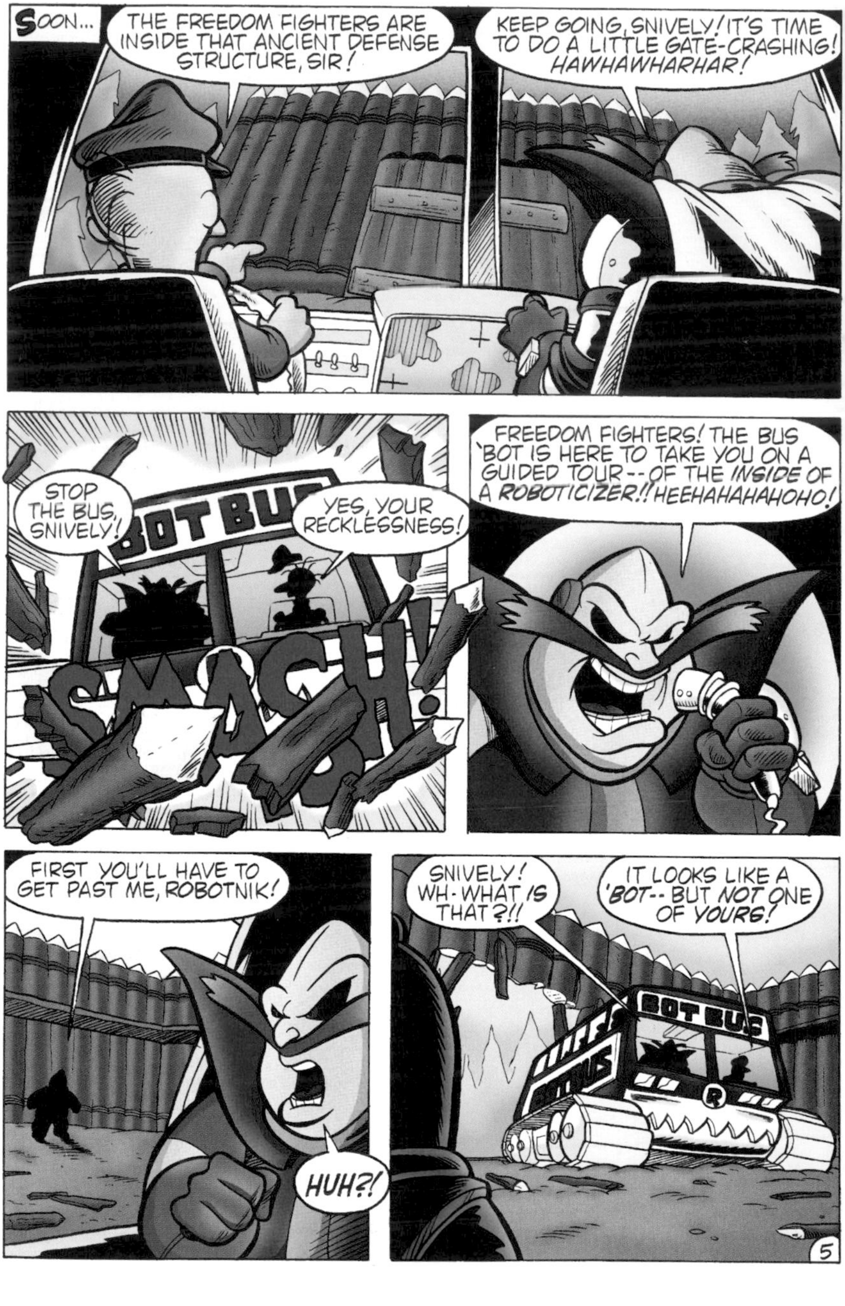
SOON...
THE FREEDOM FIGHTERS ARE INSIDE THAT ANCIENT DEFENSE STRUCTURE, SIR!
KEEP GOING, SNIVELY! IT'S TIME TO DO A LITTLE GATE-CRASHING! HAWHAWHARHAR!
STOP THE BUS, SNIVELY!
YES, YOUR RECKLESSNESS!
BOT BUS
SMASH!
FREEDOM FIGHTERS! THE BUS 'BOT IS HERE TO TAKE YOU ON A GUIDED TOUR -- OF THE INSIDE OF A ROBOTICIZER!! HEEHAHAHAHOHO!
FIRST YOU'LL HAVE TO GET PAST ME, ROBOTNIK!
HUH?!
SNIVELY! WH-WHAT IS THAT?!!
IT LOOKS LIKE A 'BOT-- BUT NOT ONE OF YOURS!
BOT BUS

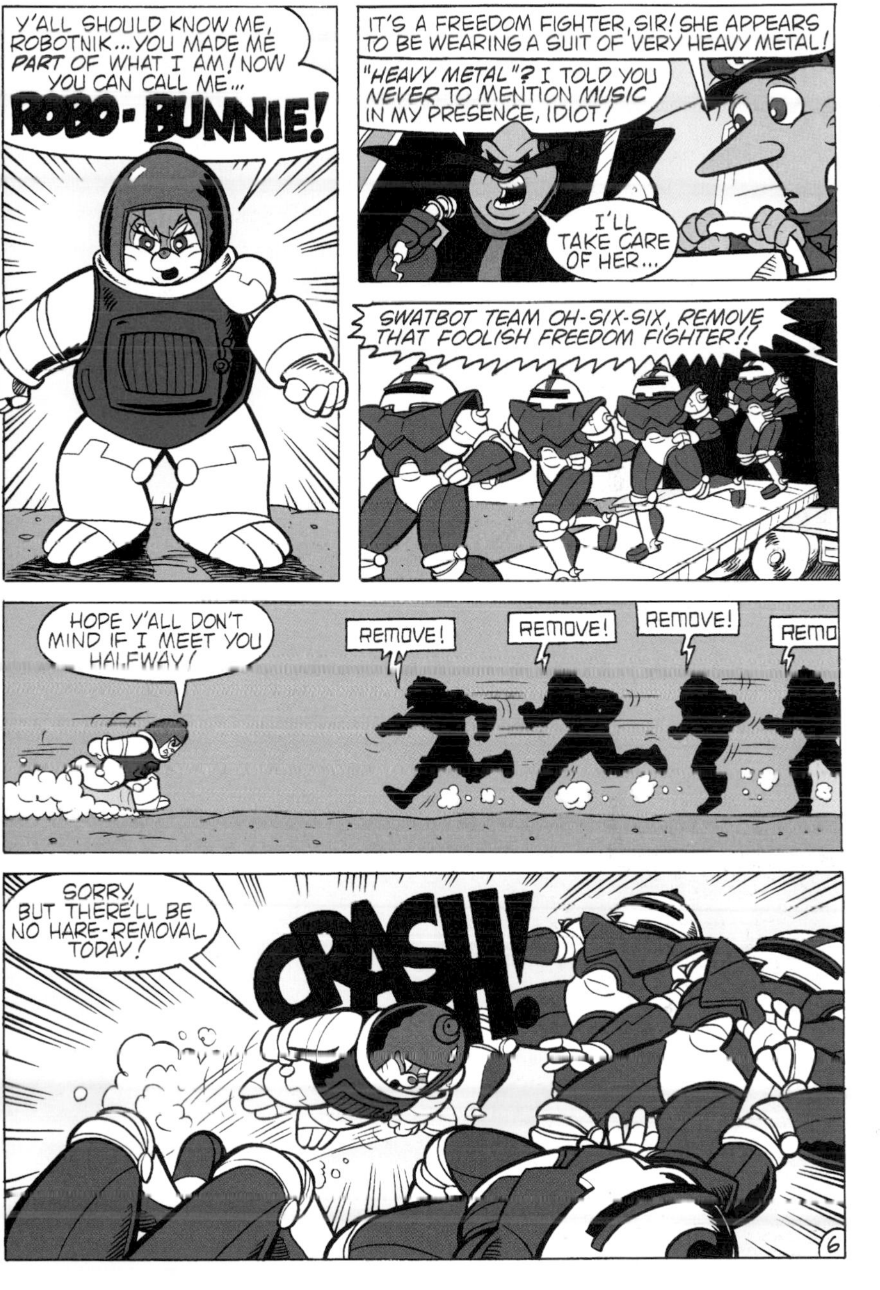

Y'ALL SHOULD KNOW ME, ROBOTNIK... YOU MADE ME PART OF WHAT I AM! NOW YOU CAN CALL ME... ROBO-BUNNIE!
IT'S A FREEDOM FIGHTER, SIR! SHE APPEARS TO BE WEARING A SUIT OF VERY HEAVY METAL!
"HEAVY METAL"? I TOLD YOU NEVER TO MENTION MUSIC IN MY PRESENCE, IDIOT!
I'LL TAKE CARE OF HER...
SWATBOT TEAM OH-SIX-SIX, REMOVE THAT FOOLISH FREEDOM FIGHTER!!
HOPE Y'ALL DON'T MIND IF I MEET YOU HALFWAY!
REMOVE!
REMOVE!
REMOVE!
REMO
SORRY, BUT THERE'LL BE NO HARE-REMOVAL TODAY!
CRASH!

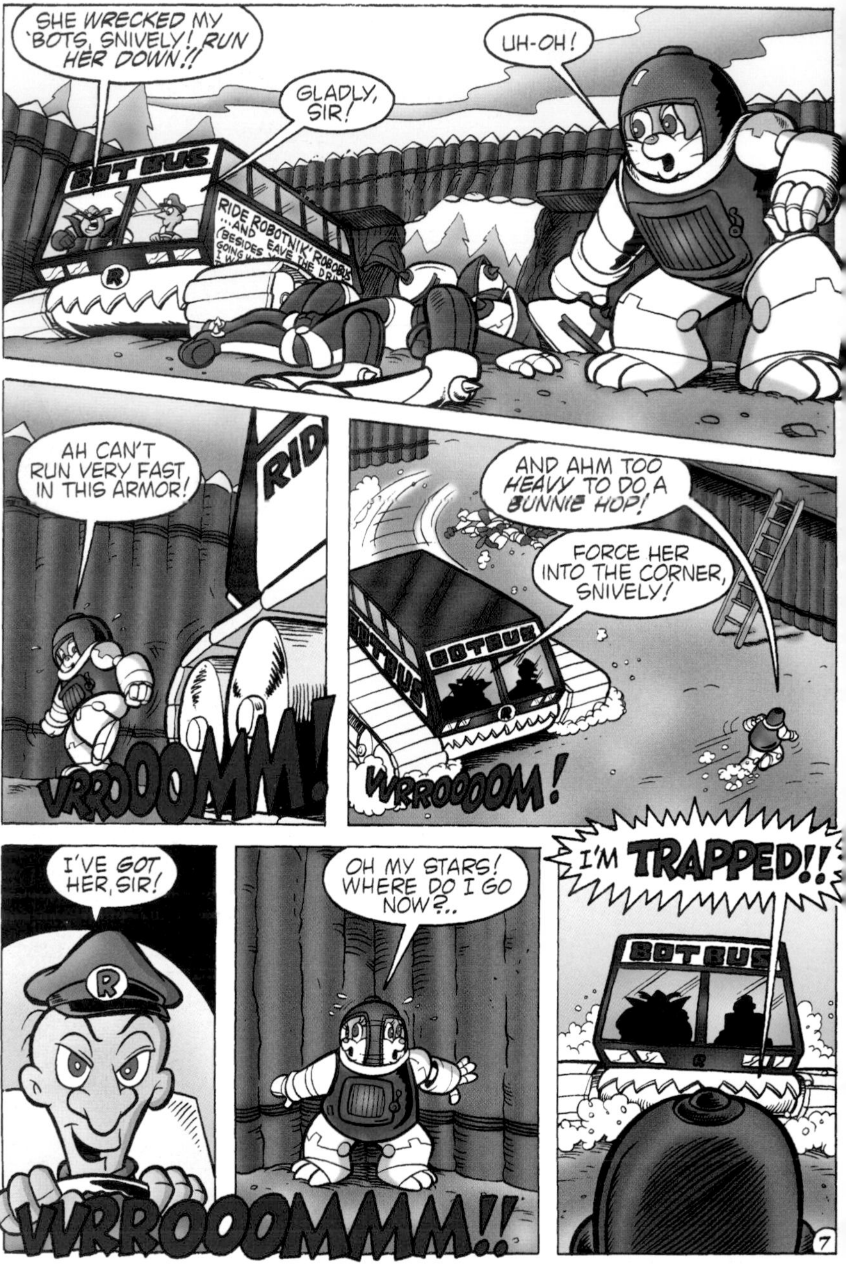
SHE WRECKED MY 'BOTS, SNIVELY! RUN HER DOWN!!
GLADLY, SIR!
UH-OH!
BOT BUS
AH CAN'T RUN VERY FAST IN THIS ARMOR!
RID
VRROOOMM!
AND AHM TOO HEAVY TO DO A BUNNIE HOP!
FORCE HER INTO THE CORNER, SNIVELY!
BOT BUS
WRROOOOOM!
I'VE GOT HER, SIR!
OH MY STARS! WHERE DO I GO NOW?..
I'M TRAPPED!!
BOT BUS
VVRROOOMMMM!!

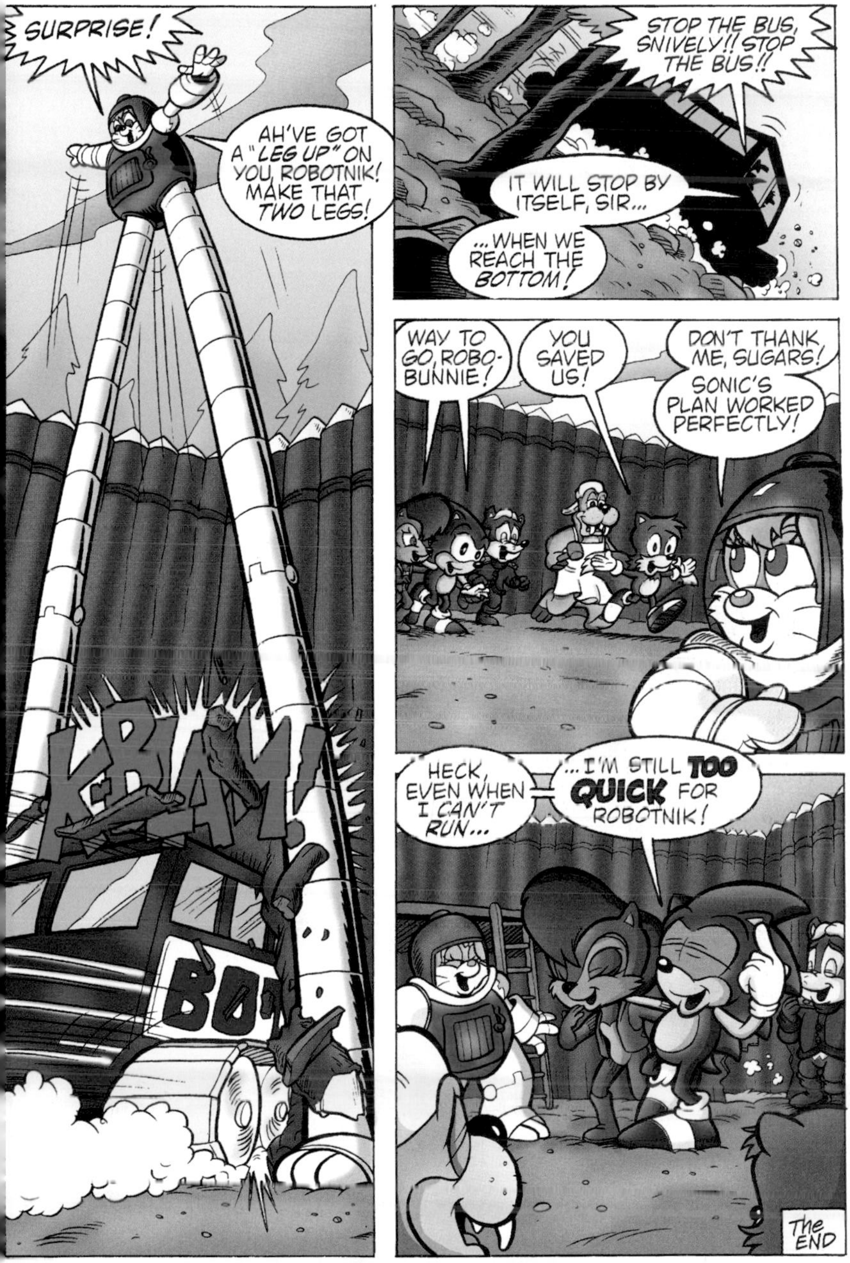
SURPRISE!
AH'VE GOT A "LEG UP" ON YOU, ROBOTNIK! MAKE THAT TWO LEGS!
K-BAM!
BOT
STOP THE BUS, SNIVELY!! STOP THE BUS!!
IT WILL STOP BY ITSELF, SIR...
...WHEN WE REACH THE BOTTOM!
WAY TO GO, ROBO-BUNNIE!
YOU SAVED US!
DON'T THANK ME, SUGARS!
SONIC'S PLAN WORKED PERFECTLY!
HECK, EVEN WHEN I CAN'T RUN...
...I'M STILL TOO QUICK FOR ROBOTNIK!
The END

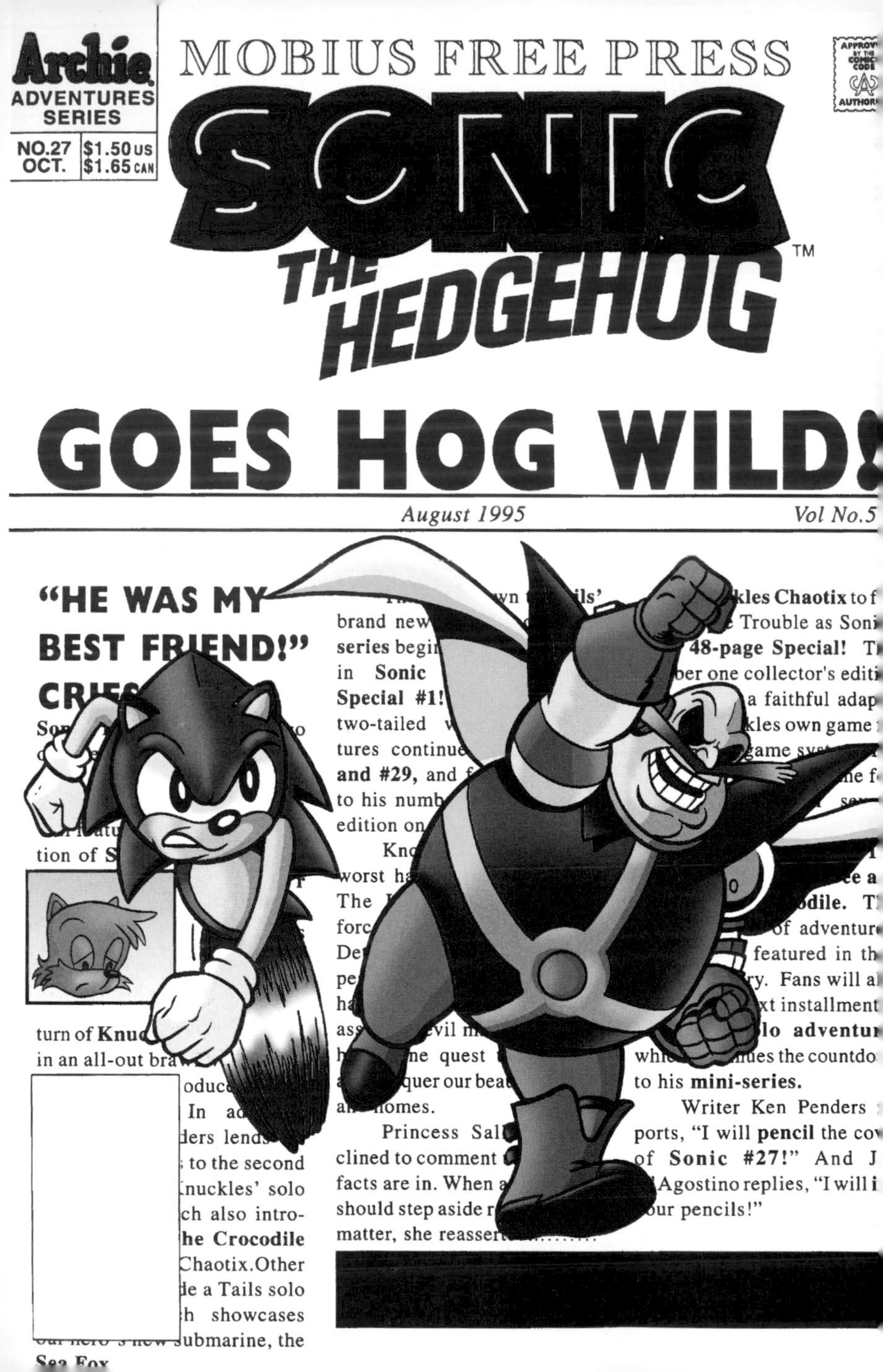
Archie ADVENTURES SERIES
NO.27 OCT.
$1.50 US
$1.65 CAN
MOBIUS FREE PRESS
SONIC THE HEDGEHOG™
GOES HOG WILD!
August 1995
Vol No.5
"HE WAS MY BEST FRIEND!" CRIES
brand new
series begi
in Sonic
Special #1!
two-tailed
tures continue
and #29, and
to his numb
edition on
worst h
The
forc
De
pe
ha
ass vil m
h ne quest
a quer our bea
al homes.
Princess Sal
clined to comment
facts are in. When a
should step aside r
matter, she reassert........
kles Chaotix to f
Trouble as Soni
48-page Special! T
ber one collector's editi
a faithful adap
kles own game
game sys
he f
ce a
odile. T
of adventur
featured in th
ry. Fans will a
xt installment
lo adventu
whi ues the countdo
to his mini-series.
Writer Ken Penders
ports, "I will pencil the co
of Sonic #27!" And J
Agostino replies, "I will i
our pencils!"
tion of S
turn of Knu
in an all-out bra
oduc
In ad
ders lends
to the second
nuckles' solo
ch also intro-
he Crocodile
Chaotix.Other
de a Tails solo
h showcases
ubmarine, the
Sea Fox

LATE AT NIGHT, DEEP IN THE BOWELS OF *ROBOTROPOLIS*...

YOU *SURE* IT'S SAFE, *SLEUTH DAWGGY-DAWG?*

LONG *ENOUGH* FOR US TO SEND WORD, *KICKS-A-LOT!*

AMAZING *ROBOTNIK* HASN'T CAUGHT ON TO OUR *CODE!*

YEP! JUST THINKS *VANDALS* ARE *MESSING UP* HIS CITY!

WAIT A MINUTE! WHAT ARE YOU *DOING?*

YOU *ALREADY* SPRAY-PAINTED THE *MESSAGE!*

WELL, I *DIDN'T* WANT OL' *IVO* TO THINK WE WERE ANYTHING *BUT* VANDALS!

SONIC & SALLY

GOOD THINKING, SLEUTH!

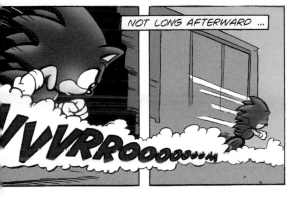

NOT LONG AFTERWARD ...

VVVRROOOooooM

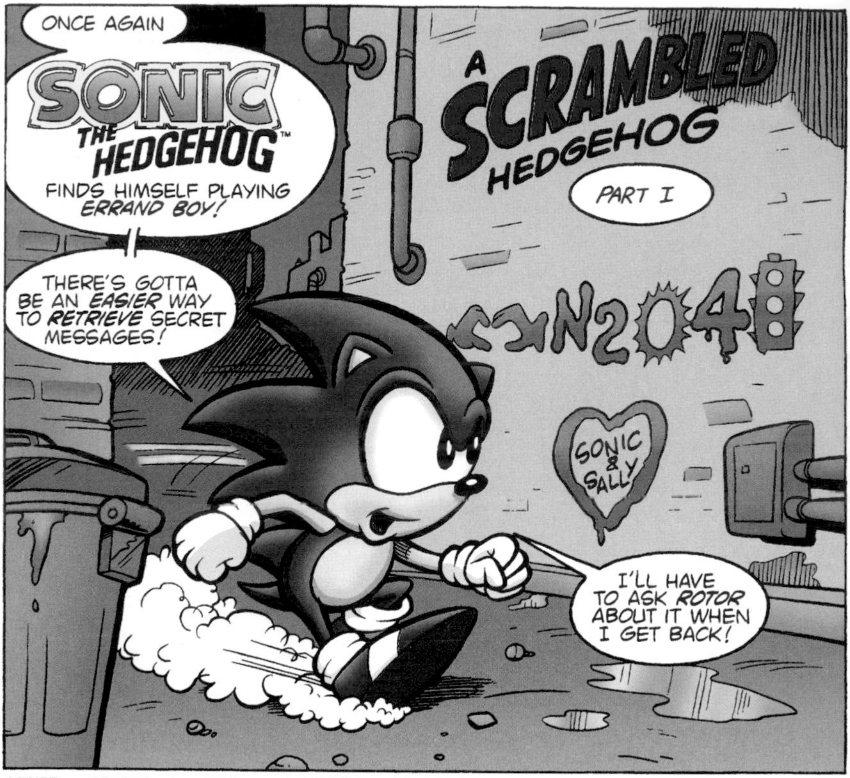
ONCE AGAIN
SONIC THE HEDGEHOG™
FINDS HIMSELF PLAYING ERRAND BOY!
A SCRAMBLED HEDGEHOG
PART I
THERE'S GOTTA BE AN EASIER WAY TO RETRIEVE SECRET MESSAGES!
SONIC & SALLY
I'LL HAVE TO ASK ROTOR ABOUT IT WHEN I GET BACK!

SCRIPT: KEN PENDERS PENCILS: ART MAWHINNEY INKS: RICH KOSLOWSKI LETTERING: MINDY EISMAN COLORING: BARRY GROSSMAN EDITOR: SCOTT FULOP MANAGING EDITOR: VICTOR GORELICK EDITOR-IN-CHIEF: RICHARD GOLDWATER

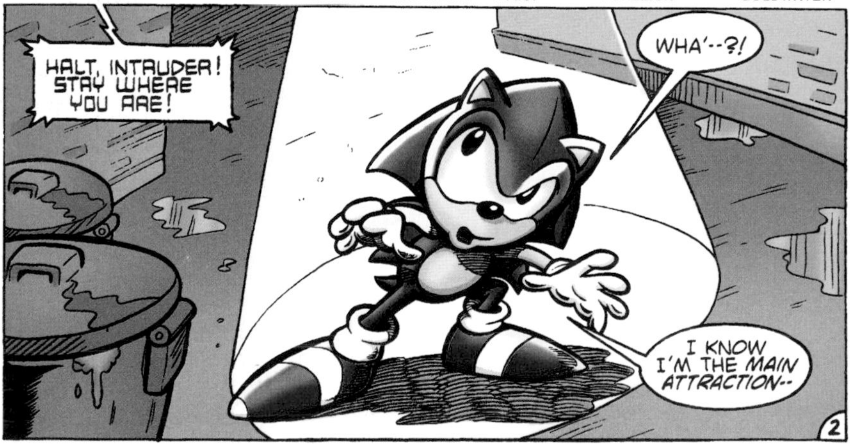
HALT, INTRUDER! STAY WHERE YOU ARE!
WHA'--?!
I KNOW I'M THE MAIN ATTRACTION--

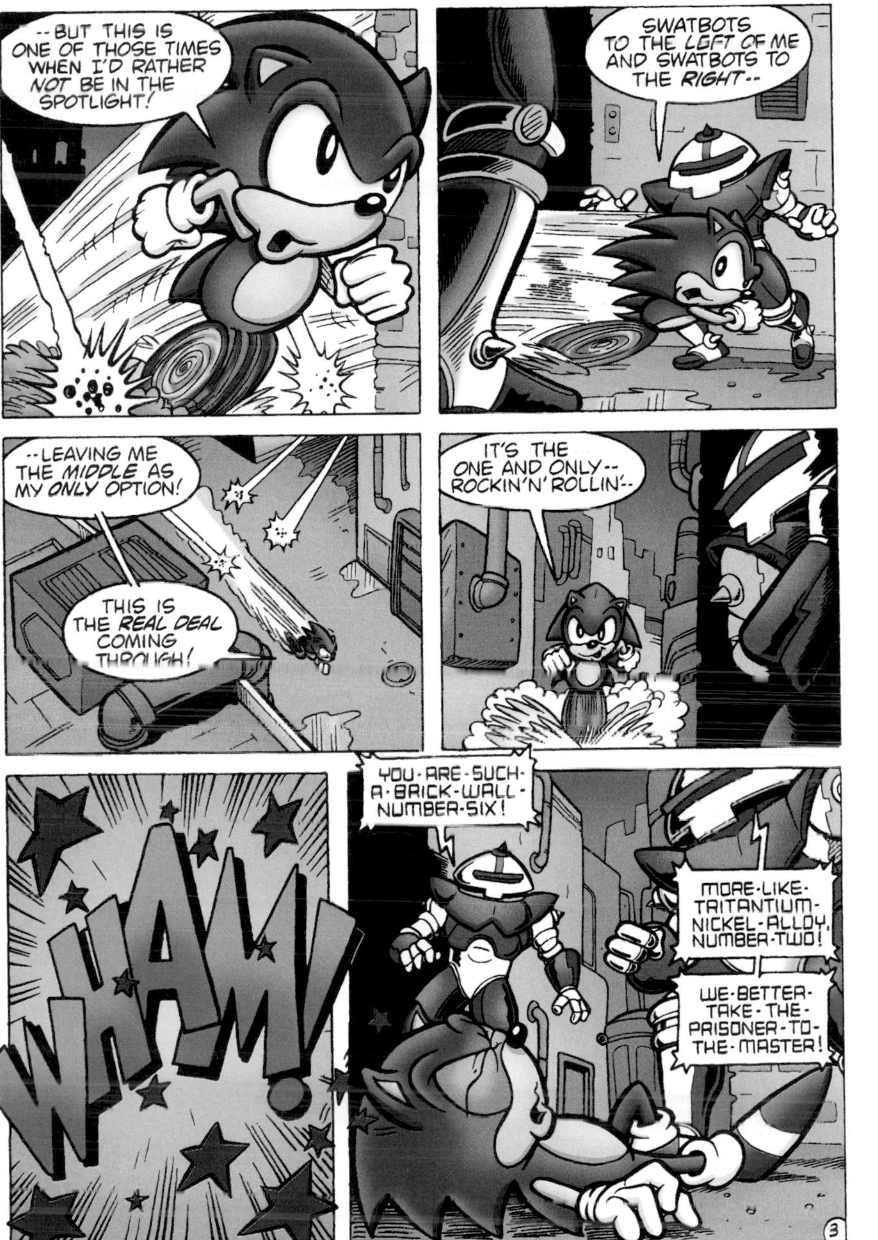
--BUT THIS IS ONE OF THOSE TIMES WHEN I'D RATHER NOT BE IN THE SPOTLIGHT!
SWATBOTS TO THE LEFT OF ME AND SWATBOTS TO THE RIGHT--
--LEAVING ME THE MIDDLE AS MY ONLY OPTION!
THIS IS THE REAL DEAL COMING THROUGH!
IT'S THE ONE AND ONLY--ROCKIN'N' ROLLIN'--
WHAM!
YOU-ARE-SUCH-A-BRICK-WALL-NUMBER-SIX!
MORE-LIKE-TRITANTIUM-NICKEL-ALLOY, NUMBER-TWO!
WE-BETTER-TAKE-THE-PRISONER-TO-THE-MASTER!
3

IT'S ABOUT TIME!

WHA--?

JUST RELAX--

WHERE AM I?

ANYBODY GOT THE NUMBER OF THE *TRUCK* THAT HIT ME?

OOOOOOOOO...

TAKE YOUR *TIME* WAKING, HEDGEHOG! NOW THAT I HAVE YOU, I CAN AFFORD TO BE *PATIENT!* BUT NOT *TOO* PATIENT! AFTER ALL--

--I HAVE A LOT OF *SCHEMES* TO FOIL AND *ENEMIES* TO *CRUSH!*

HEDGEHOG? *WHAT* HEDGEHOG? I'M--

--I'M--

--I'M *NOT SURE WHO I AM!*

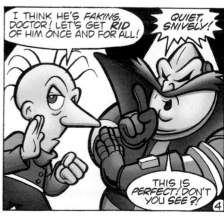

I THINK HE'S *FAKING,* DOCTOR! LET'S GET *RID* OF HIM ONCE AND FOR ALL!

QUIET, SNIVELY!

THIS IS *PERFECT!* DON'T YOU *SEE?!*

4

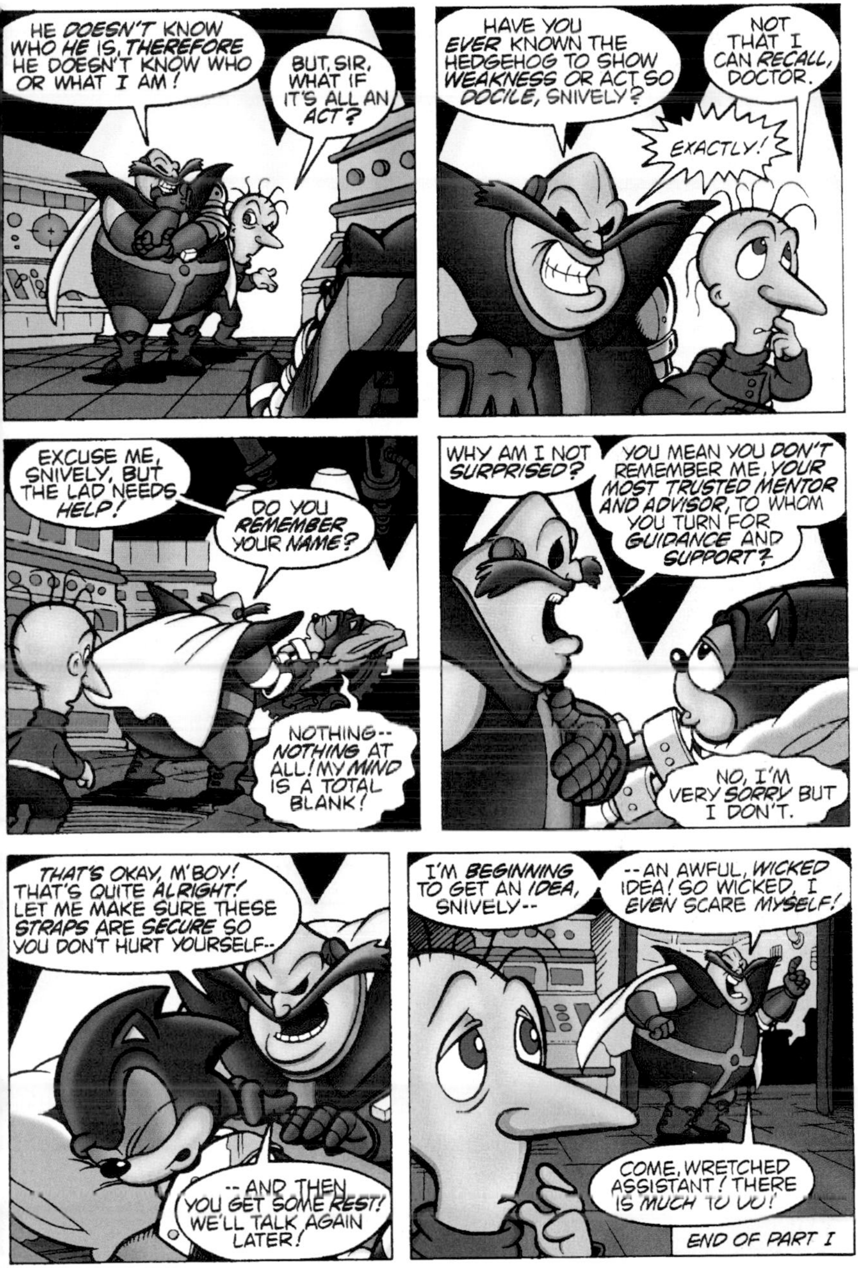
HE DOESN'T KNOW WHO HE IS, THEREFORE HE DOESN'T KNOW WHO OR WHAT I AM!
BUT, SIR, WHAT IF IT'S ALL AN ACT?
HAVE YOU EVER KNOWN THE HEDGEHOG TO SHOW WEAKNESS OR ACT SO DOCILE, SNIVELY?
NOT THAT I CAN RECALL, DOCTOR.
EXACTLY!
EXCUSE ME, SNIVELY, BUT THE LAD NEEDS HELP!
DO YOU REMEMBER YOUR NAME?
NOTHING-- NOTHING AT ALL! MY MIND IS A TOTAL BLANK!
WHY AM I NOT SURPRISED?
YOU MEAN YOU DON'T REMEMBER ME, YOUR MOST TRUSTED MENTOR AND ADVISOR, TO WHOM YOU TURN FOR GUIDANCE AND SUPPORT?
NO, I'M VERY SORRY BUT I DON'T.
THAT'S OKAY, M'BOY! THAT'S QUITE ALRIGHT! LET ME MAKE SURE THESE STRAPS ARE SECURE SO YOU DON'T HURT YOURSELF--
-- AND THEN YOU GET SOME REST! WE'LL TALK AGAIN LATER!
I'M BEGINNING TO GET AN IDEA, SNIVELY--
-- AN AWFUL, WICKED IDEA! SO WICKED, I EVEN SCARE MYSELF!
COME, WRETCHED ASSISTANT! THERE IS MUCH TO DO!
END OF PART I

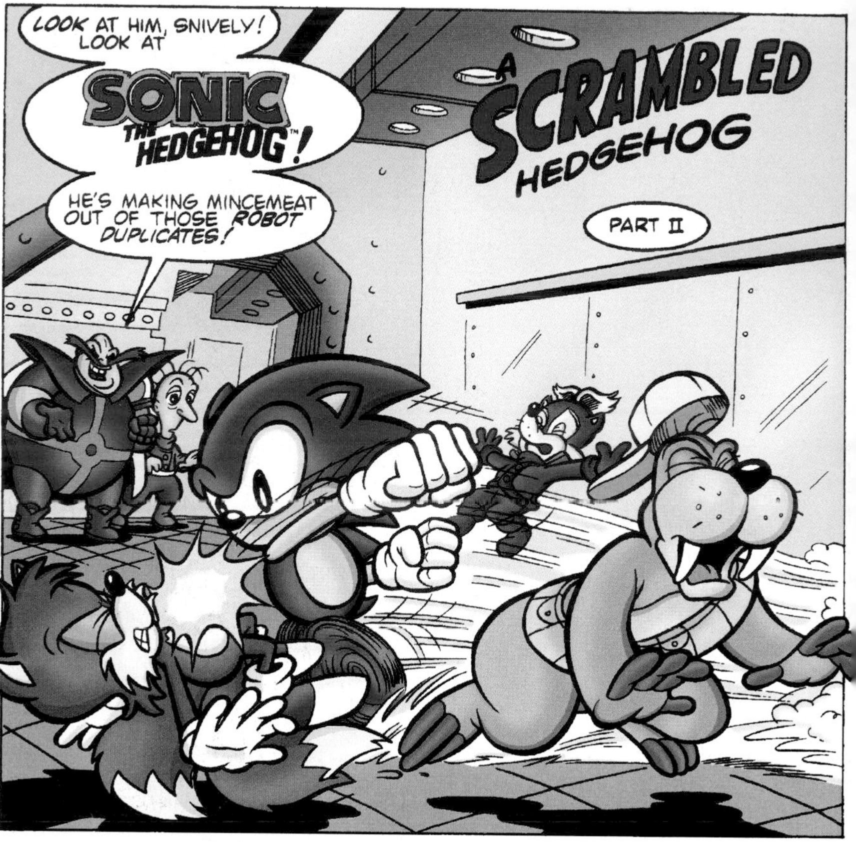
LOOK AT HIM, SNIVELY! LOOK AT
SONIC THE HEDGEHOG™!
A SCRAMBLED HEDGEHOG
PART II
HE'S MAKING MINCEMEAT OUT OF THOSE ROBOT DUPLICATES!

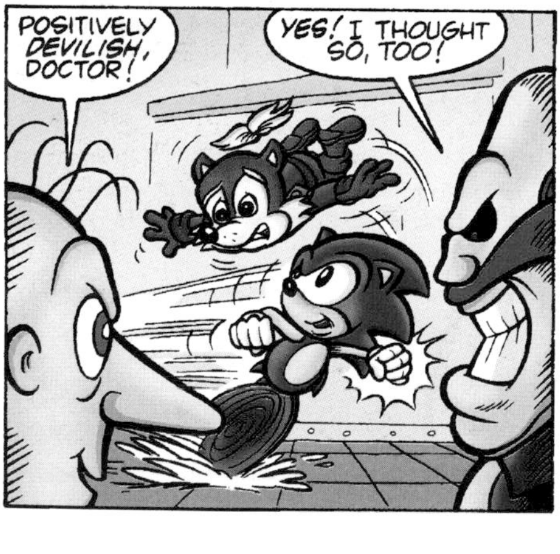
POSITIVELY DEVILISH, DOCTOR!
YES! I THOUGHT SO, TOO!

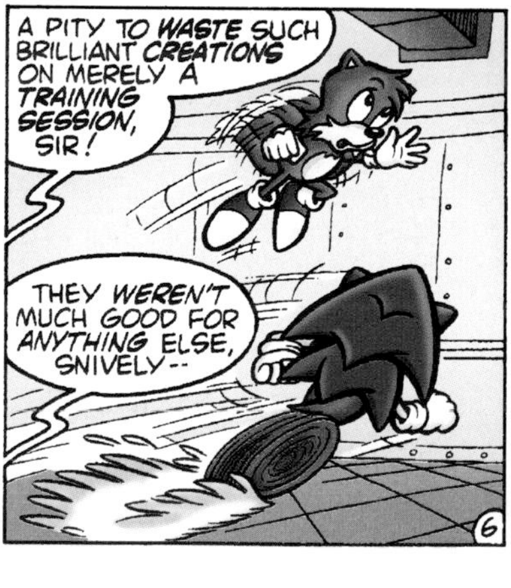
A PITY TO WASTE SUCH BRILLIANT CREATIONS ON MERELY A TRAINING SESSION, SIR!
THEY WEREN'T MUCH GOOD FOR ANYTHING ELSE, SNIVELY--

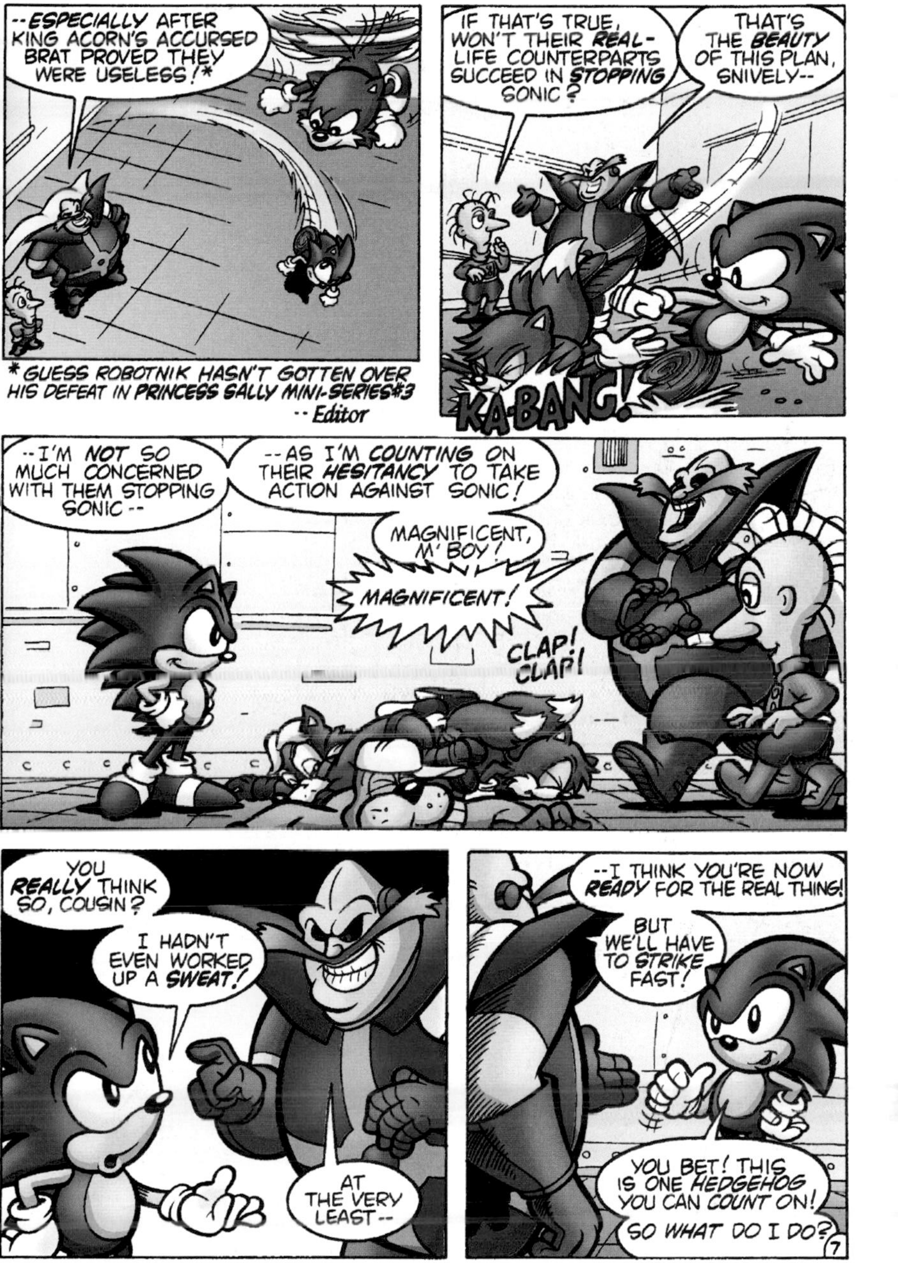
--ESPECIALLY AFTER KING ACORN'S ACCURSED BRAT PROVED THEY WERE USELESS!*
* GUESS ROBOTNIK HASN'T GOTTEN OVER HIS DEFEAT IN PRINCESS SALLY MINI-SERIES #3 --Editor
IF THAT'S TRUE, WON'T THEIR REAL-LIFE COUNTERPARTS SUCCEED IN STOPPING SONIC?
THAT'S THE BEAUTY OF THIS PLAN, SNIVELY--
KA-BANG!
--I'M NOT SO MUCH CONCERNED WITH THEM STOPPING SONIC--
--AS I'M COUNTING ON THEIR HESITANCY TO TAKE ACTION AGAINST SONIC!
MAGNIFICENT, M' BOY!
MAGNIFICENT!
CLAP! CLAP!
YOU REALLY THINK SO, COUSIN?
I HADN'T EVEN WORKED UP A SWEAT!
AT THE VERY LEAST--
--I THINK YOU'RE NOW READY FOR THE REAL THING!
BUT WE'LL HAVE TO STRIKE FAST!
YOU BET! THIS IS ONE HEDGEHOG YOU CAN COUNT ON!
SO WHAT DO I DO?
7

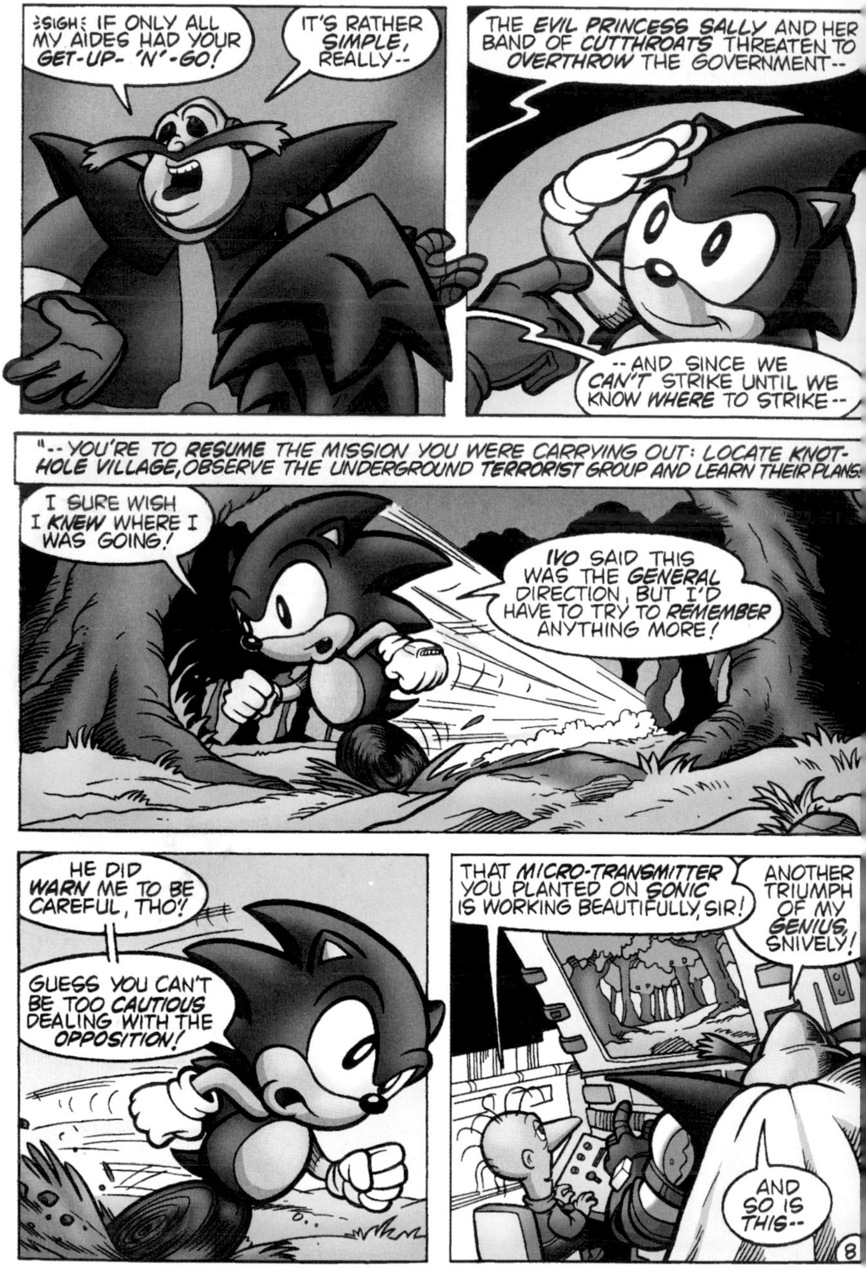

:SIGH: IF ONLY ALL MY AIDES HAD YOUR GET-UP-'N'-GO!
IT'S RATHER SIMPLE, REALLY--
THE EVIL PRINCESS SALLY AND HER BAND OF CUTTHROATS THREATEN TO OVERTHROW THE GOVERNMENT--
--AND SINCE WE CAN'T STRIKE UNTIL WE KNOW WHERE TO STRIKE--
"--YOU'RE TO RESUME THE MISSION YOU WERE CARRYING OUT: LOCATE KNOTHOLE VILLAGE, OBSERVE THE UNDERGROUND TERRORIST GROUP AND LEARN THEIR PLANS!"
I SURE WISH I KNEW WHERE I WAS GOING!
IVO SAID THIS WAS THE GENERAL DIRECTION, BUT I'D HAVE TO TRY TO REMEMBER ANYTHING MORE!
HE DID WARN ME TO BE CAREFUL, THO'!
GUESS YOU CAN'T BE TOO CAUTIOUS DEALING WITH THE OPPOSITION!
THAT MICRO-TRANSMITTER YOU PLANTED ON SONIC IS WORKING BEAUTIFULLY, SIR!
ANOTHER TRIUMPH OF MY GENIUS, SNIVELY!
AND SO IS THIS--

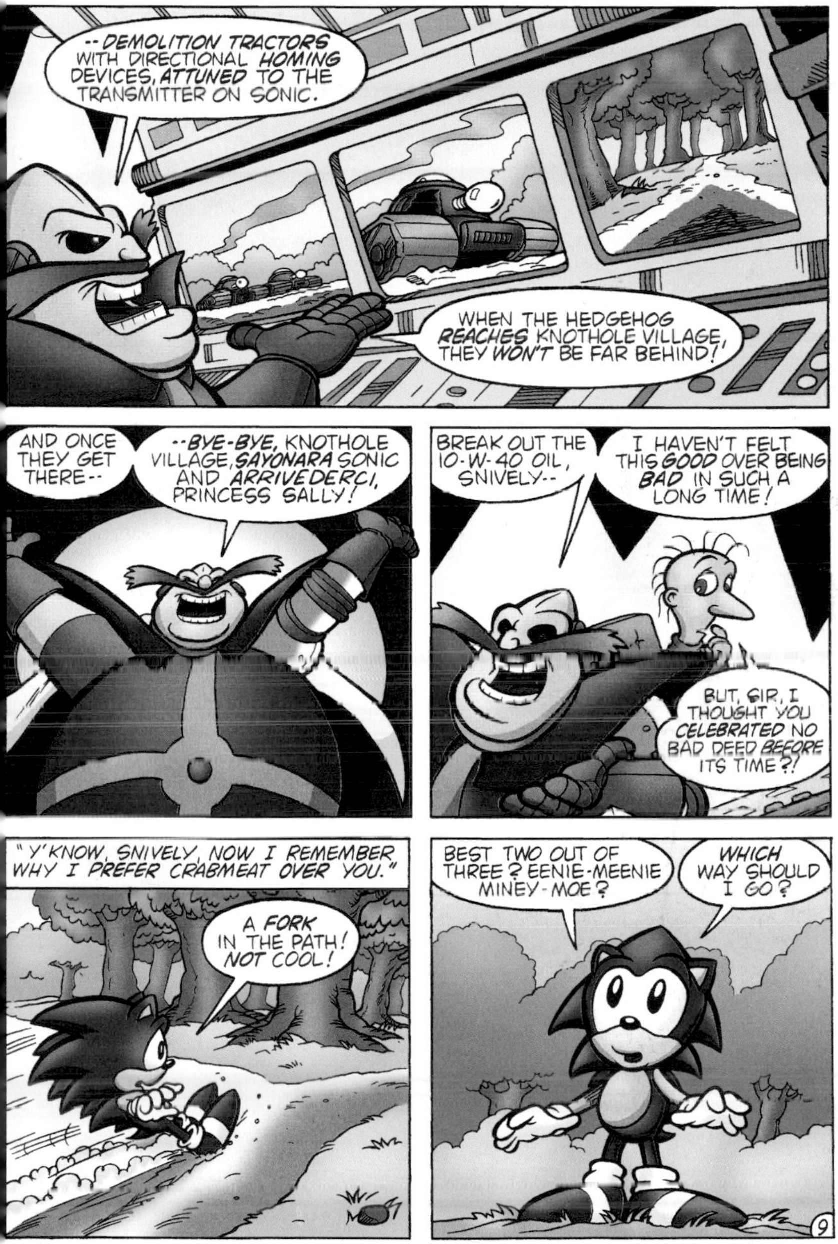
--DEMOLITION TRACTORS WITH DIRECTIONAL HOMING DEVICES, ATTUNED TO THE TRANSMITTER ON SONIC.
WHEN THE HEDGEHOG REACHES KNOTHOLE VILLAGE, THEY WON'T BE FAR BEHIND!
AND ONCE THEY GET THERE--
--BYE-BYE, KNOTHOLE VILLAGE, SAYONARA SONIC AND ARRIVEDERCI, PRINCESS SALLY!
BREAK OUT THE 10-W-40 OIL, SNIVELY--
I HAVEN'T FELT THIS GOOD OVER BEING BAD IN SUCH A LONG TIME!
BUT, SIR, I THOUGHT YOU CELEBRATED NO BAD DEED BEFORE ITS TIME?!
"Y'KNOW, SNIVELY, NOW I REMEMBER WHY I PREFER CRABMEAT OVER YOU."
A FORK IN THE PATH! NOT COOL!
BEST TWO OUT OF THREE? EENIE-MEENIE MINEY-MOE?
WHICH WAY SHOULD I GO?
9

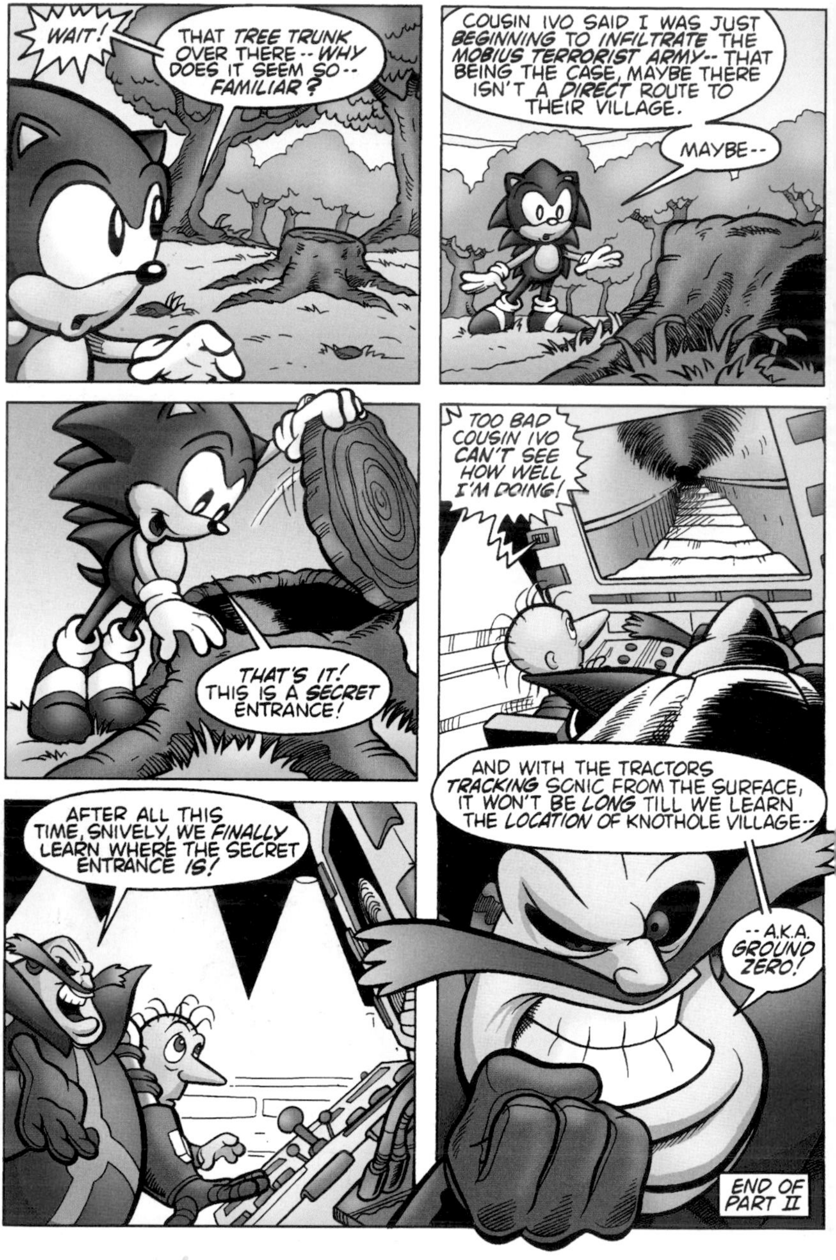
WAIT!
THAT TREE TRUNK OVER THERE--WHY DOES IT SEEM SO--FAMILIAR?
COUSIN IVO SAID I WAS JUST BEGINNING TO INFILTRATE THE MOBIUS TERRORIST ARMY--THAT BEING THE CASE, MAYBE THERE ISN'T A DIRECT ROUTE TO THEIR VILLAGE.
MAYBE--
THAT'S IT! THIS IS A SECRET ENTRANCE!
TOO BAD COUSIN IVO CAN'T SEE HOW WELL I'M DOING!
AFTER ALL THIS TIME, SNIVELY, WE FINALLY LEARN WHERE THE SECRET ENTRANCE IS!
AND WITH THE TRACTORS TRACKING SONIC FROM THE SURFACE, IT WON'T BE LONG TILL WE LEARN THE LOCATION OF KNOTHOLE VILLAGE--
--A.K.A. GROUND ZERO!
END OF PART II

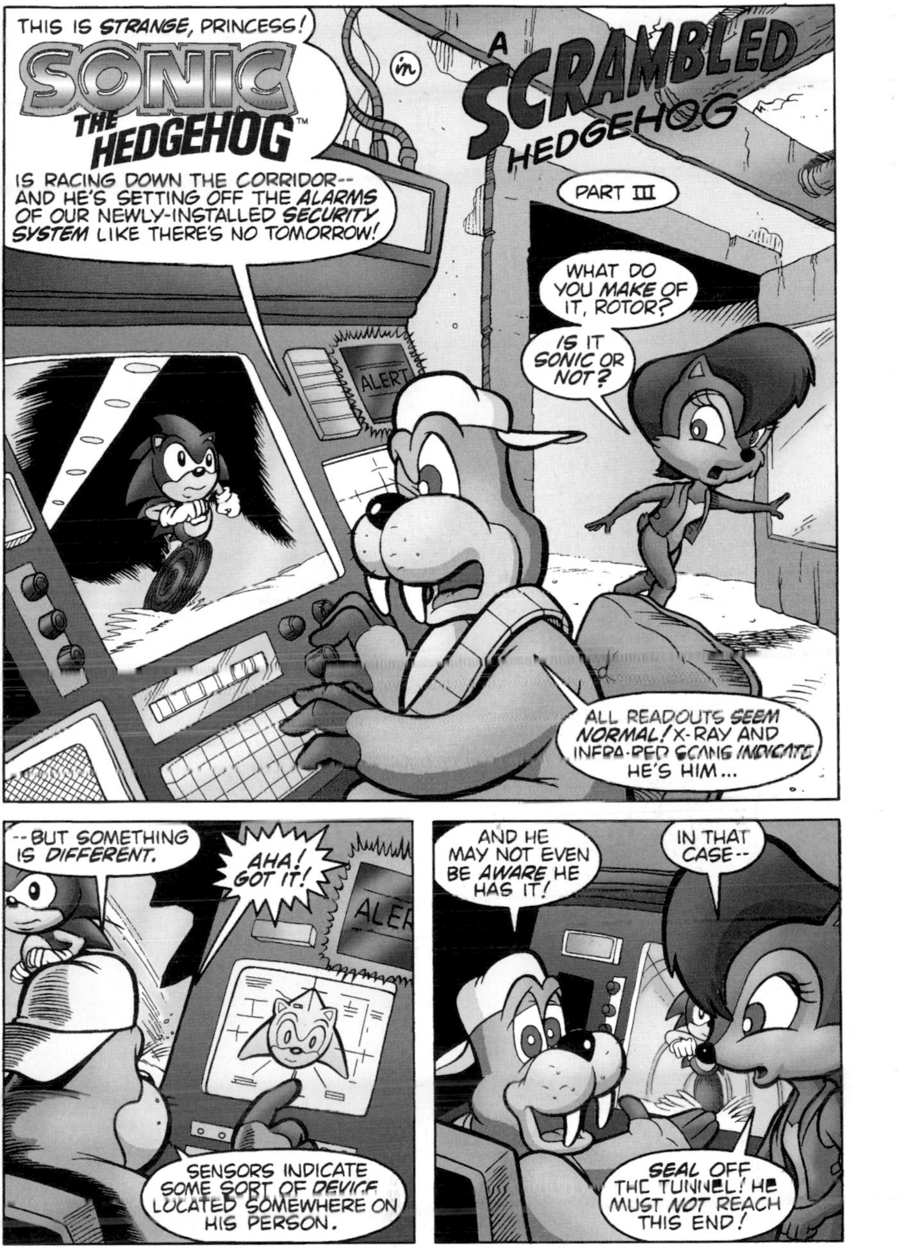
THIS IS STRANGE, PRINCESS!
SONIC THE HEDGEHOG™
in
A SCRAMBLED HEDGEHOG
PART III
IS RACING DOWN THE CORRIDOR-- AND HE'S SETTING OFF THE ALARMS OF OUR NEWLY-INSTALLED SECURITY SYSTEM LIKE THERE'S NO TOMORROW!
WHAT DO YOU MAKE OF IT, ROTOR?
IS IT SONIC OR NOT?
ALERT
ALL READOUTS SEEM NORMAL! X-RAY AND INFRA-RED SCANS INDICATE HE'S HIM...
--BUT SOMETHING IS DIFFERENT.
AHA! GOT IT!
SENSORS INDICATE SOME SORT OF DEVICE LOCATED SOMEWHERE ON HIS PERSON.
AND HE MAY NOT EVEN BE AWARE HE HAS IT!
IN THAT CASE--
SEAL OFF THE TUNNEL! HE MUST NOT REACH THIS END!

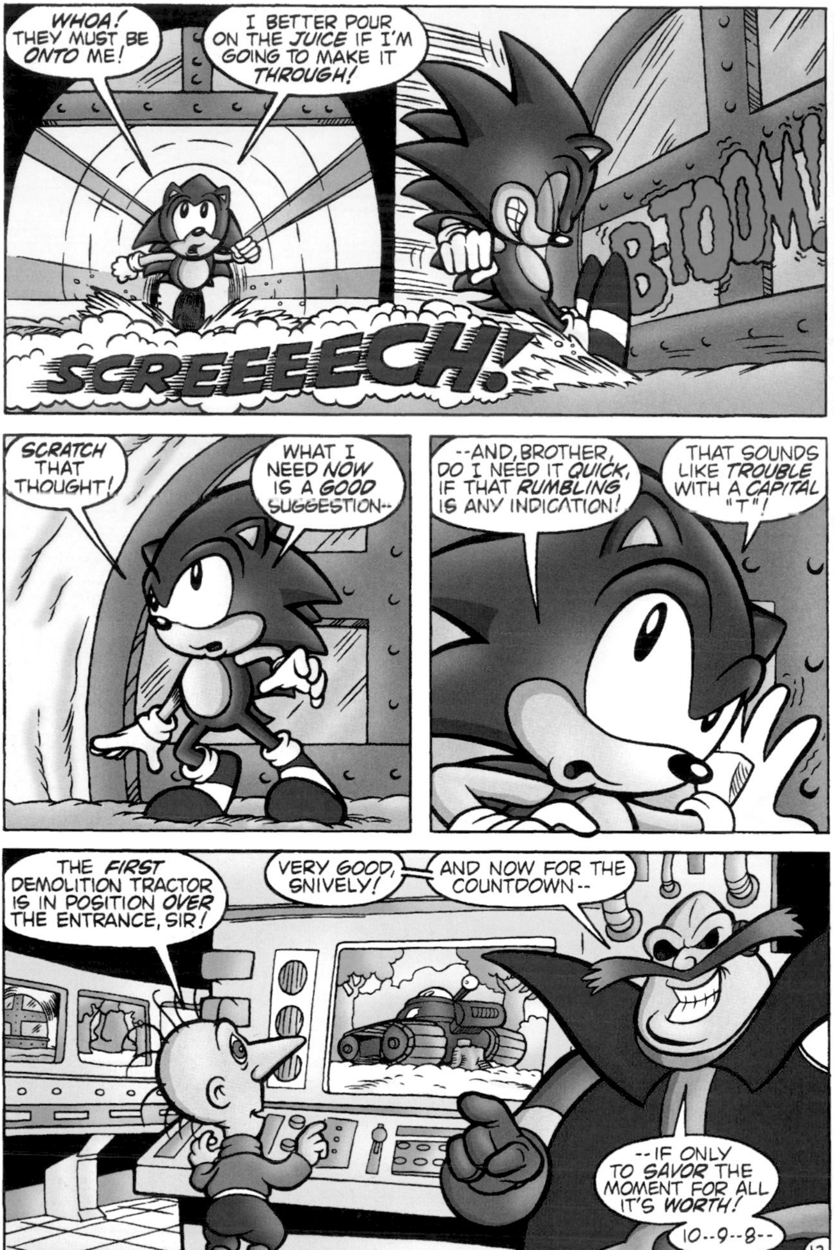
WHOA! THEY MUST BE ONTO ME!
I BETTER POUR ON THE JUICE IF I'M GOING TO MAKE IT THROUGH!
B-TOOM!
SCREEEEECH!
SCRATCH THAT THOUGHT!
WHAT I NEED NOW IS A GOOD SUGGESTION--
--AND, BROTHER, DO I NEED IT QUICK, IF THAT RUMBLING IS ANY INDICATION!
THAT SOUNDS LIKE TROUBLE WITH A CAPITAL "T"!
THE FIRST DEMOLITION TRACTOR IS IN POSITION OVER THE ENTRANCE, SIR!
VERY GOOD, SNIVELY!
AND NOW FOR THE COUNTDOWN--
--IF ONLY TO SAVOR THE MOMENT FOR ALL IT'S WORTH!
10--9--8--
12

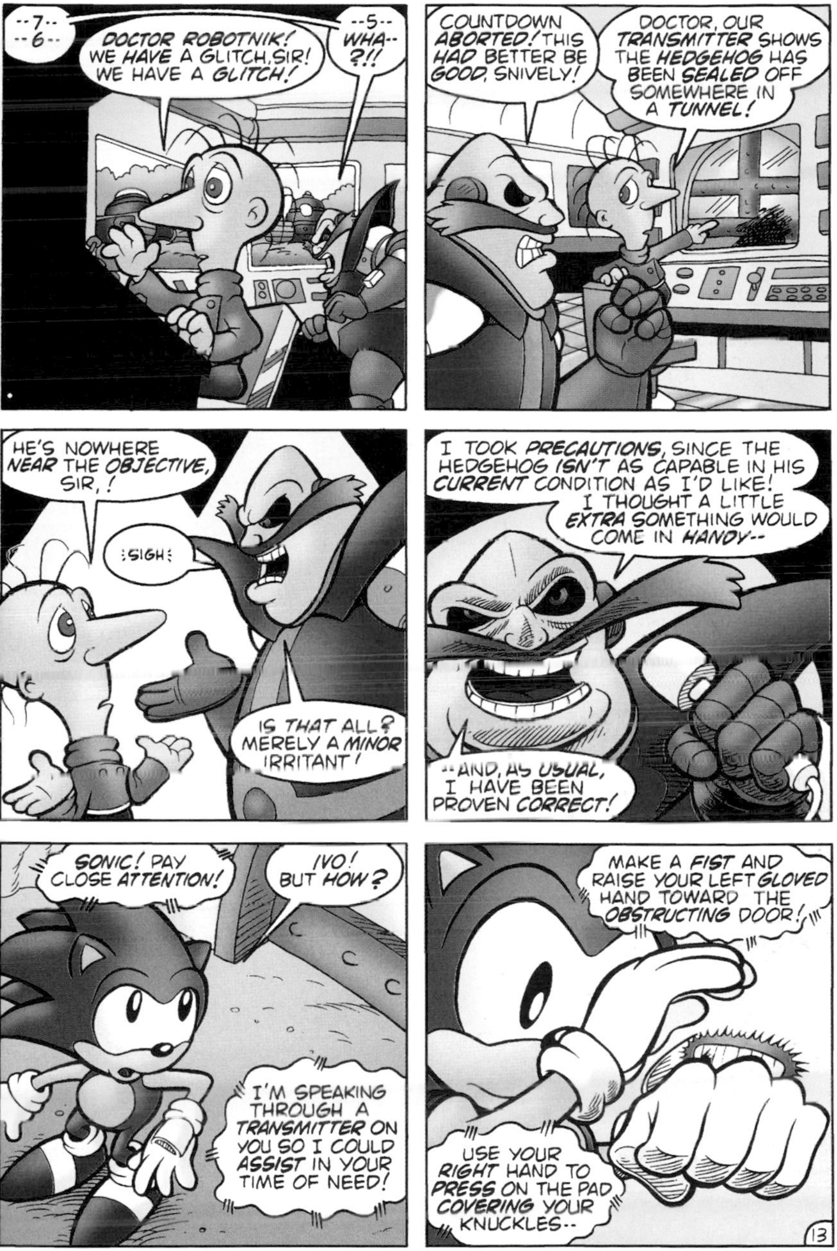
--7--
--6--
DOCTOR ROBOTNIK! WE HAVE A GLITCH, SIR! WE HAVE A GLITCH!
--5--
WHA-- ?!!
COUNTDOWN ABORTED! THIS HAD BETTER BE GOOD, SNIVELY!
DOCTOR, OUR TRANSMITTER SHOWS THE HEDGEHOG HAS BEEN SEALED OFF SOMEWHERE IN A TUNNEL!
HE'S NOWHERE NEAR THE OBJECTIVE, SIR, !
:SIGH:
IS THAT ALL? MERELY A MINOR IRRITANT!
I TOOK PRECAUTIONS, SINCE THE HEDGEHOG ISN'T AS CAPABLE IN HIS CURRENT CONDITION AS I'D LIKE! I THOUGHT A LITTLE EXTRA SOMETHING WOULD COME IN HANDY--
--AND, AS USUAL, I HAVE BEEN PROVEN CORRECT!
SONIC! PAY CLOSE ATTENTION!
IVO! BUT HOW?
I'M SPEAKING THROUGH A TRANSMITTER ON YOU SO I COULD ASSIST IN YOUR TIME OF NEED!
MAKE A FIST AND RAISE YOUR LEFT GLOVED HAND TOWARD THE OBSTRUCTING DOOR!
USE YOUR RIGHT HAND TO PRESS ON THE PAD COVERING YOUR KNUCKLES--

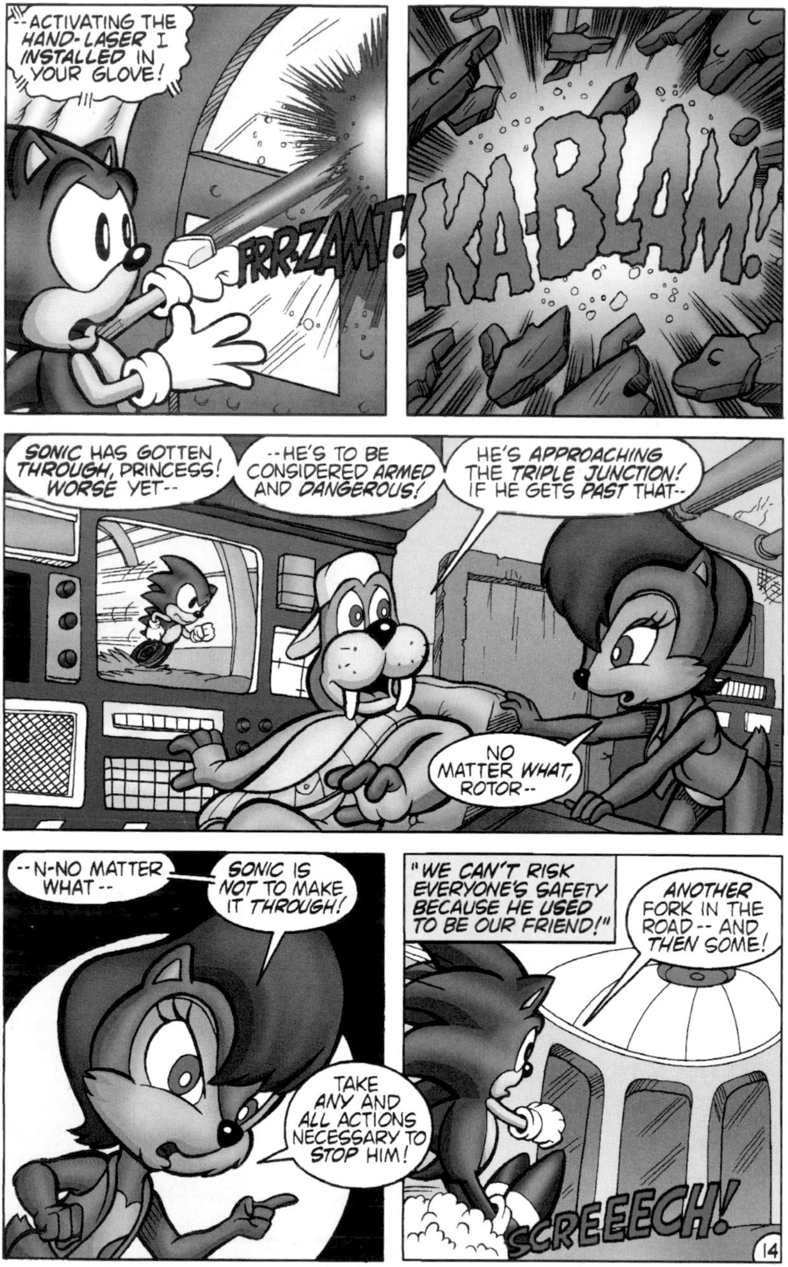
--ACTIVATING THE HAND-LASER I INSTALLED IN YOUR GLOVE!
FRRZAMT!
KA-BLAM!
SONIC HAS GOTTEN THROUGH, PRINCESS! WORSE YET--
--HE'S TO BE CONSIDERED ARMED AND DANGEROUS!
HE'S APPROACHING THE TRIPLE JUNCTION! IF HE GETS PAST THAT--
NO MATTER WHAT, ROTOR--
--N-NO MATTER WHAT--
SONIC IS NOT TO MAKE IT THROUGH!
TAKE ANY AND ALL ACTIONS NECESSARY TO STOP HIM!
"WE CAN'T RISK EVERYONE'S SAFETY BECAUSE HE USED TO BE OUR FRIEND!"
ANOTHER FORK IN THE ROAD -- AND THEN SOME!
SCREEECH!
14

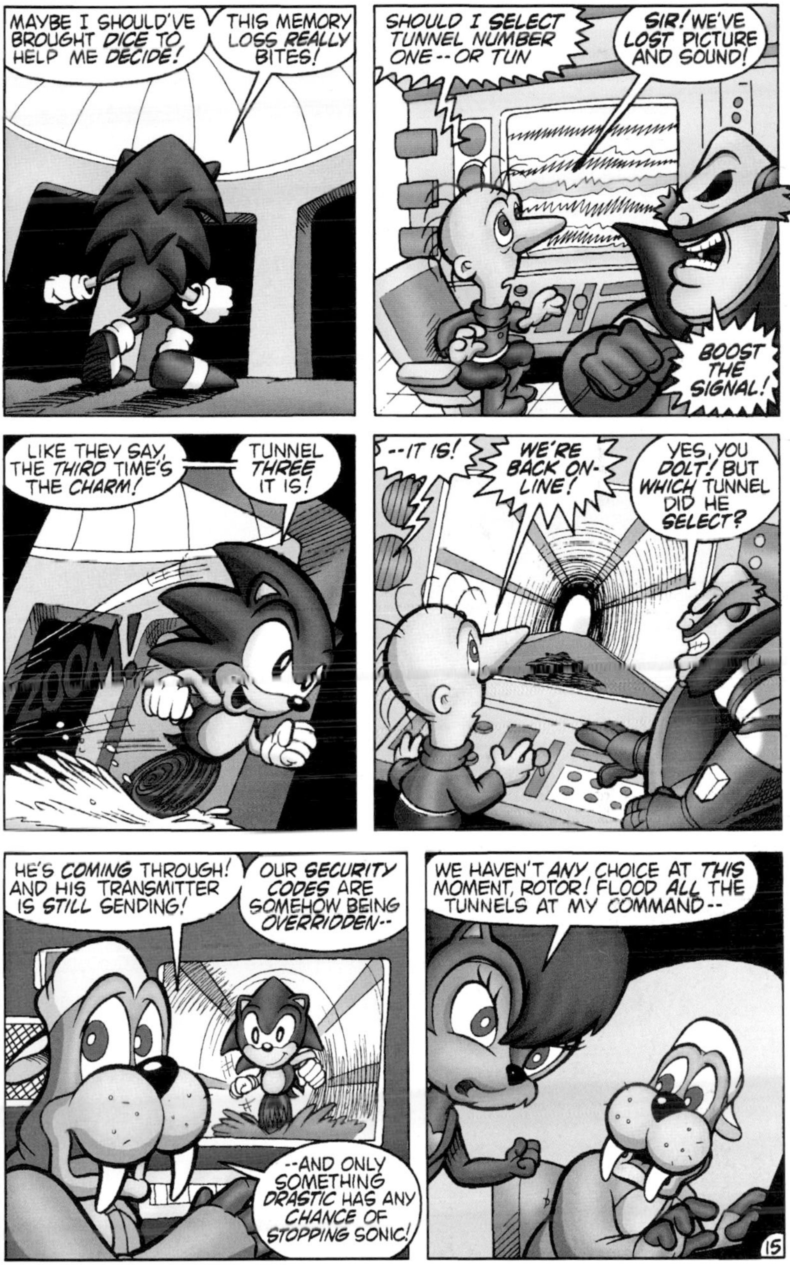
MAYBE I SHOULD'VE BROUGHT DICE TO HELP ME DECIDE!
THIS MEMORY LOSS REALLY BITES!
SHOULD I SELECT TUNNEL NUMBER ONE--OR TUN
SIR! WE'VE LOST PICTURE AND SOUND!
BOOST THE SIGNAL!
LIKE THEY SAY, THE THIRD TIME'S THE CHARM!
TUNNEL THREE IT IS!
ZOOM!
--IT IS!
WE'RE BACK ON-LINE!
YES, YOU DOLT! BUT WHICH TUNNEL DID HE SELECT?
HE'S COMING THROUGH! AND HIS TRANSMITTER IS STILL SENDING!
OUR SECURITY CODES ARE SOMEHOW BEING OVERRIDDEN--
--AND ONLY SOMETHING DRASTIC HAS ANY CHANCE OF STOPPING SONIC!
WE HAVEN'T ANY CHOICE AT THIS MOMENT, ROTOR! FLOOD ALL THE TUNNELS AT MY COMMAND--
15

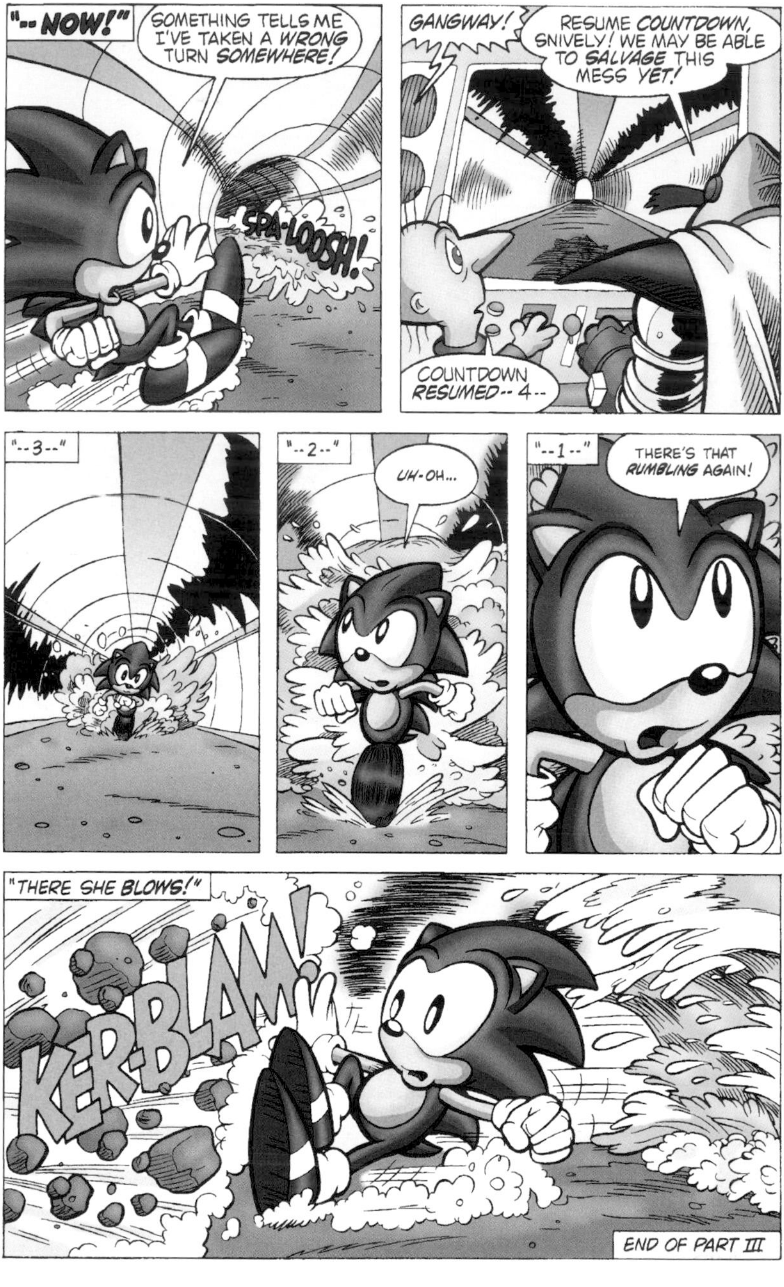
"-- NOW!"
SOMETHING TELLS ME I'VE TAKEN A WRONG TURN SOMEWHERE!
SPA-LOOSH!
GANGWAY!
RESUME COUNTDOWN, SNIVELY! WE MAY BE ABLE TO SALVAGE THIS MESS YET!
COUNTDOWN RESUMED-- 4--
"--3--"
"--2--"
UH-OH...
"--1--"
THERE'S THAT RUMBLING AGAIN!
"THERE SHE BLOWS!"
KER-BLAM!
END OF PART III

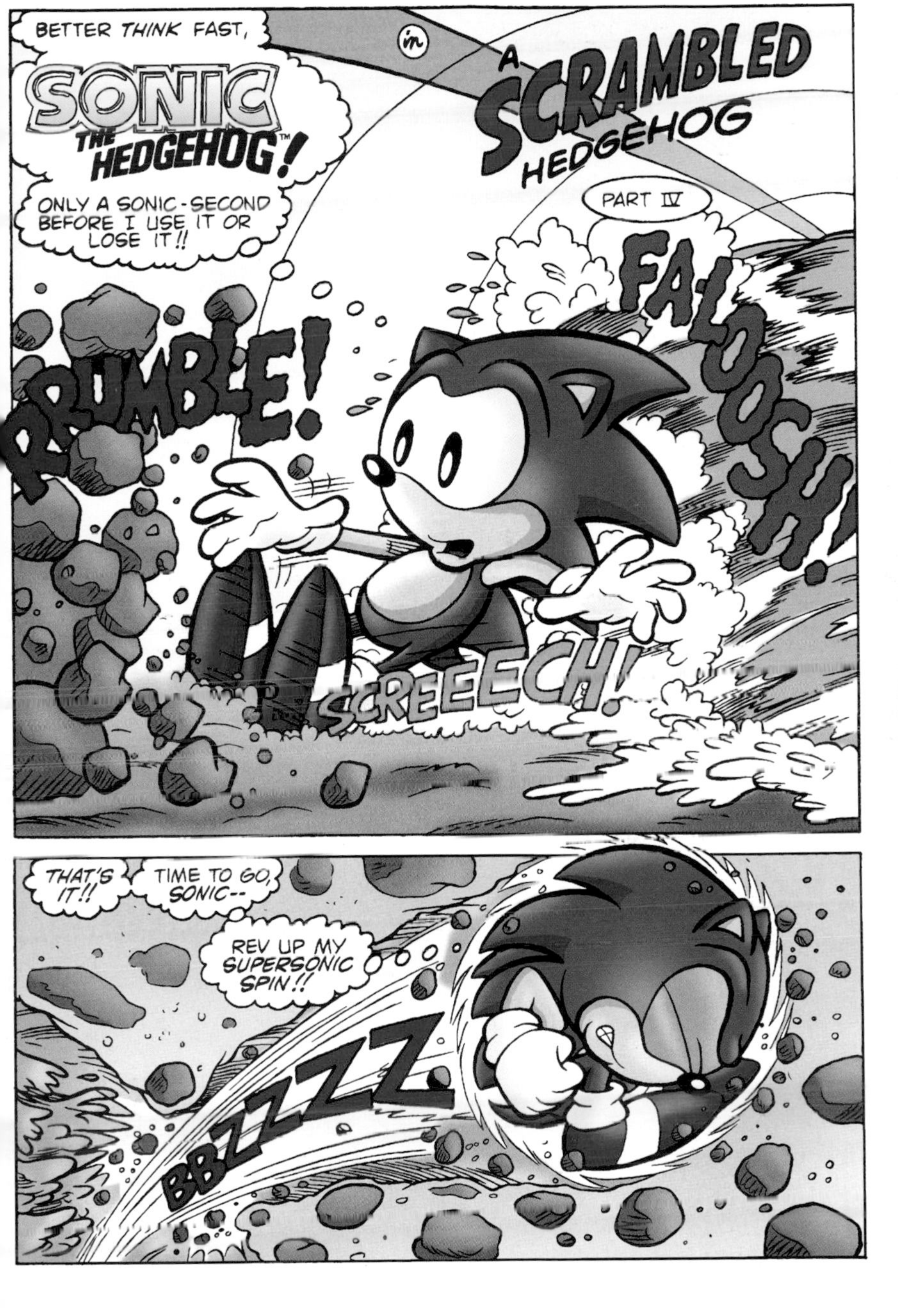
BETTER THINK FAST,
SONIC THE HEDGEHOG™!
in
A SCRAMBLED HEDGEHOG
PART IV
ONLY A SONIC-SECOND BEFORE I USE IT OR LOSE IT!!
RRUMBLE!
FA-LOOSH!!
SCREEECH!
THAT'S IT!!
TIME TO GO, SONIC--
REV UP MY SUPERSONIC SPIN!!
BBZZZZZ

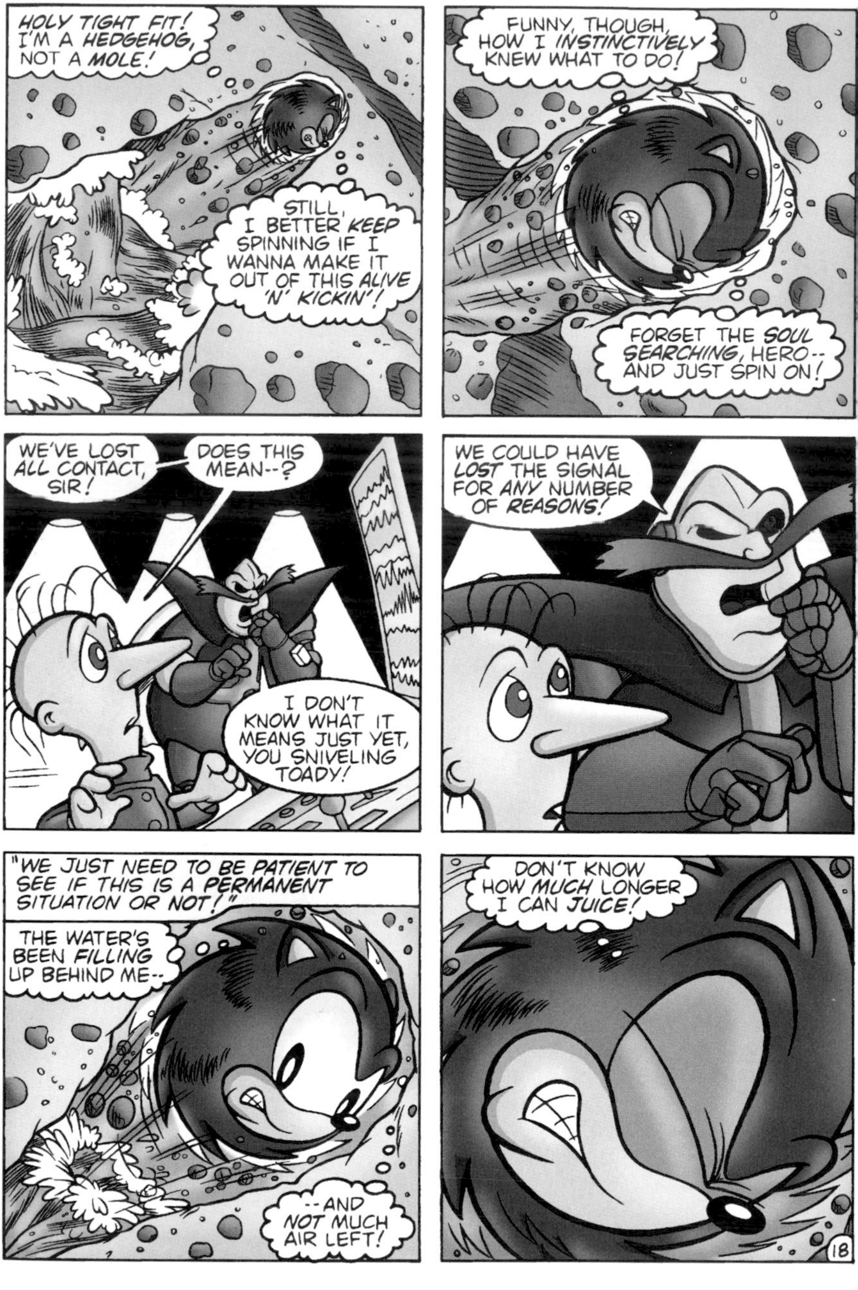
HOLY TIGHT FIT! I'M A HEDGEHOG, NOT A MOLE!
STILL, I BETTER KEEP SPINNING IF I WANNA MAKE IT OUT OF THIS ALIVE 'N' KICKIN'!
FUNNY, THOUGH, HOW I INSTINCTIVELY KNEW WHAT TO DO!
FORGET THE SOUL SEARCHING, HERO-- AND JUST SPIN ON!
WE'VE LOST ALL CONTACT, SIR!
DOES THIS MEAN--?
I DON'T KNOW WHAT IT MEANS JUST YET, YOU SNIVELING TOADY!
WE COULD HAVE LOST THE SIGNAL FOR ANY NUMBER OF REASONS!
"WE JUST NEED TO BE PATIENT TO SEE IF THIS IS A PERMANENT SITUATION OR NOT!"
THE WATER'S BEEN FILLING UP BEHIND ME--
--AND NOT MUCH AIR LEFT!
DON'T KNOW HOW MUCH LONGER I CAN JUICE!
18

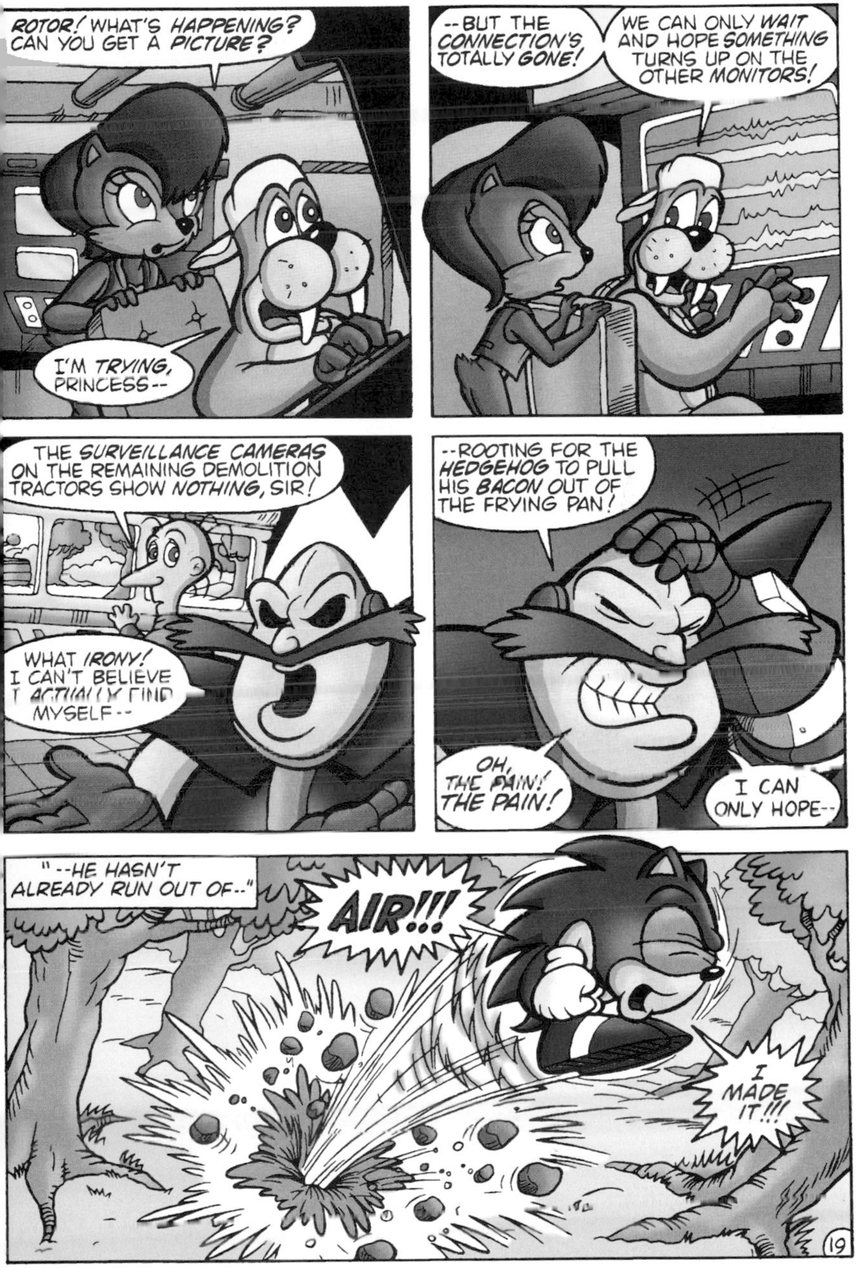
ROTOR! WHAT'S HAPPENING? CAN YOU GET A PICTURE?
I'M TRYING, PRINCESS--
--BUT THE CONNECTION'S TOTALLY GONE!
WE CAN ONLY WAIT AND HOPE SOMETHING TURNS UP ON THE OTHER MONITORS!
THE SURVEILLANCE CAMERAS ON THE REMAINING DEMOLITION TRACTORS SHOW NOTHING, SIR!
WHAT IRONY! I CAN'T BELIEVE I ACTUALLY FIND MYSELF--
--ROOTING FOR THE HEDGEHOG TO PULL HIS BACON OUT OF THE FRYING PAN!
OH, THE PAIN! THE PAIN!
I CAN ONLY HOPE--
"--HE HASN'T ALREADY RUN OUT OF--"
AIR!!!
I MADE IT!!!

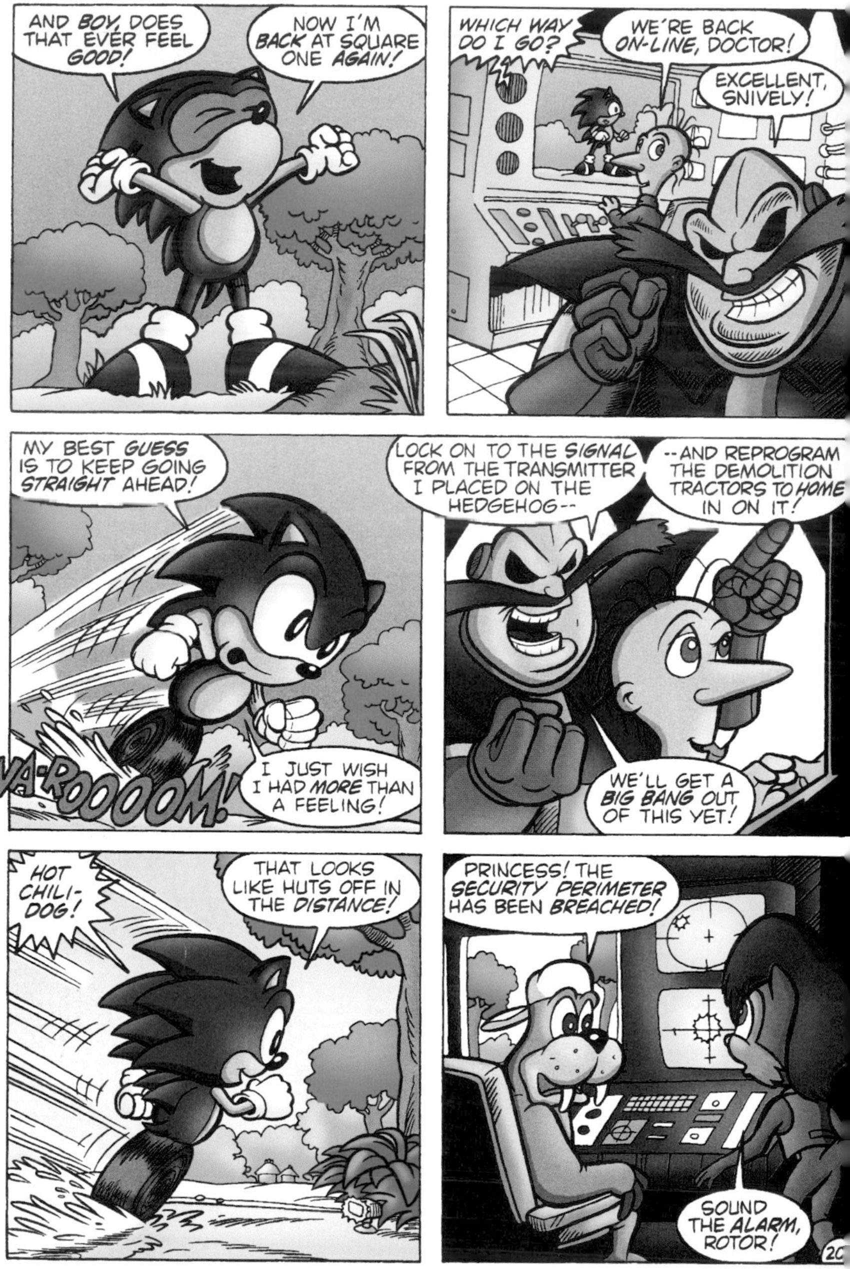
AND BOY, DOES THAT EVER FEEL GOOD!
NOW I'M BACK AT SQUARE ONE AGAIN!
WHICH WAY DO I GO?
WE'RE BACK ON-LINE, DOCTOR!
EXCELLENT, SNIVELY!
MY BEST GUESS IS TO KEEP GOING STRAIGHT AHEAD!
VA-ROOOOOM!
I JUST WISH I HAD MORE THAN A FEELING!
LOCK ON TO THE SIGNAL FROM THE TRANSMITTER I PLACED ON THE HEDGEHOG--
--AND REPROGRAM THE DEMOLITION TRACTORS TO HOME IN ON IT!
WE'LL GET A BIG BANG OUT OF THIS YET!
HOT CHILI-DOG!
THAT LOOKS LIKE HUTS OFF IN THE DISTANCE!
PRINCESS! THE SECURITY PERIMETER HAS BEEN BREACHED!
SOUND THE ALARM, ROTOR!

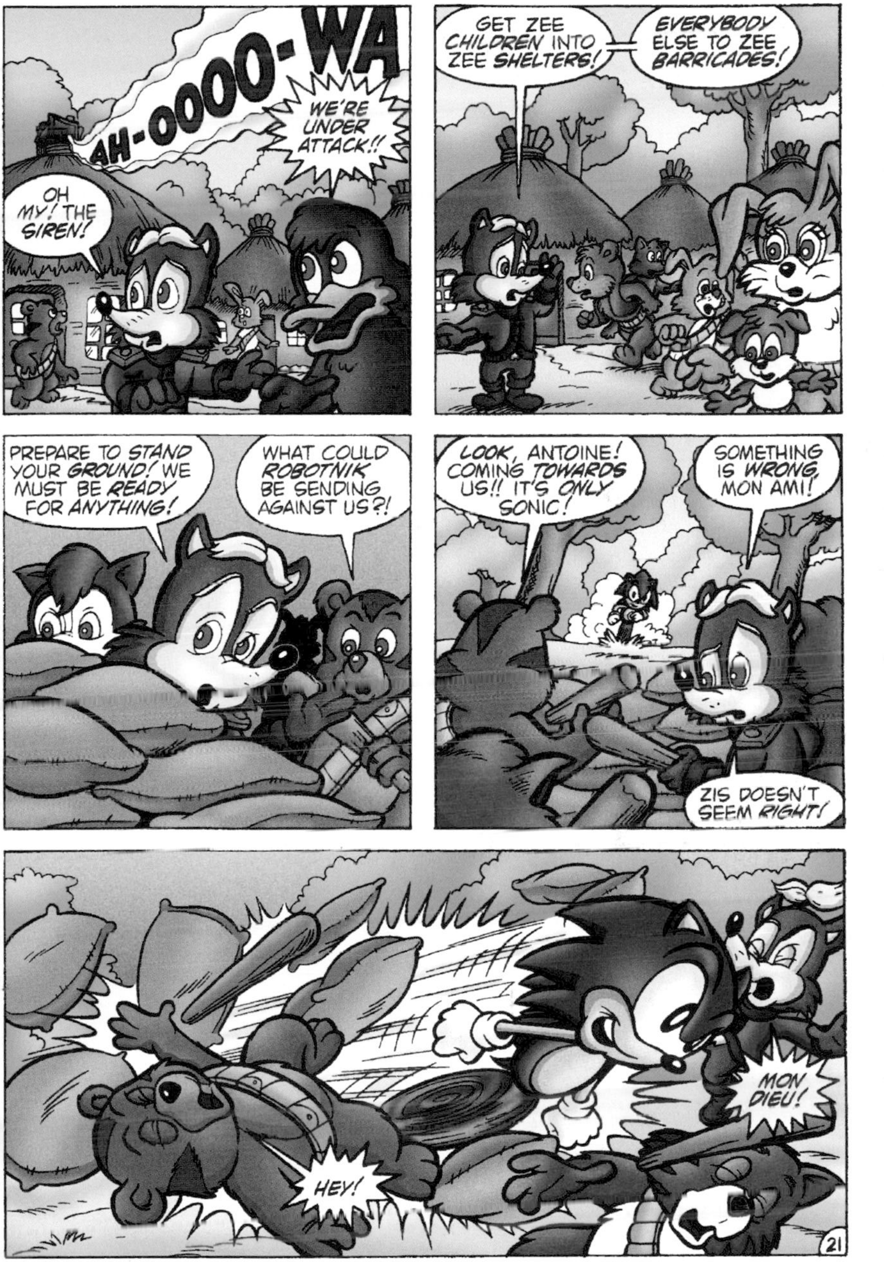
AH-OOOO-WA
WE'RE UNDER ATTACK!!
OH MY! THE SIREN!
GET ZEE CHILDREN INTO ZEE SHELTERS!
EVERYBODY ELSE TO ZEE BARRICADES!
PREPARE TO STAND YOUR GROUND! WE MUST BE READY FOR ANYTHING!
WHAT COULD ROBOTNIK BE SENDING AGAINST US?!
LOOK, ANTOINE! COMING TOWARDS US!! IT'S ONLY SONIC!
SOMETHING IS WRONG, MON AMI!
ZIS DOESN'T SEEM RIGHT!
MON DIEU!
HEY!

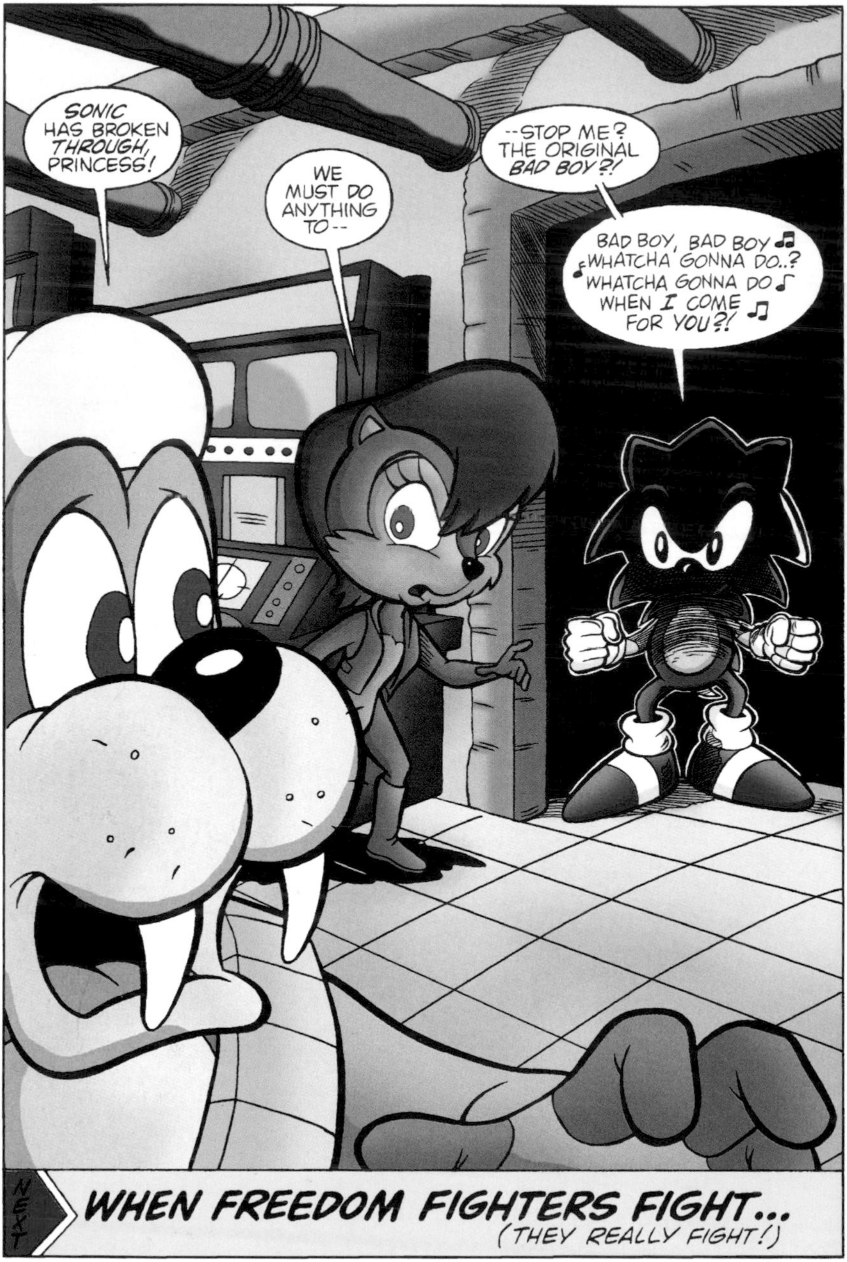
SONIC HAS BROKEN THROUGH, PRINCESS!
WE MUST DO ANYTHING TO--
--STOP ME? THE ORIGINAL BAD BOY?!
BAD BOY, BAD BOY ♫ WHATCHA GONNA DO..? WHATCHA GONNA DO ♪ WHEN I COME FOR YOU?! ♫
NEXT
WHEN FREEDOM FIGHTERS FIGHT...
(THEY REALLY FIGHT!)

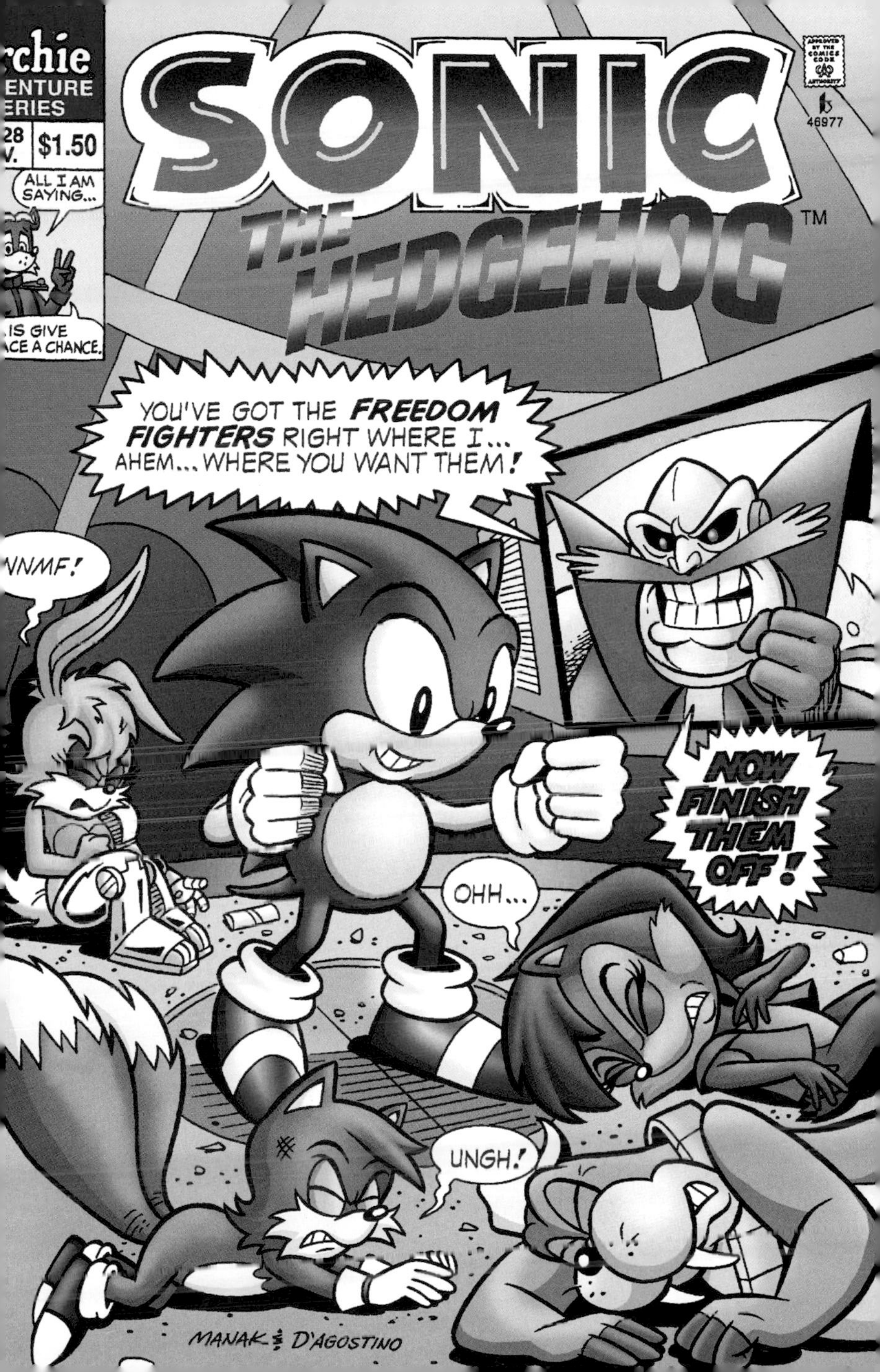

rchie
ENTURE
ERIES
28
V.
$1.50
ALL I AM SAYING...
IS GIVE
CE A CHANCE.
SONIC
THE HEDGEHOG
TM
46977
YOU'VE GOT THE FREEDOM FIGHTERS RIGHT WHERE I... AHEM... WHERE YOU WANT THEM!
NNMF!
NOW FINISH THEM OFF!
OHH...
UNGH!
MANAK & D'AGOSTINO

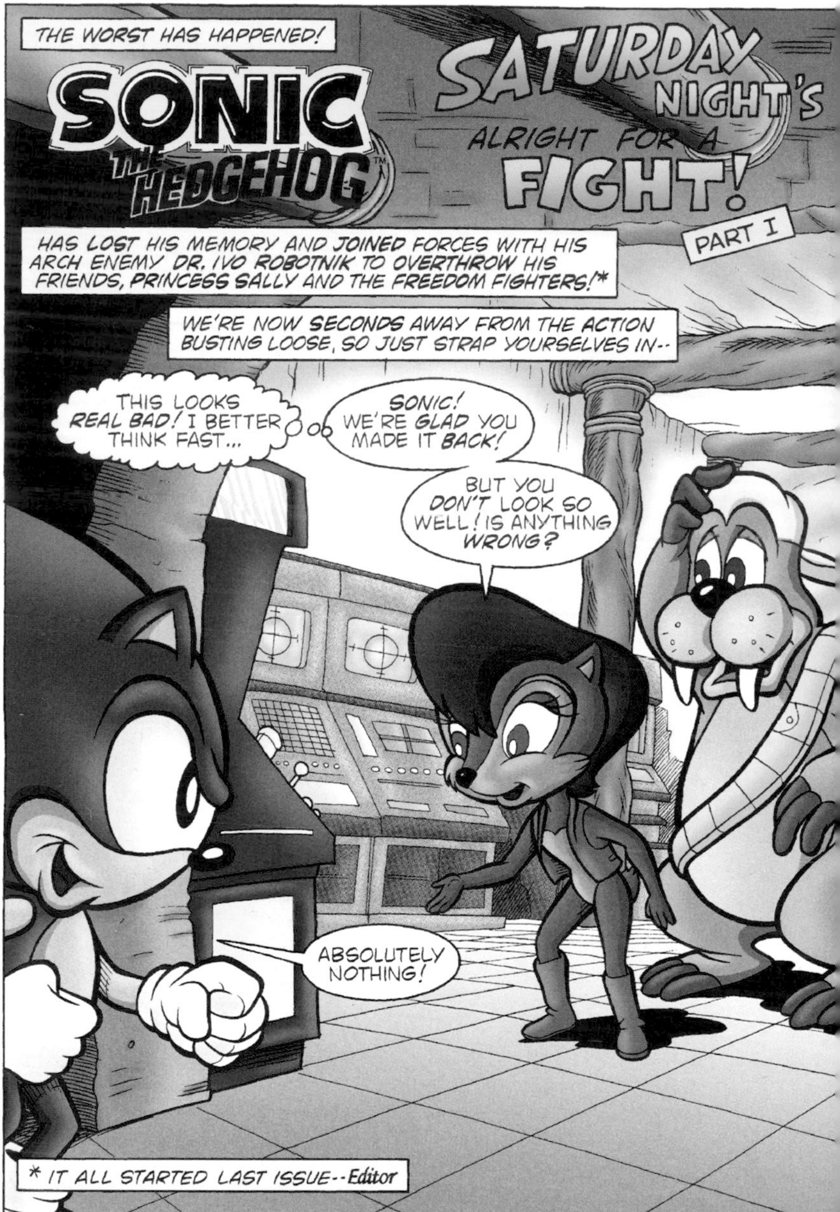
THE WORST HAS HAPPENED!
SONIC THE HEDGEHOG™
SATURDAY NIGHT'S ALRIGHT FOR A FIGHT!
PART I
HAS LOST HIS MEMORY AND JOINED FORCES WITH HIS ARCH ENEMY DR. IVO ROBOTNIK TO OVERTHROW HIS FRIENDS, PRINCESS SALLY AND THE FREEDOM FIGHTERS!*
WE'RE NOW SECONDS AWAY FROM THE ACTION BUSTING LOOSE, SO JUST STRAP YOURSELVES IN--
THIS LOOKS REAL BAD! I BETTER THINK FAST...
SONIC! WE'RE GLAD YOU MADE IT BACK!
BUT YOU DON'T LOOK SO WELL! IS ANYTHING WRONG?
ABSOLUTELY NOTHING!
* IT ALL STARTED LAST ISSUE--Editor

SCRIPT:	PENCILS:	INKS:	LETTERING:	COLORING:	EDITOR:	MANAGING EDITOR:	EDITOR-IN-CH
KEN PENDERS	ART MAWHINNEY	RICH KOSLOWSKI	MINDY EISMAN	BARRY GROSSMAN	SCOTT FULOP	VICTOR GORELICK	RICHARD GOLDWATE

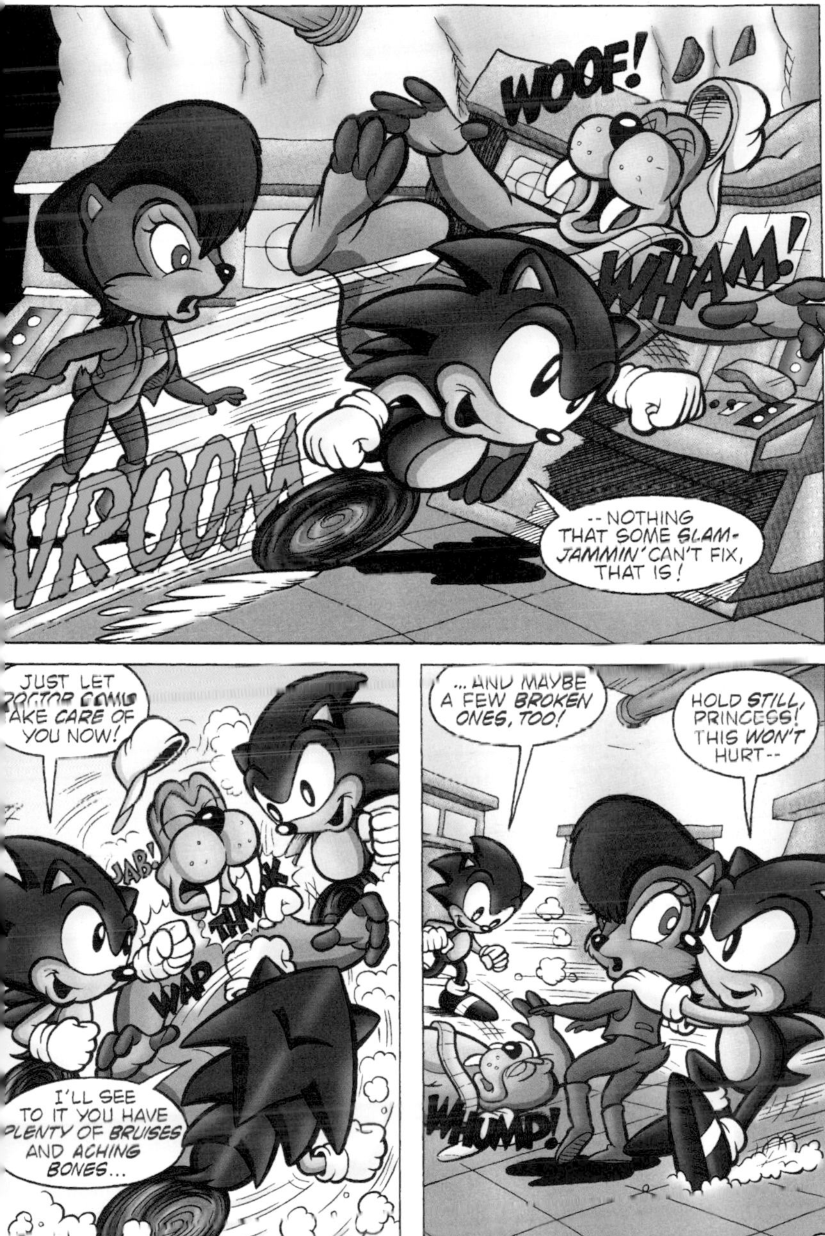
WOOF!
WHAM!
VROOM
--NOTHING THAT SOME SLAM-JAMMIN' CAN'T FIX, THAT IS!
JUST LET DOCTOR SONIC TAKE CARE OF YOU NOW!
JAB!
WAP
I'LL SEE TO IT YOU HAVE PLENTY OF BRUISES AND ACHING BONES...
...AND MAYBE A FEW BROKEN ONES, TOO!
HOLD STILL, PRINCESS! THIS WON'T HURT--
WHUMP!

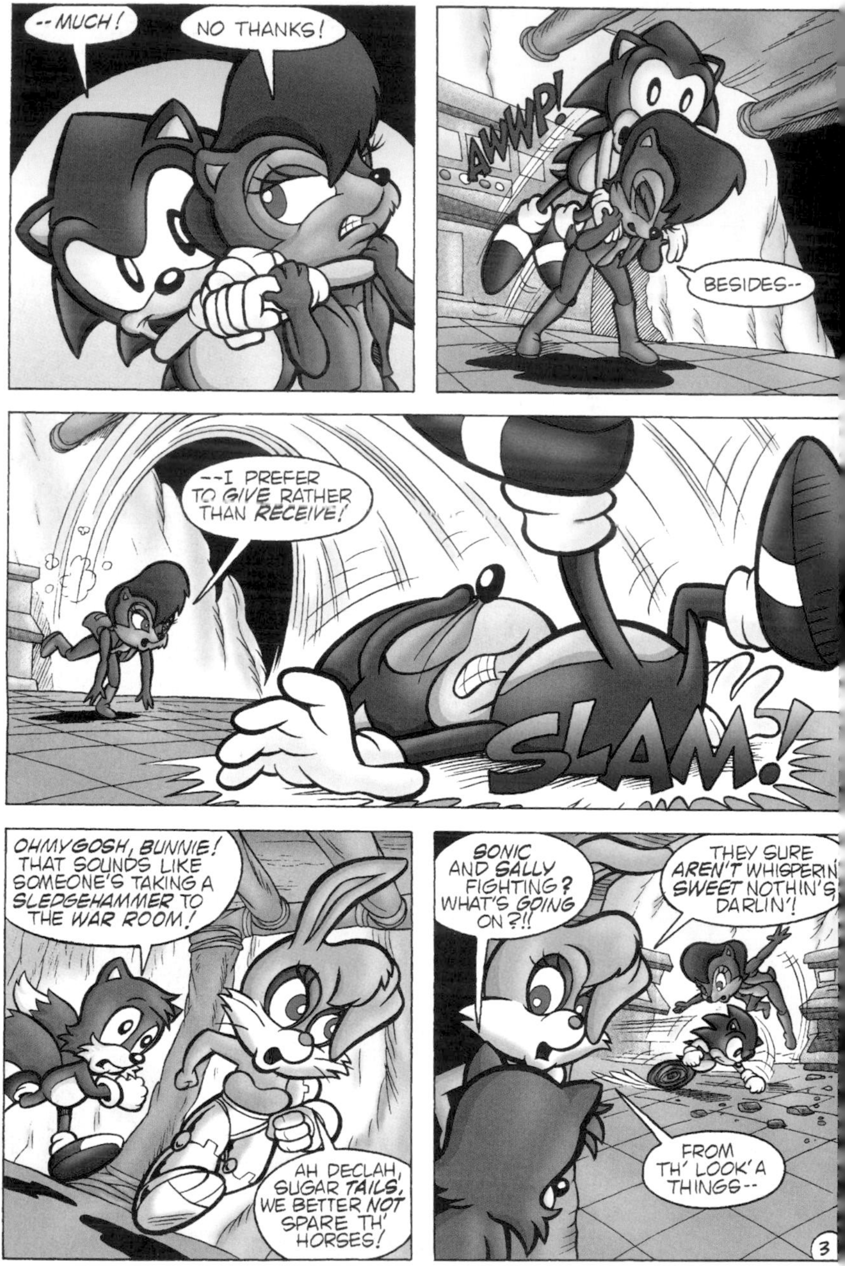
--MUCH!
NO THANKS!
AWWP!
BESIDES--
--I PREFER TO GIVE RATHER THAN RECEIVE!
SLAM!
OHMYGOSH, BUNNIE! THAT SOUNDS LIKE SOMEONE'S TAKING A SLEDGEHAMMER TO THE WAR ROOM!
AH DECLAH, SUGAR TAILS, WE BETTER NOT SPARE TH' HORSES!
SONIC AND SALLY FIGHTING? WHAT'S GOING ON?!!
THEY SURE AREN'T WHISPERIN' SWEET NOTHIN'S, DARLIN'!
FROM TH' LOOK'A THINGS--
3

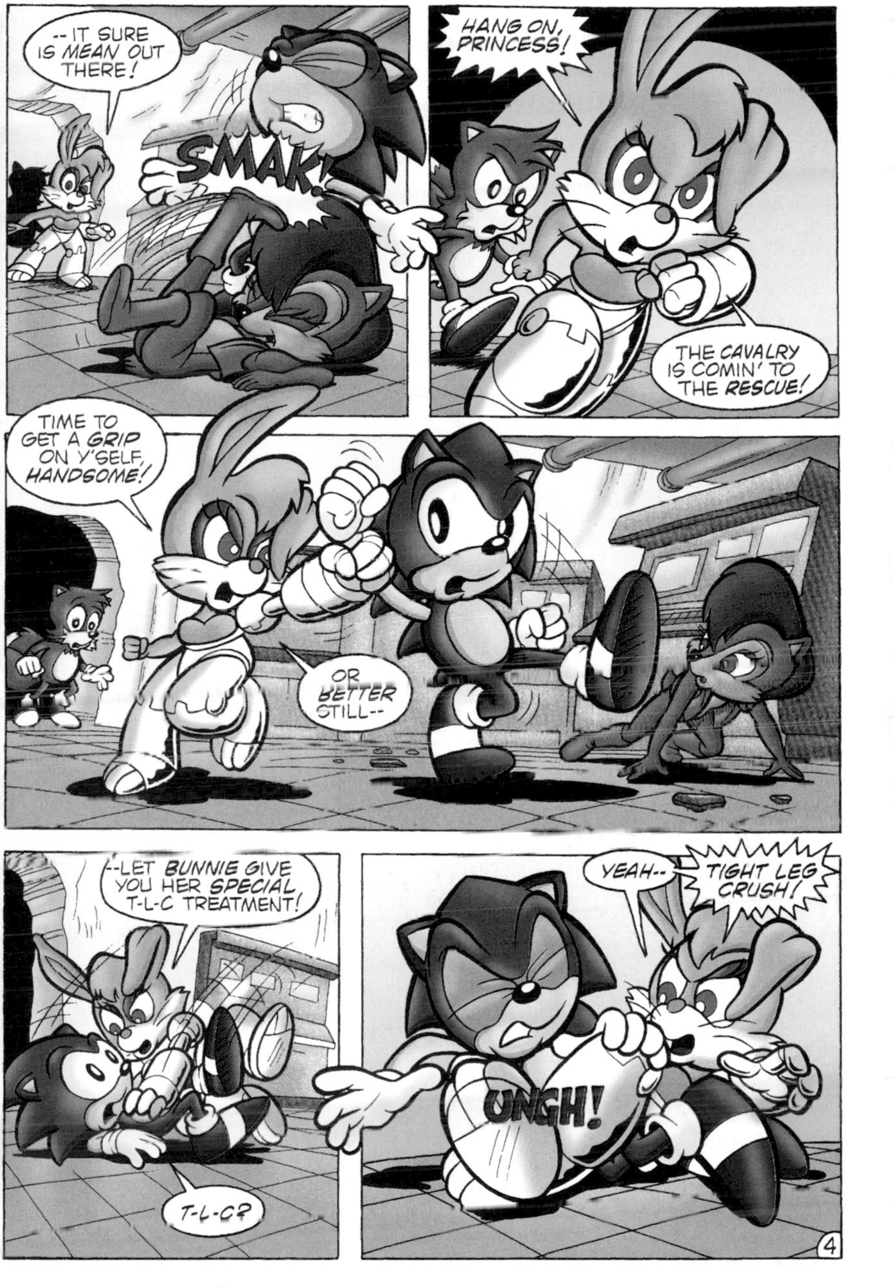

-- IT SURE IS MEAN OUT THERE!
SMAK!
HANG ON, PRINCESS!
THE CAVALRY IS COMIN' TO THE RESCUE!
TIME TO GET A GRIP ON Y'SELF, HANDSOME!
OR BETTER STILL--
--LET BUNNIE GIVE YOU HER SPECIAL T-L-C TREATMENT!
T-L-C?
YEAH--
TIGHT LEG CRUSH!
UNGH!

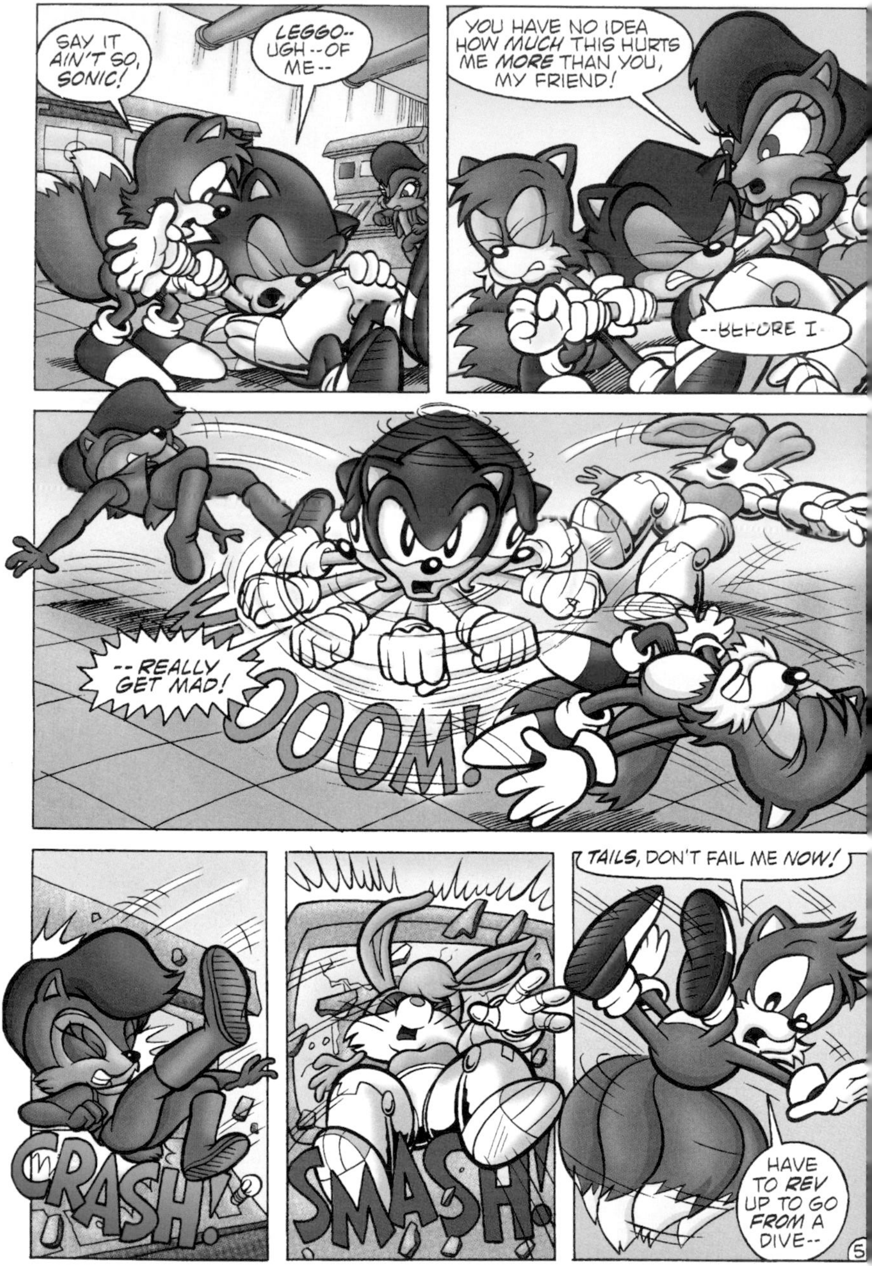
SAY IT AIN'T SO, SONIC!
LEGGO.. UGH--OF ME--
YOU HAVE NO IDEA HOW MUCH THIS HURTS ME MORE THAN YOU, MY FRIEND!
--BEFORE I-
--REALLY GET MAD!
WOOOM!
CRASH!
SMASH!
TAILS, DON'T FAIL ME NOW!
HAVE TO REV UP TO GO FROM A DIVE--

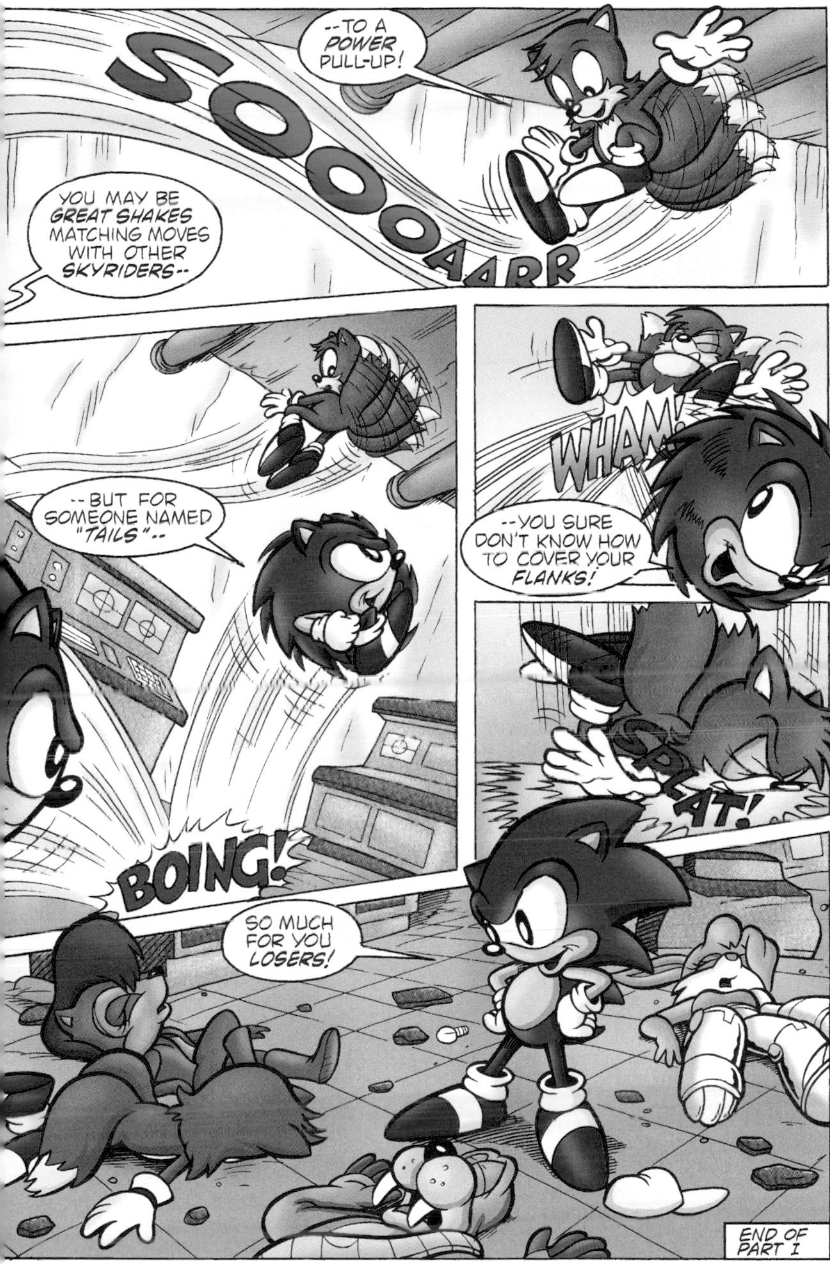

SOOOOAARR
--TO A POWER PULL-UP!
YOU MAY BE GREAT SHAKES MATCHING MOVES WITH OTHER SKYRIDERS--
--BUT FOR SOMEONE NAMED "TAILS"--
WHAM!
--YOU SURE DON'T KNOW HOW TO COVER YOUR FLANKS!
SPLAT!
BOING!
SO MUCH FOR YOU LOSERS!
END OF PART I

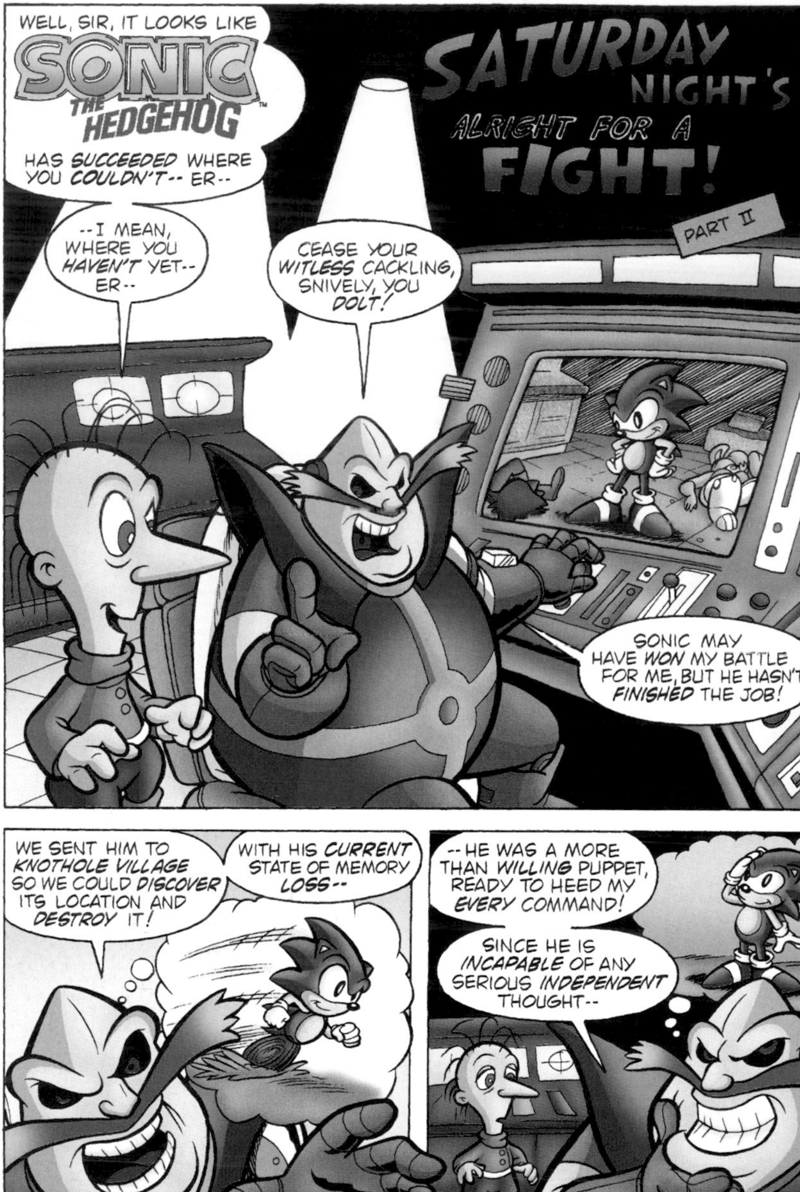
WELL, SIR, IT LOOKS LIKE
SONIC THE HEDGEHOG
HAS SUCCEEDED WHERE YOU COULDN'T-- ER--
SATURDAY NIGHT'S ALRIGHT FOR A FIGHT!
PART II
--I MEAN, WHERE YOU HAVEN'T YET-- ER--
CEASE YOUR WITLESS CACKLING, SNIVELY, YOU DOLT!
SONIC MAY HAVE WON MY BATTLE FOR ME, BUT HE HASN'T FINISHED THE JOB!
WE SENT HIM TO KNOTHOLE VILLAGE SO WE COULD DISCOVER ITS LOCATION AND DESTROY IT!
WITH HIS CURRENT STATE OF MEMORY LOSS--
--HE WAS A MORE THAN WILLING PUPPET, READY TO HEED MY EVERY COMMAND!
SINCE HE IS INCAPABLE OF ANY SERIOUS INDEPENDENT THOUGHT--

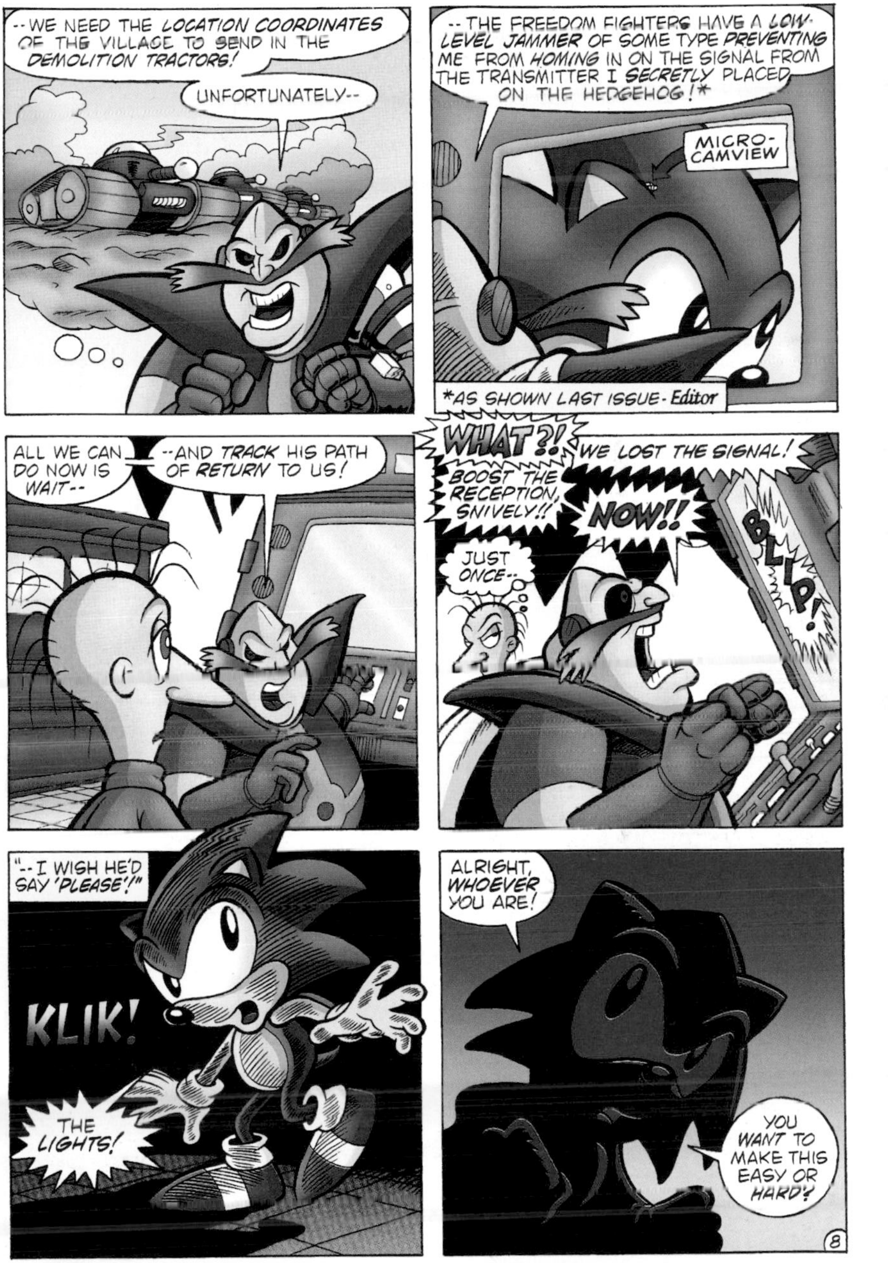
--WE NEED THE LOCATION COORDINATES OF THE VILLAGE TO SEND IN THE DEMOLITION TRACTORS!
UNFORTUNATELY--
--THE FREEDOM FIGHTERS HAVE A LOW-LEVEL JAMMER OF SOME TYPE PREVENTING ME FROM HOMING IN ON THE SIGNAL FROM THE TRANSMITTER I SECRETLY PLACED ON THE HEDGEHOG!*
MICRO-CAMVIEW
*AS SHOWN LAST ISSUE-Editor
ALL WE CAN DO NOW IS WAIT--
--AND TRACK HIS PATH OF RETURN TO US!
WHAT?!
WE LOST THE SIGNAL!
BOOST THE RECEPTION, SNIVELY!!
NOW!!
JUST ONCE--
BLLIP!
"--I WISH HE'D SAY 'PLEASE'!"
KLIK!
THE LIGHTS!
ALRIGHT, WHOEVER YOU ARE!
YOU WANT TO MAKE THIS EASY OR HARD?

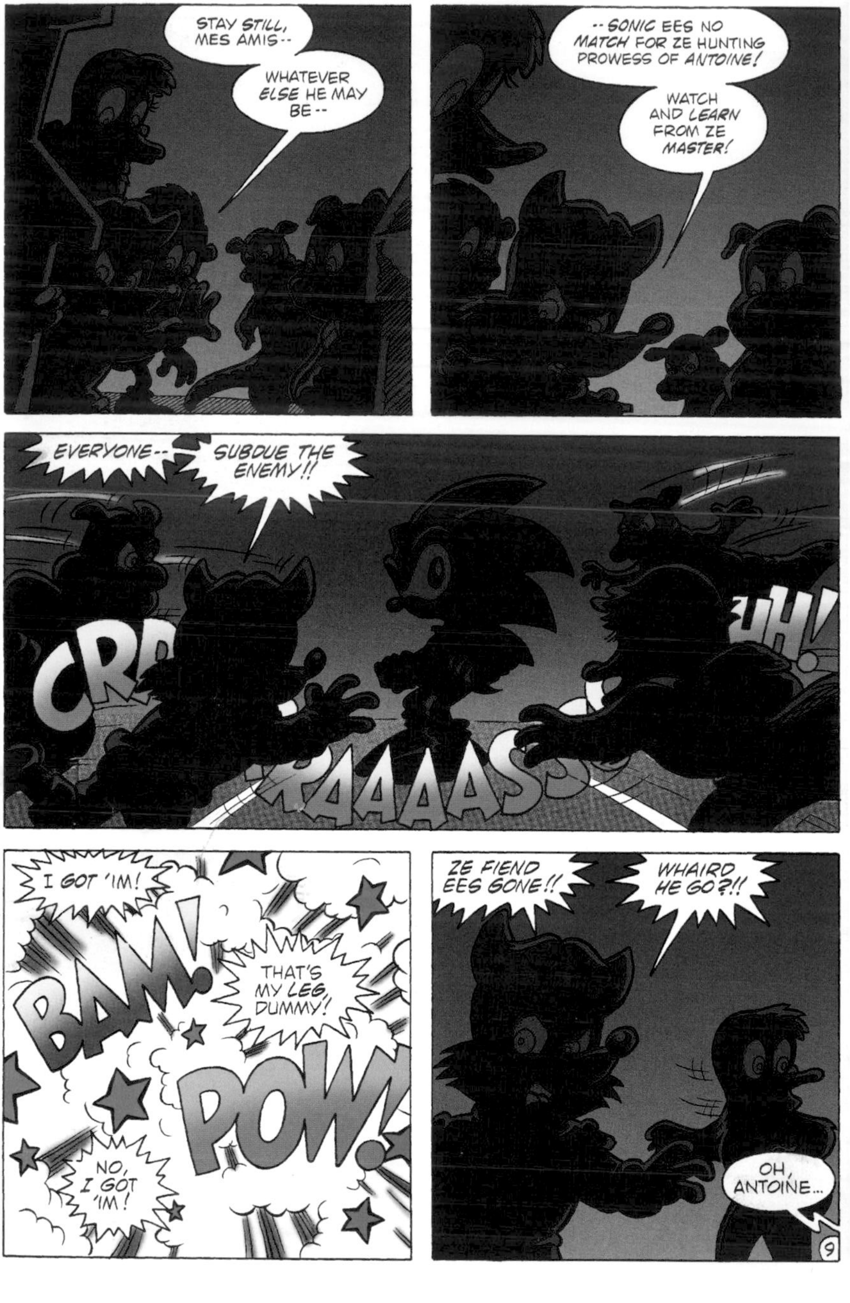
STAY STILL, MES AMIS--
WHATEVER ELSE HE MAY BE--
--SONIC EES NO MATCH FOR ZE HUNTING PROWESS OF ANTOINE!
WATCH AND LEARN FROM ZE MASTER!
EVERYONE--
SUBDUE THE ENEMY!!
CRRAAAASSH!
I GOT 'IM!
BAM!
THAT'S MY LEG, DUMMY!
POW!
NO, I GOT 'IM!
ZE FIEND EES GONE!!
WHAIRD HE GO?!!
OH, ANTOINE...
9

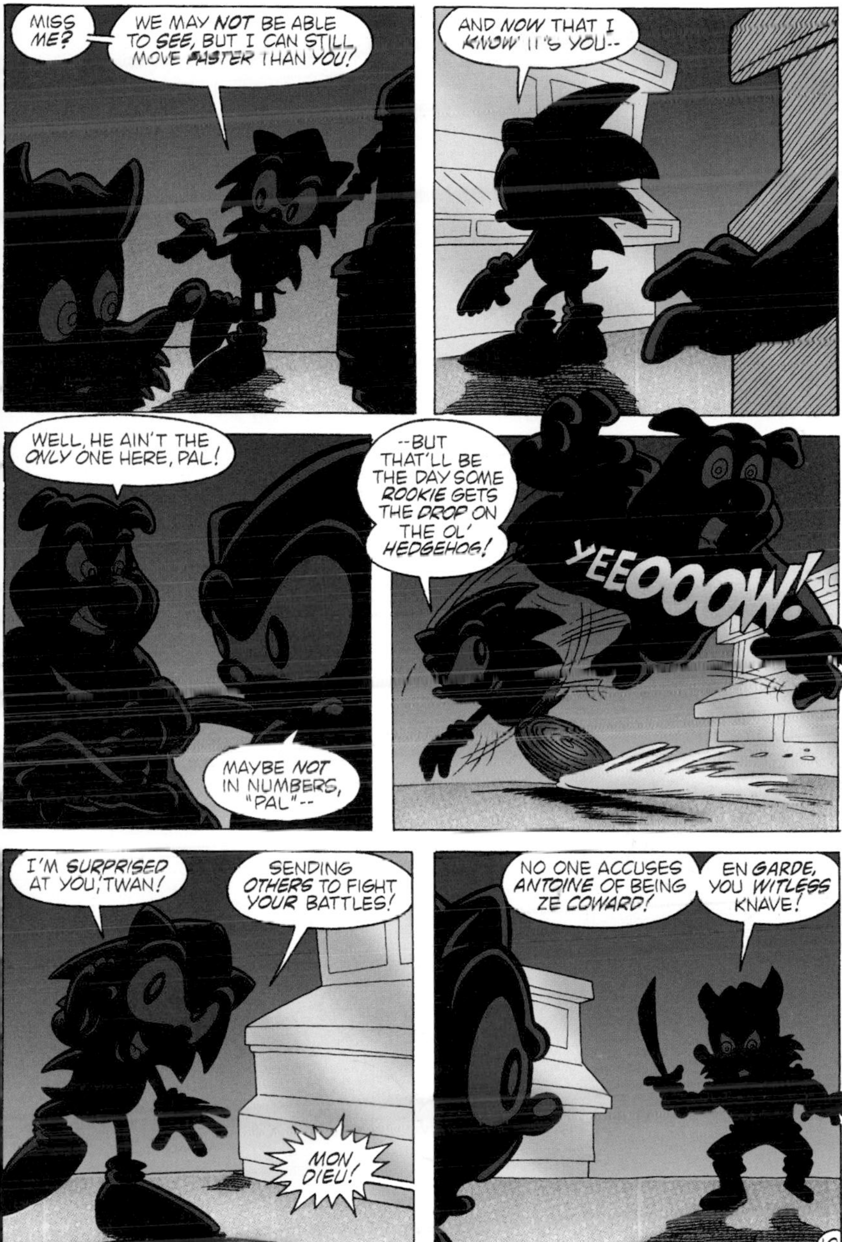
MISS ME?
WE MAY NOT BE ABLE TO SEE, BUT I CAN STILL MOVE FASTER THAN YOU!
AND NOW THAT I KNOW IT'S YOU--
WELL, HE AIN'T THE ONLY ONE HERE, PAL!
MAYBE NOT IN NUMBERS, "PAL"--
--BUT THAT'LL BE THE DAY SOME ROOKIE GETS THE DROP ON THE OL' HEDGEHOG!
YEEOOOOW!
I'M SURPRISED AT YOU, TWAN!
SENDING OTHERS TO FIGHT YOUR BATTLES!
MON DIEU!
NO ONE ACCUSES ANTOINE OF BEING ZE COWARD!
EN GARDE, YOU WITLESS KNAVE!

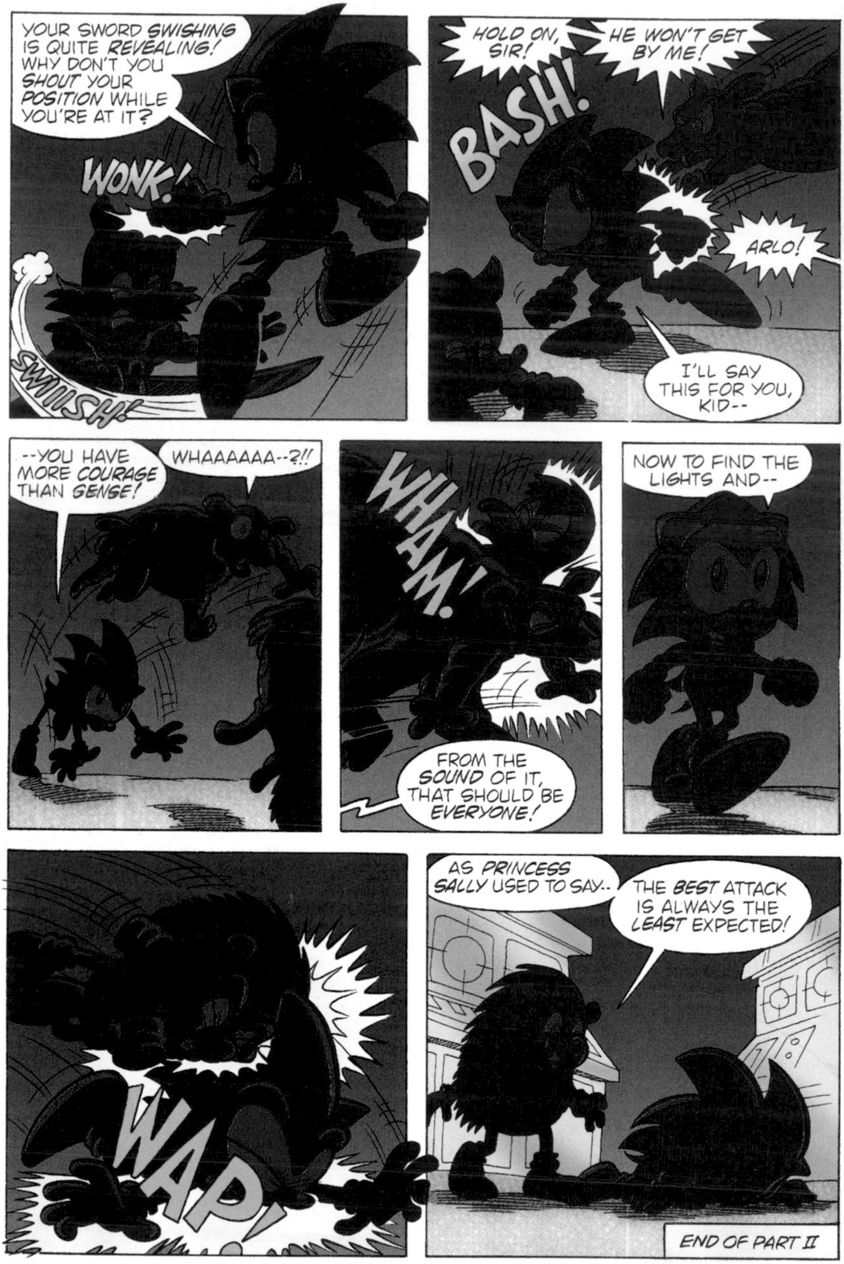
YOUR SWORD SWISHING IS QUITE REVEALING! WHY DON'T YOU SHOUT YOUR POSITION WHILE YOU'RE AT IT?
WONK!
SWIIISH!
HOLD ON, SIR!
HE WON'T GET BY ME!
BASH!
ARLO!
I'LL SAY THIS FOR YOU, KID--
--YOU HAVE MORE COURAGE THAN SENSE!
WHAAAAAA--?!!
WHAM!
FROM THE SOUND OF IT, THAT SHOULD BE EVERYONE!
NOW TO FIND THE LIGHTS AND--
WAP!
AS PRINCESS SALLY USED TO SAY..
THE BEST ATTACK IS ALWAYS THE LEAST EXPECTED!
END OF PART II

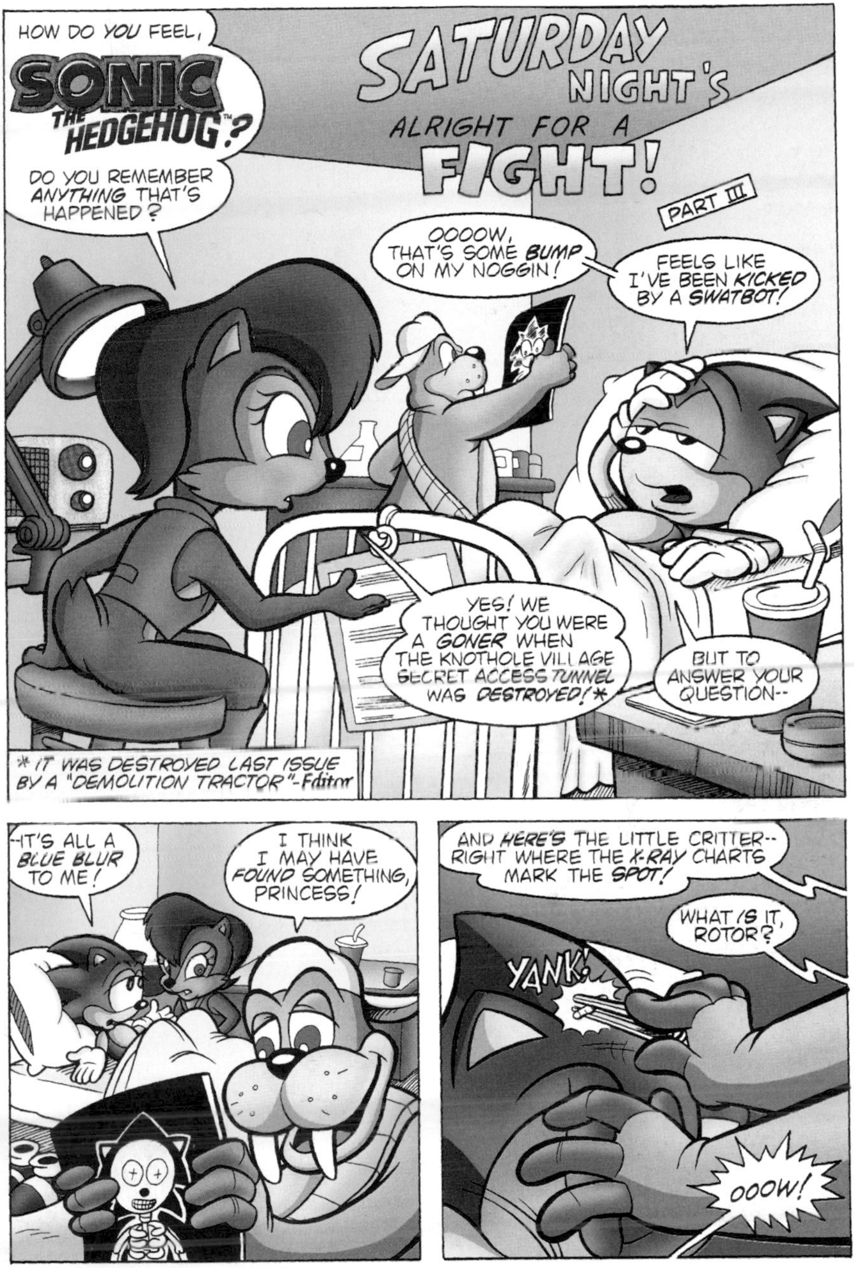

HOW DO YOU FEEL,
SONIC THE HEDGEHOG™?
DO YOU REMEMBER ANYTHING THAT'S HAPPENED?
SATURDAY NIGHT'S ALRIGHT FOR A FIGHT!
PART III
OOOOW, THAT'S SOME BUMP ON MY NOGGIN!
FEELS LIKE I'VE BEEN KICKED BY A SWATBOT!
YES! WE THOUGHT YOU WERE A GONER WHEN THE KNOTHOLE VILLAGE SECRET ACCESS TUNNEL WAS DESTROYED!*
BUT TO ANSWER YOUR QUESTION--
* IT WAS DESTROYED LAST ISSUE BY A "DEMOLITION TRACTOR" -Editor
--IT'S ALL A BLUE BLUR TO ME!
I THINK I MAY HAVE FOUND SOMETHING, PRINCESS!
AND HERE'S THE LITTLE CRITTER-- RIGHT WHERE THE X-RAY CHARTS MARK THE SPOT!
WHAT IS IT, ROTOR?
YANK!
OOOW!

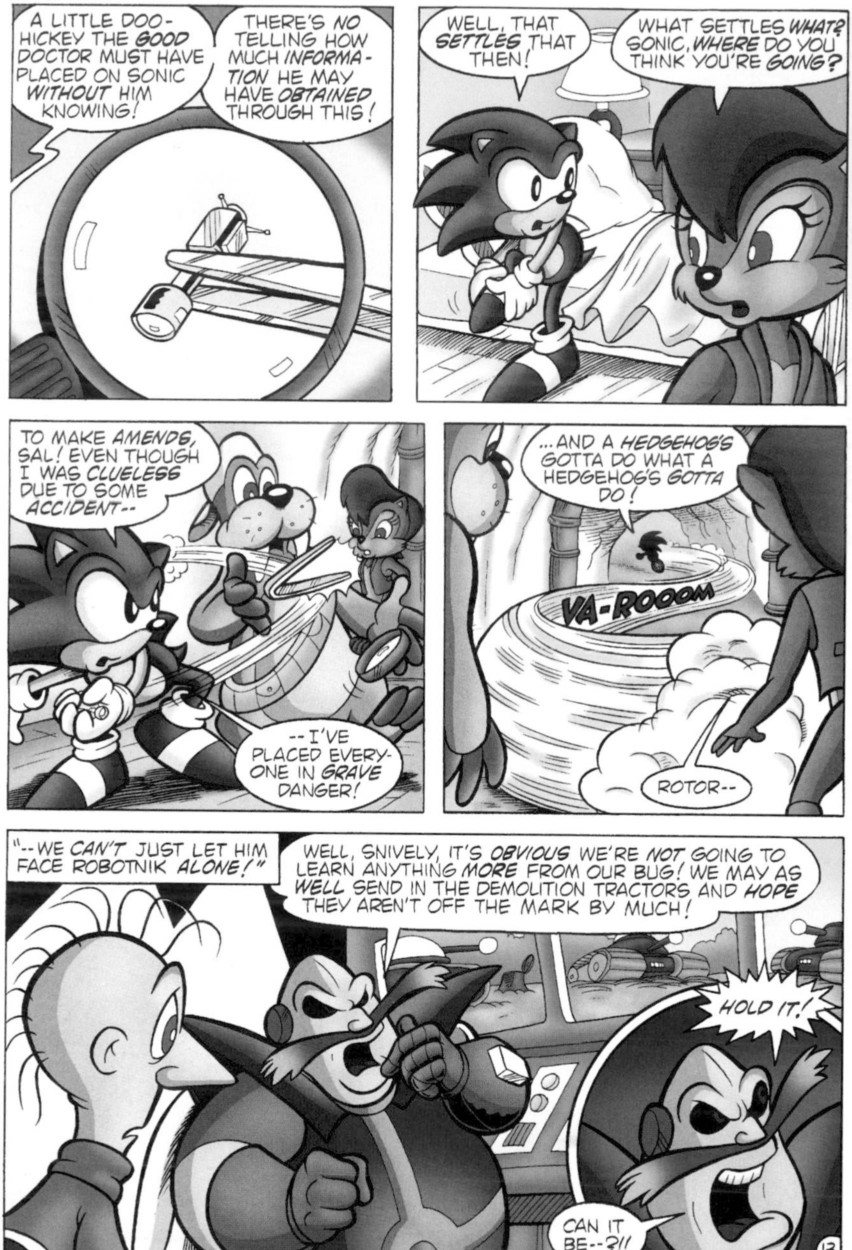
A LITTLE DOO-HICKEY THE GOOD DOCTOR MUST HAVE PLACED ON SONIC WITHOUT HIM KNOWING!
THERE'S NO TELLING HOW MUCH INFORMA-TION HE MAY HAVE OBTAINED THROUGH THIS!
WELL, THAT SETTLES THAT THEN!
WHAT SETTLES WHAT? SONIC, WHERE DO YOU THINK YOU'RE GOING?
TO MAKE AMENDS, SAL! EVEN THOUGH I WAS CLUELESS DUE TO SOME ACCIDENT--
--I'VE PLACED EVERY-ONE IN GRAVE DANGER!
...AND A HEDGEHOG'S GOTTA DO WHAT A HEDGEHOG'S GOTTA DO!
VA-ROOOM
ROTOR--
"--WE CAN'T JUST LET HIM FACE ROBOTNIK ALONE!"
WELL, SNIVELY, IT'S OBVIOUS WE'RE NOT GOING TO LEARN ANYTHING MORE FROM OUR BUG! WE MAY AS WELL SEND IN THE DEMOLITION TRACTORS AND HOPE THEY AREN'T OFF THE MARK BY MUCH!
HOLD IT!
CAN IT BE--?!!
13

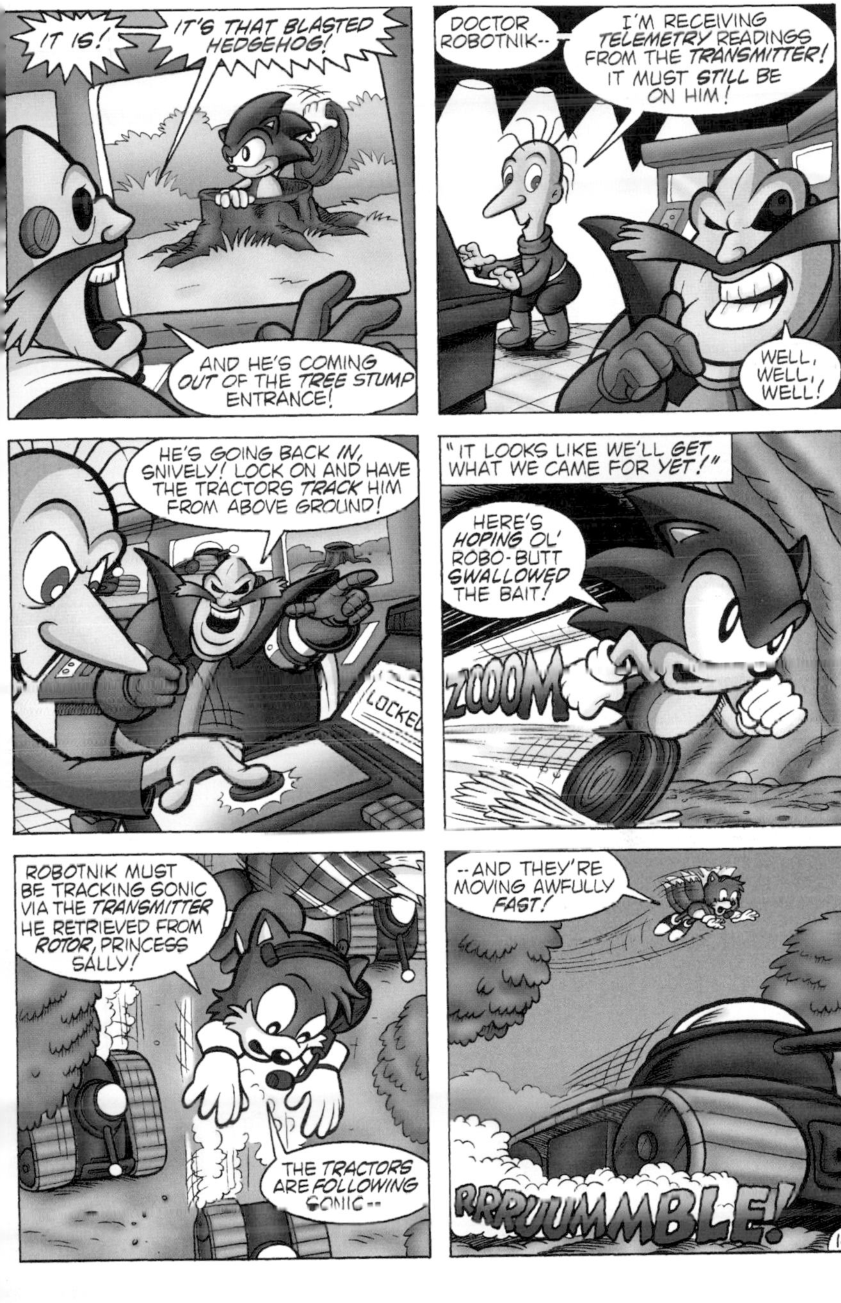
IT IS!
IT'S THAT BLASTED HEDGEHOG!
AND HE'S COMING OUT OF THE TREE STUMP ENTRANCE!
DOCTOR ROBOTNIK--
I'M RECEIVING TELEMETRY READINGS FROM THE TRANSMITTER! IT MUST STILL BE ON HIM!
WELL, WELL, WELL!
HE'S GOING BACK IN, SNIVELY! LOCK ON AND HAVE THE TRACTORS TRACK HIM FROM ABOVE GROUND!
LOCKED
"IT LOOKS LIKE WE'LL GET WHAT WE CAME FOR YET!"
HERE'S HOPING OL' ROBO-BUTT SWALLOWED THE BAIT!
ZOOOM
ROBOTNIK MUST BE TRACKING SONIC VIA THE TRANSMITTER HE RETRIEVED FROM ROTOR, PRINCESS SALLY!
THE TRACTORS ARE FOLLOWING SONIC--
--AND THEY'RE MOVING AWFULLY FAST!
RRRUUMMBLE!
14

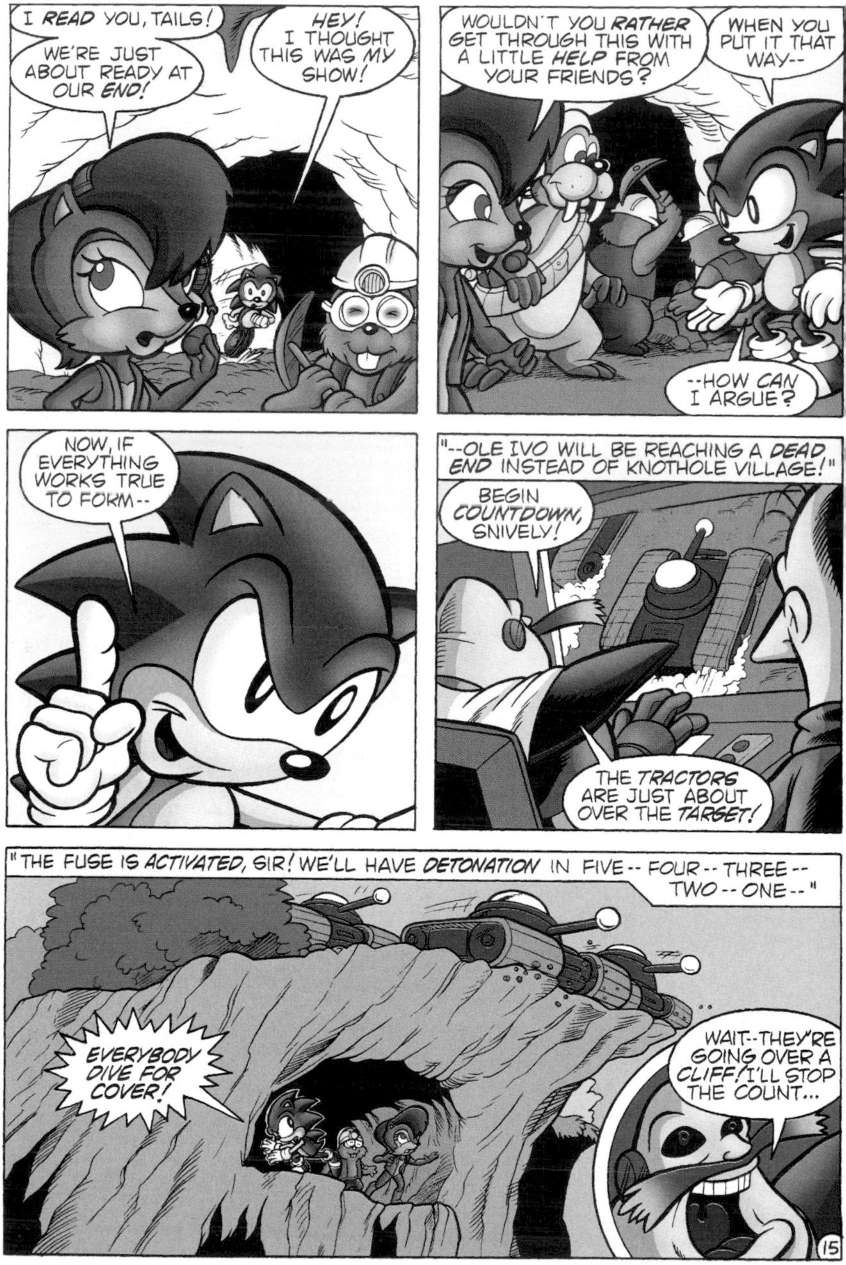
I READ YOU, TAILS!
WE'RE JUST ABOUT READY AT OUR END!
HEY! I THOUGHT THIS WAS MY SHOW!
WOULDN'T YOU RATHER GET THROUGH THIS WITH A LITTLE HELP FROM YOUR FRIENDS?
WHEN YOU PUT IT THAT WAY--
--HOW CAN I ARGUE?
NOW, IF EVERYTHING WORKS TRUE TO FORM--
"--OLE IVO WILL BE REACHING A DEAD END INSTEAD OF KNOTHOLE VILLAGE!"
BEGIN COUNTDOWN, SNIVELY!
THE TRACTORS ARE JUST ABOUT OVER THE TARGET!
"THE FUSE IS ACTIVATED, SIR! WE'LL HAVE DETONATION IN FIVE-- FOUR-- THREE-- TWO-- ONE--"
EVERYBODY DIVE FOR COVER!
WAIT--THEY'RE GOING OVER A CLIFF! I'LL STOP THE COUNT...
15

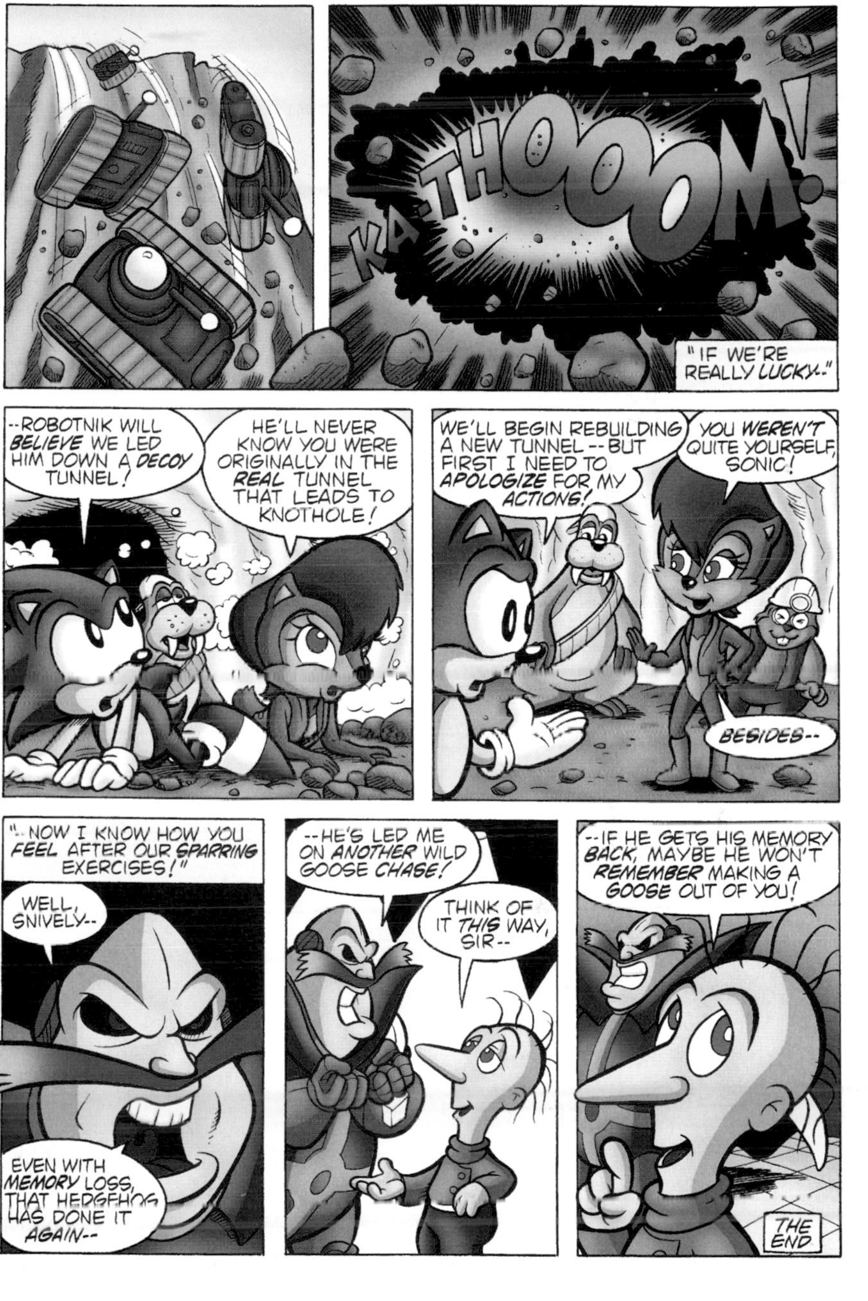
KA-THOOOM!
"IF WE'RE REALLY LUCKY--"
--ROBOTNIK WILL BELIEVE WE LED HIM DOWN A DECOY TUNNEL!
HE'LL NEVER KNOW YOU WERE ORIGINALLY IN THE REAL TUNNEL THAT LEADS TO KNOTHOLE!
WE'LL BEGIN REBUILDING A NEW TUNNEL -- BUT FIRST I NEED TO APOLOGIZE FOR MY ACTIONS!
YOU WEREN'T QUITE YOURSELF, SONIC!
BESIDES--
"--NOW I KNOW HOW YOU FEEL AFTER OUR SPARRING EXERCISES!"
WELL, SNIVELY--
EVEN WITH MEMORY LOSS, THAT HEDGEHOG HAS DONE IT AGAIN--
--HE'S LED ME ON ANOTHER WILD GOOSE CHASE!
THINK OF IT THIS WAY, SIR--
--IF HE GETS HIS MEMORY BACK, MAYBE HE WON'T REMEMBER MAKING A GOOSE OUT OF YOU!
THE END

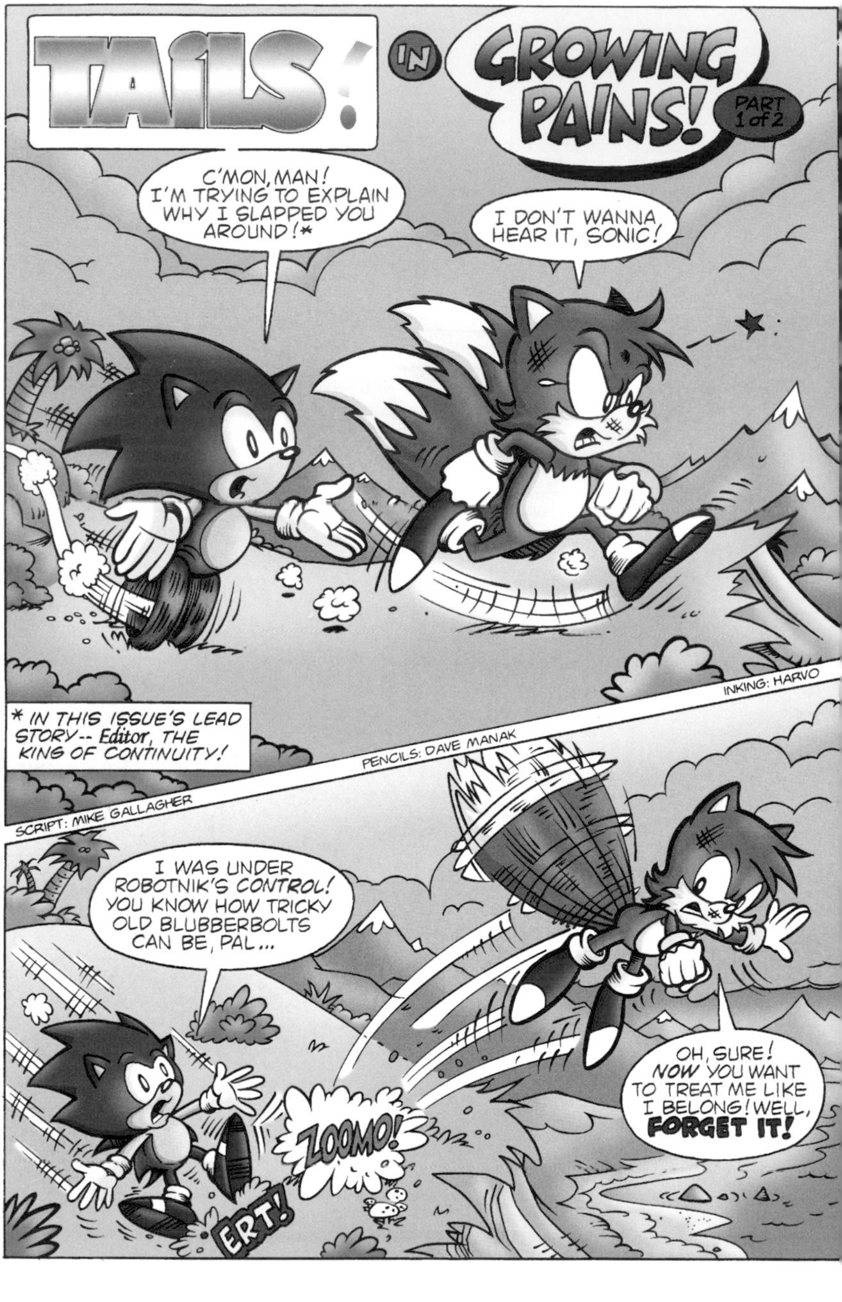
TAILS! IN GROWING PAINS! PART 1 of 2
C'MON, MAN! I'M TRYING TO EXPLAIN WHY I SLAPPED YOU AROUND!*
I DON'T WANNA HEAR IT, SONIC!
* IN THIS ISSUE'S LEAD STORY-- Editor, THE KING OF CONTINUITY!
INKING: HARVO
PENCILS: DAVE MANAK
SCRIPT: MIKE GALLAGHER
I WAS UNDER ROBOTNIK'S CONTROL! YOU KNOW HOW TRICKY OLD BLUBBERBOLTS CAN BE, PAL...
OH, SURE! NOW YOU WANT TO TREAT ME LIKE I BELONG! WELL, FORGET IT!
ZOOMO!
ERT!

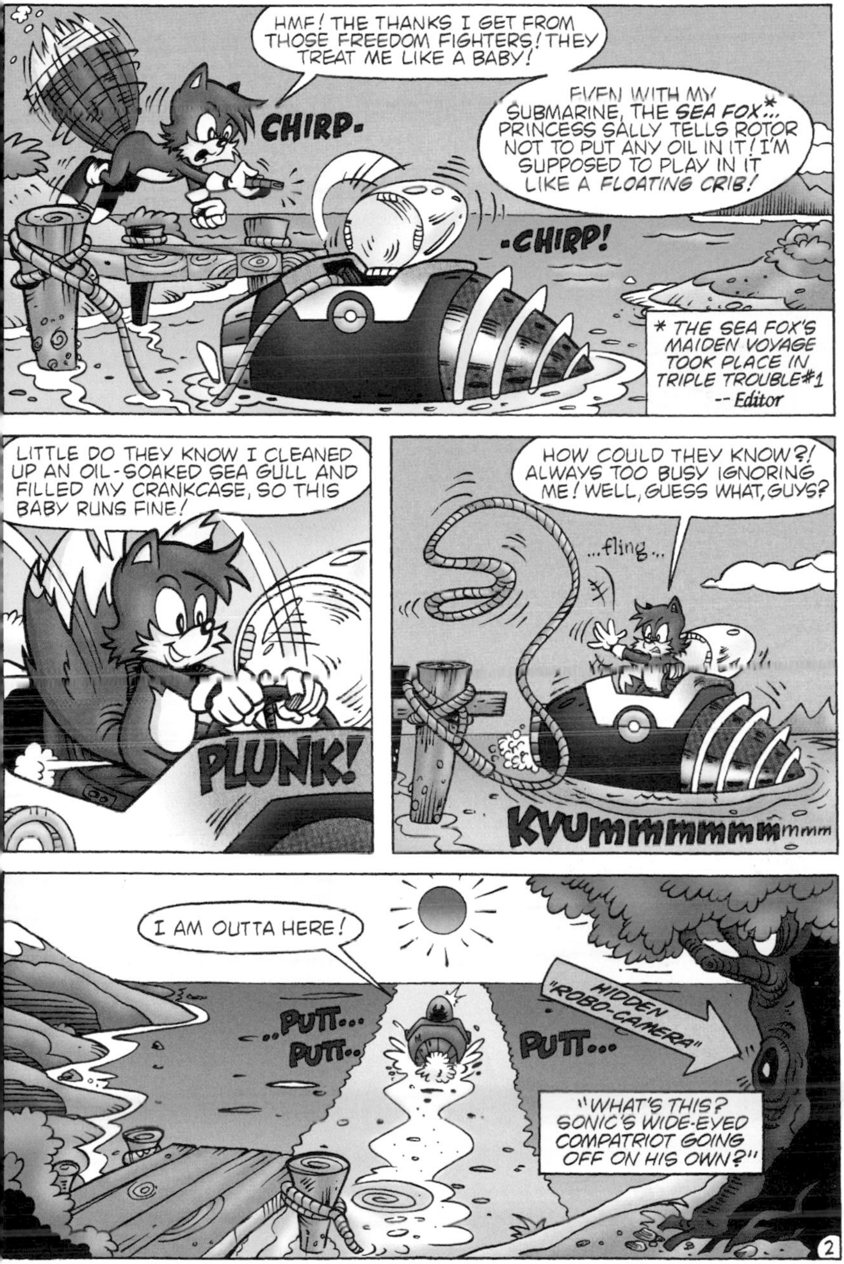
HMF! THE THANKS I GET FROM THOSE FREEDOM FIGHTERS! THEY TREAT ME LIKE A BABY!
CHIRP-
EVEN WITH MY SUBMARINE, THE SEA FOX*... PRINCESS SALLY TELLS ROTOR NOT TO PUT ANY OIL IN IT! I'M SUPPOSED TO PLAY IN IT LIKE A FLOATING CRIB!
-CHIRP!
* THE SEA FOX'S MAIDEN VOYAGE TOOK PLACE IN TRIPLE TROUBLE #1 -- Editor
LITTLE DO THEY KNOW I CLEANED UP AN OIL-SOAKED SEA GULL AND FILLED MY CRANKCASE, SO THIS BABY RUNS FINE!
PLUNK!
HOW COULD THEY KNOW?! ALWAYS TOO BUSY IGNORING ME! WELL, GUESS WHAT, GUYS?
...fling...
KVUMMMMMMMMmmm
I AM OUTTA HERE!
...PUTT... PUTT...
PUTT...
HIDDEN "ROBO-CAMERA"
"WHAT'S THIS? SONIC'S WIDE-EYED COMPATRIOT GOING OFF ON HIS OWN?"

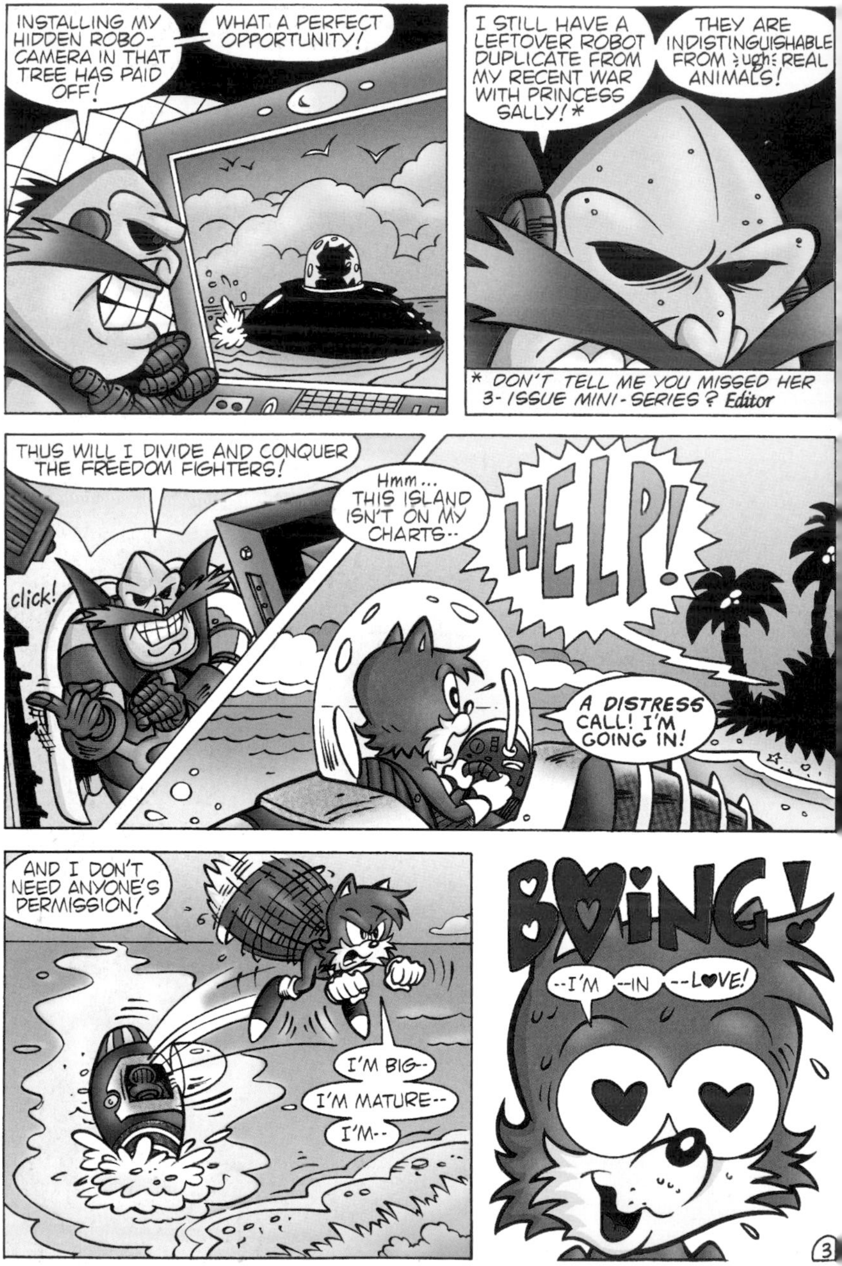

INSTALLING MY HIDDEN ROBO-CAMERA IN THAT TREE HAS PAID OFF!
WHAT A PERFECT OPPORTUNITY!
I STILL HAVE A LEFTOVER ROBOT DUPLICATE FROM MY RECENT WAR WITH PRINCESS SALLY! *
THEY ARE INDISTINGUISHABLE FROM ugh REAL ANIMALS!
* DON'T TELL ME YOU MISSED HER 3-ISSUE MINI-SERIES? Editor
THUS WILL I DIVIDE AND CONQUER THE FREEDOM FIGHTERS!
click!
Hmm... THIS ISLAND ISN'T ON MY CHARTS--
HELP!
A DISTRESS CALL! I'M GOING IN!
AND I DON'T NEED ANYONE'S PERMISSION!
I'M BIG--
I'M MATURE--
I'M--
BOING!
--I'M --IN --LOVE!

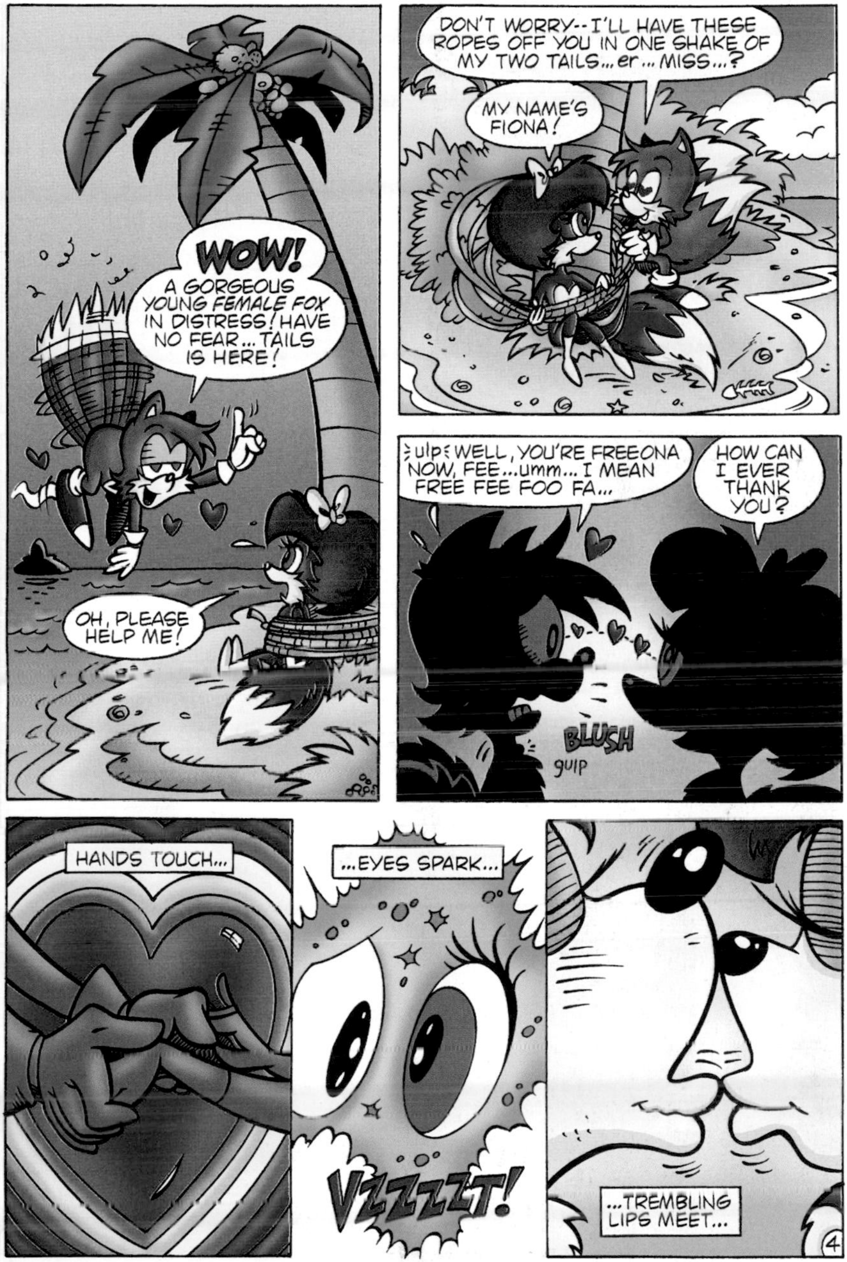
WOW!
A GORGEOUS YOUNG FEMALE FOX IN DISTRESS! HAVE NO FEAR... TAILS IS HERE!
OH, PLEASE HELP ME!
DON'T WORRY-- I'LL HAVE THESE ROPES OFF YOU IN ONE SHAKE OF MY TWO TAILS... er ... MISS...?
MY NAME'S FIONA!
ulp WELL, YOU'RE FREEONA NOW, FEE...umm... I MEAN FREE FEE FOO FA...
HOW CAN I EVER THANK YOU?
BLUSH
gulp
HANDS TOUCH...
...EYES SPARK...
VZZZZT!
...TREMBLING LIPS MEET...
4

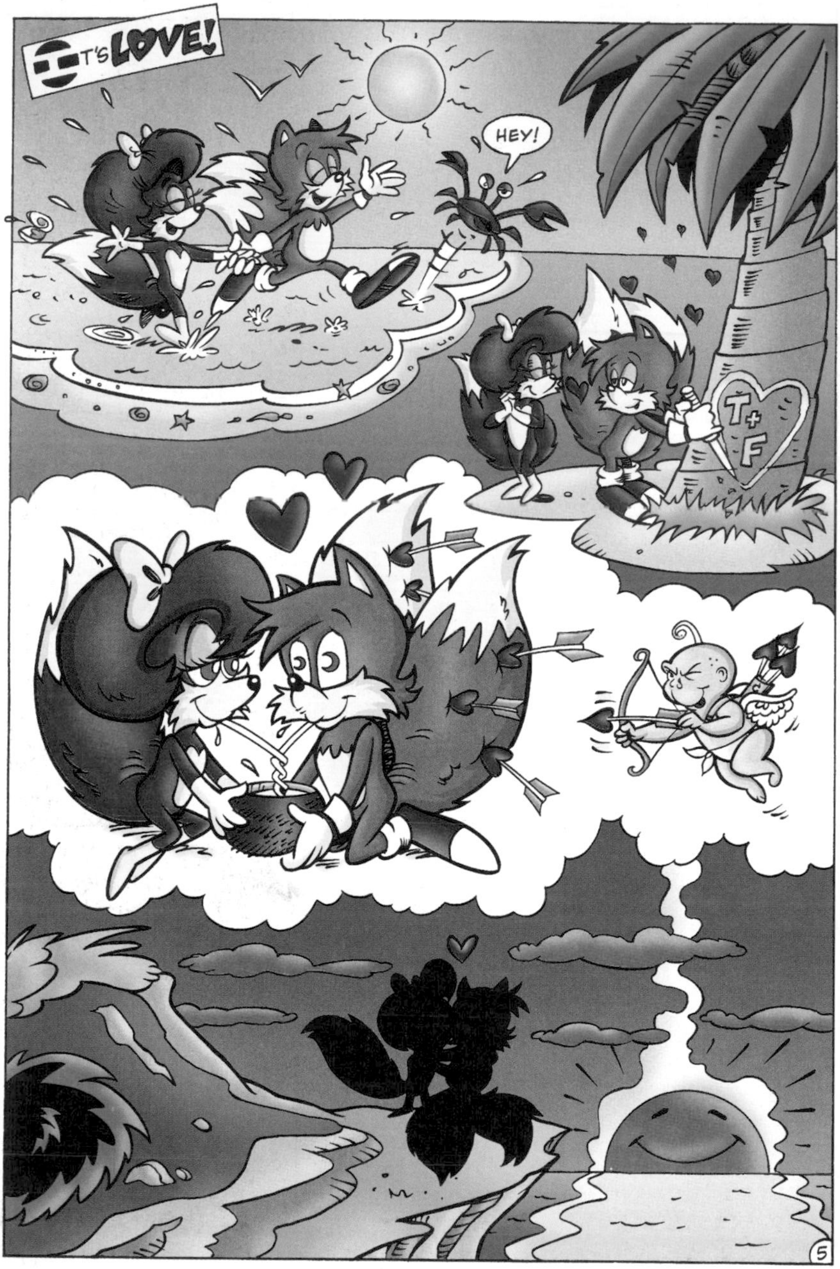
IT'S LOVE!
HEY!
T+F

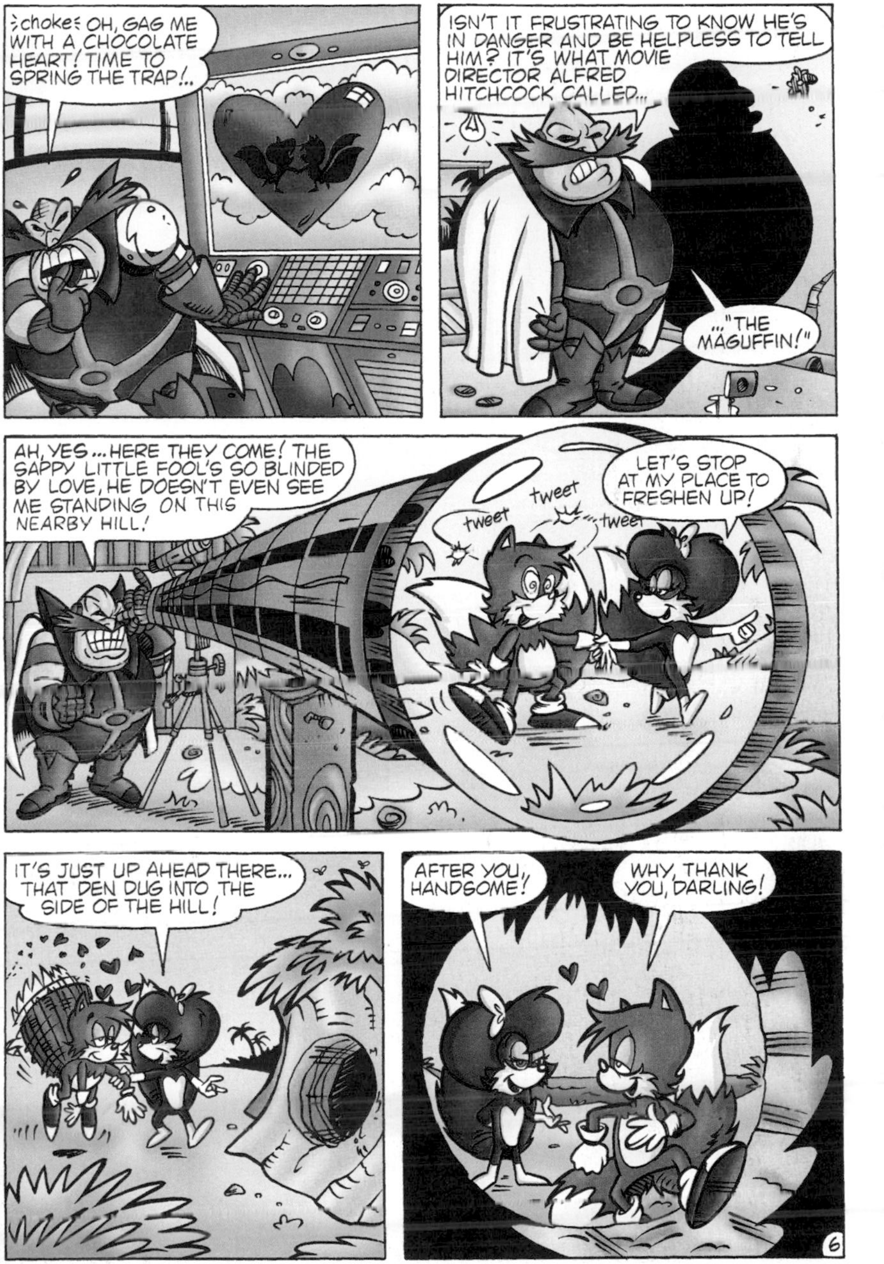

÷choke÷ OH, GAG ME WITH A CHOCOLATE HEART! TIME TO SPRING THE TRAP!..
ISN'T IT FRUSTRATING TO KNOW HE'S IN DANGER AND BE HELPLESS TO TELL HIM? IT'S WHAT MOVIE DIRECTOR ALFRED HITCHCOCK CALLED...
..."THE MAGUFFIN!"
AH, YES... HERE THEY COME! THE SAPPY LITTLE FOOL'S SO BLINDED BY LOVE, HE DOESN'T EVEN SEE ME STANDING ON THIS NEARBY HILL!
tweet
tweet
tweet
LET'S STOP AT MY PLACE TO FRESHEN UP!
IT'S JUST UP AHEAD THERE... THAT DEN DUG INTO THE SIDE OF THE HILL!
AFTER YOU, HANDSOME!
WHY, THANK YOU, DARLING!
6

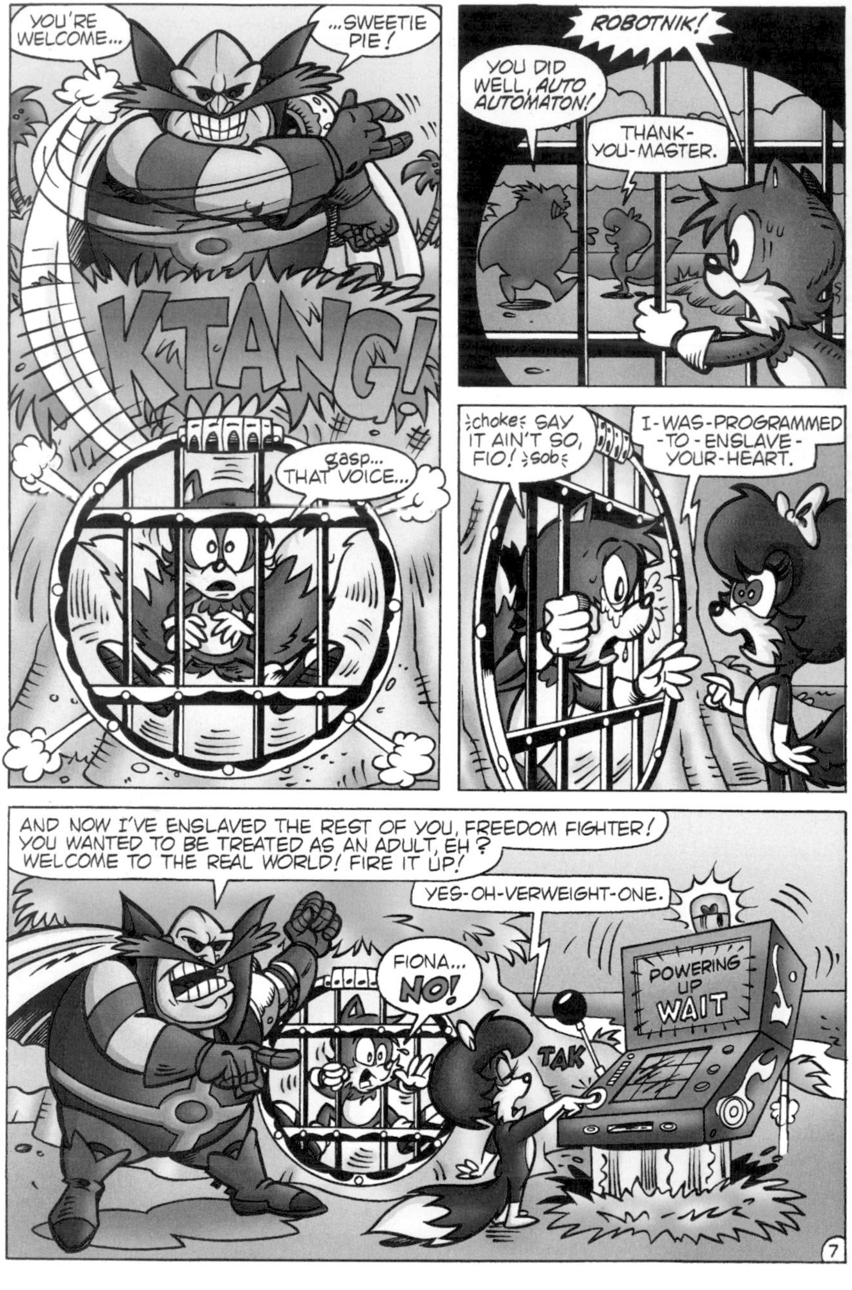
YOU'RE WELCOME...
...SWEETIE PIE!
KTANG!
gasp... THAT VOICE...
ROBOTNIK!
YOU DID WELL, AUTO AUTOMATON!
THANK-YOU-MASTER.
choke SAY IT AIN'T SO, FIO! sob
I-WAS-PROGRAMMED-TO-ENSLAVE-YOUR-HEART.
AND NOW I'VE ENSLAVED THE REST OF YOU, FREEDOM FIGHTER! YOU WANTED TO BE TREATED AS AN ADULT, EH? WELCOME TO THE REAL WORLD! FIRE IT UP!
YES-OH-VERWEIGHT-ONE.
FIONA... NO!
POWERING UP WAIT
TAK

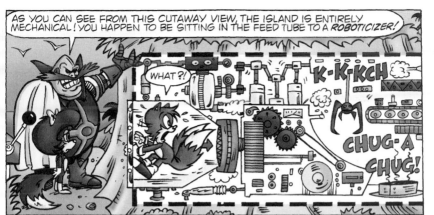

AS YOU CAN SEE FROM THIS CUTAWAY VIEW, THE ISLAND IS ENTIRELY MECHANICAL! YOU HAPPEN TO BE SITTING IN THE FEED TUBE TO A *ROBOTICIZER!*

WHAT?!

K-K-KCH

CHUG-A-CHUG!

HO HO! AND JUST FOR THE IRONY OF IT, I'LL HAVE YOUR ROBO-GIRLFRIEND THROW THE SWITCH!

SH-SHE WOULDN'T... NOT AFTER ALL WE'VE MEANT TO EACH OTHER...

SYSTEM READY

YOUR-WORD-IS-LAW-DOCTOR-ROBOTNIK!

SYSTEM ACTIVATED

CHANK

EEEEEEE!...

AH, THAT'S FUNERAL MUSIC TO MY EARS?!!!

TAILS-IS DONE-FOR!

TO BE CONTINUED NEXT ISSUE!

SONIC THE HEDGEHOG™

Welcome to a brief who's who
of the Sonic universe.
You have just read some
of the earliest
and most loved stories from the
Sonic comic. We thought
you'd like to learn a little extra
about a few of your
favorite Sonic characters.

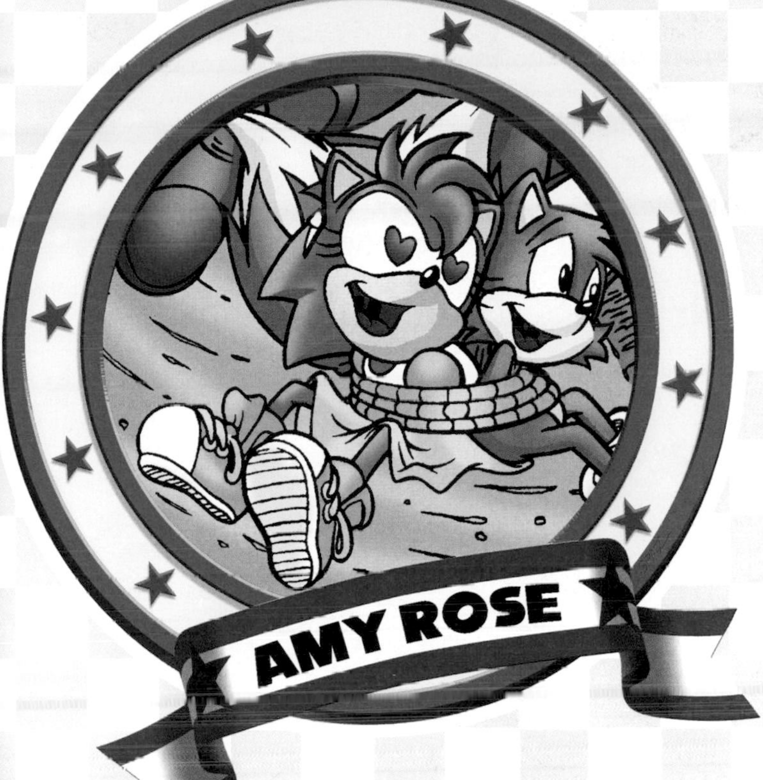
AMY ROSE

Amy Rose

After Robotnik finds some Sonic Fan Mail, he discovers the identity of Sonic's biggest fan: Amy Rose the Hedgehog! The diabolical despot kidnaps poor Amy and holds her captive, using her to lure Sonic into his most deadly trap ever! If Amy ever gets free, how will she repay her biggest hero?

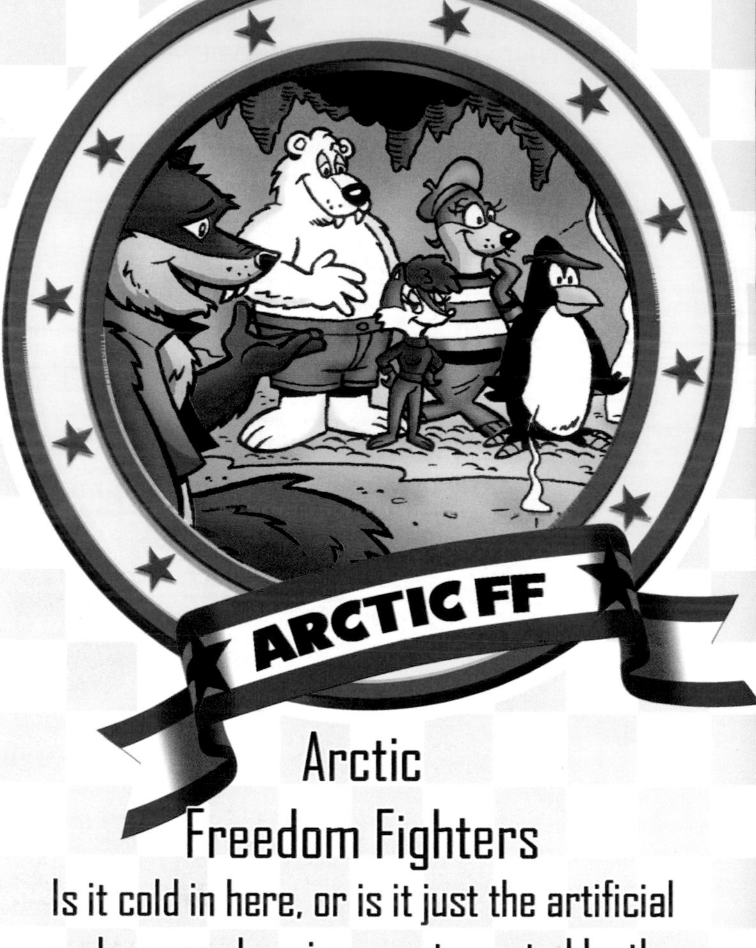
ARCTIC FF

Arctic Freedom Fighters

Is it cold in here, or is it just the artificial underground environment created by the Arctic Freedom Fighters?

This aloof band of rebels prefers to stay hidden from Robotnik instead of directly fighting against him. That is, until Sonic and the others find themselves met by a chilly reception, courtesy of Robotnik.

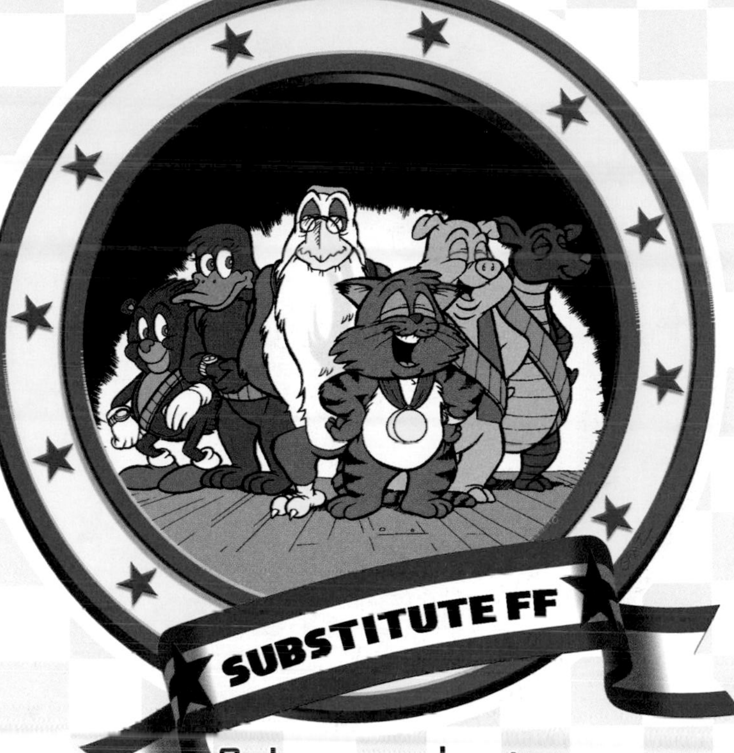
SUBSTITUTE FF

Substitute Legion of Freedom Fighters

This new band of heroes has proven themselves time and time again to be a formidable force against the evils of Dr. Robotnik. With high-flying Ceril the Eagle, brawny Hamlin Pig, courageous Arlo the Armadillo, level-headed Dylan Porcupine, medical-minded Penelope Platypus, and de-facto leader Larry Lynx, Super Jinx, there is nothing this team cannot accomplish together!

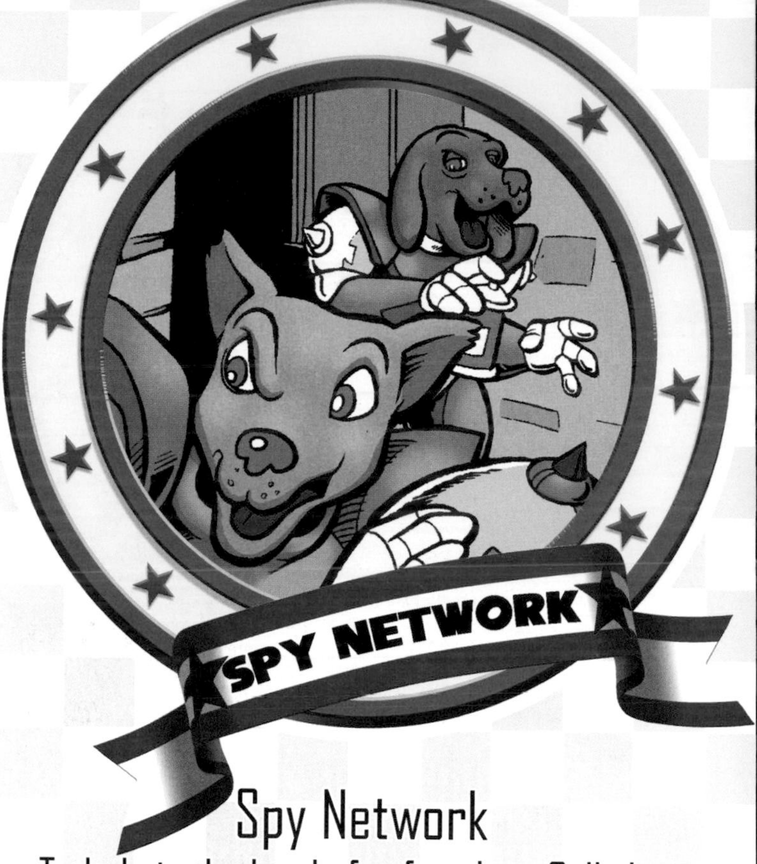
SPY NETWORK

Spy Network

To help in the battle for freedom, Sally has infiltrated Robotnik's intelligence system with the help of a group of spies from Knothole Village: two of these double agents are Sleuth Dawgy Dawg and Sir Kicks-a-lot. Who else is part of this secret network, and will they be able to help the Freedom Fighters crack through Robotnik's defenses?

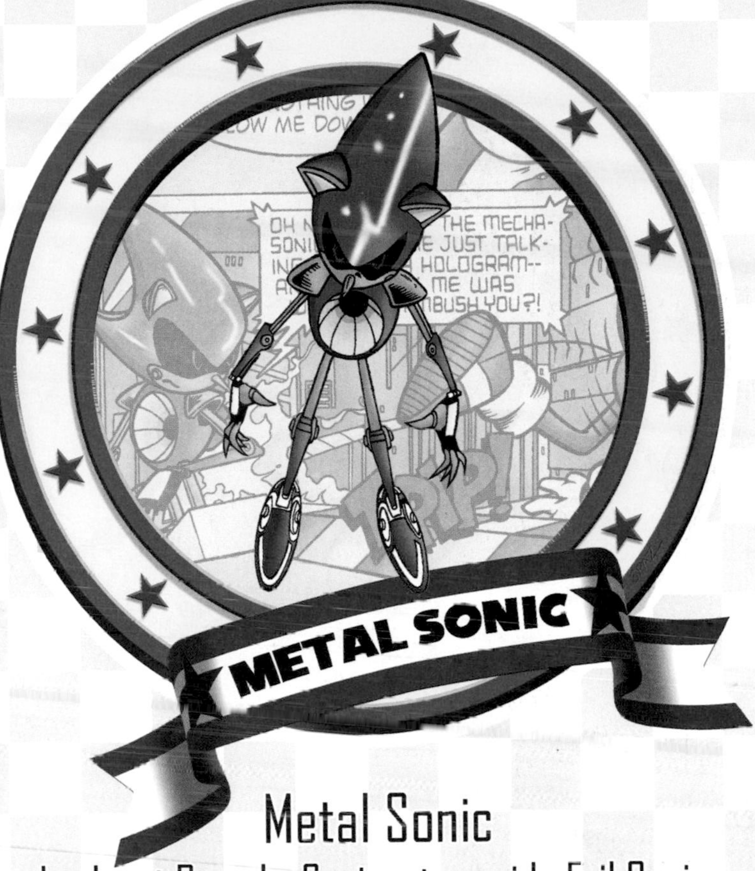
METAL SONIC

Metal Sonic

Look out Pseudo-Sonic, step aside Evil Sonic, it's time for Metal Sonic v1.0! This robotic duplicate, unlike his predecessor, is Sonic's superior in every way: faster, stronger, and more durable. Sonic will be forced to battle with this nefarious clone several times in his career, and Metal Sonic will never tire of the fight! Watch out, hero!

FIONA FOX

Fiona Fox

Ahh, true love...Or is it?! Tails finds the mysterious Fiona Fox on an island while adventuring on his new submersible (courtesy of Rotor), the Sea Fox. But what begins as a budding romance between the two foxes ends in disaster as Fiona turns out to be a robot "auto-automaton" built by none other than the evil Dr. Robotnik! This does, of course, beg the question: if this is just a robot duplicate, then where is the real Fiona Fox?

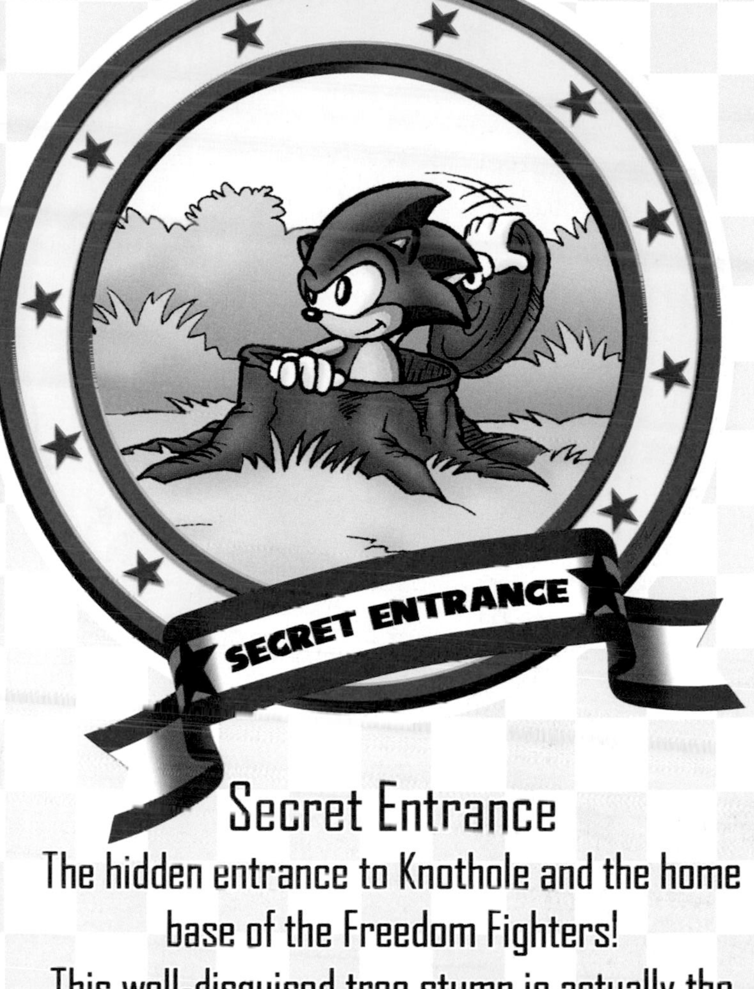
SECRET ENTRANCE

Secret Entrance

The hidden entrance to Knothole and the home base of the Freedom Fighters!
This well-disguised tree stump is actually the start of a path which snakes its way into Freedom HQ, where Sonic, Sally, and the rest hide out from Robotnik.
But now, that secret may be discovered!

KNOTHOLE

Knothole Village

And you thought the secret hideaway where the
Freedom Fighters based their operations from was
the only place where people lived! Not so!
In fact, just outside the secret base is an
entire hidden village, where the citizens of Knothole
(formerly the citizens of Mobotropolis)
reside with their families.
Luckily, Robotnik doesn't know its location...yet!

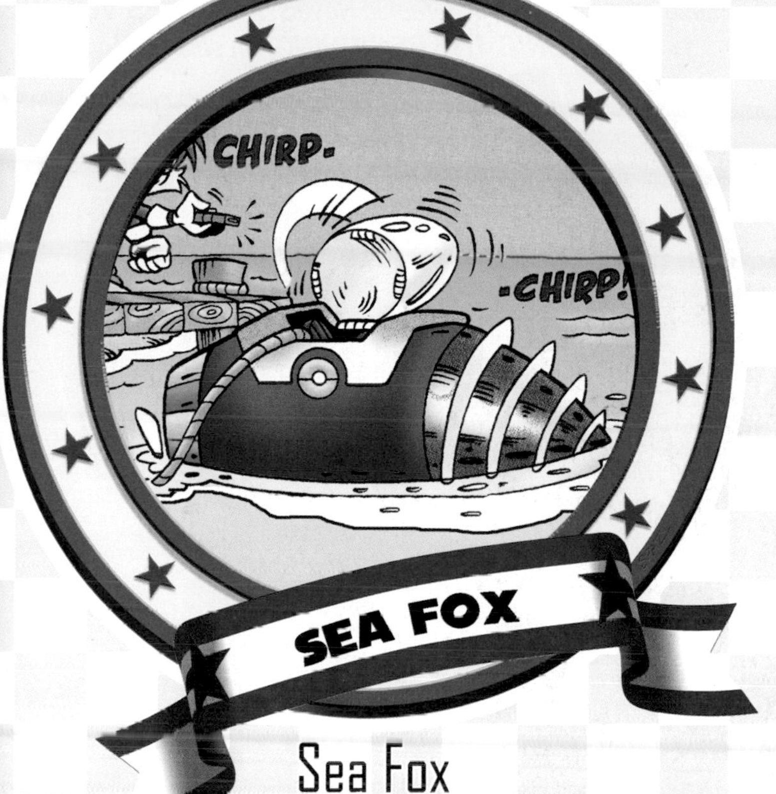
CHIRP-
-CHIRP!
SEA FOX

Sea Fox

Thanks to some handiwork on the part of Rotor, Tails now has a nifty new vehicle aside from his famous "Tornado." This water-faring vessel, dubbed the Sea Fox, was given to Tails as a gift, but originally held no oil since Sally didn't think Tails was old enough to venture out on his own. But now, the crafty fox has readied his sub and is taking it out on his own. Looks like little Tails is growing up!